# DREADNOUGHT

## APRIL DANIELS

**DIVERSIONBOOKS**

Diversion Books
A Division of Diversion Publishing Corp.
443 Park Avenue South, Suite 1008
New York, New York 10016
www.DiversionBooks.com

For more information, email info@diversionbooks.com

First Diversion Books edition January 2017.
Print ISBN: 978-1-68230-068-8
eBook ISBN: 978-1-68230-067-1

For the girls still in hiding.

# CHAPTER ONE

This is taking too long. I just want to pay for the shit and go. It's not like I'm breaking the law or anything—except it totally feels like I'm breaking the law. It'd be really cool to be able to do this without shame, without hopping on a train to ride halfway across the city first. Finally, I get to the front of the line and drop the nail polish on the counter. The cashier rings me up with a smile that makes me curdle inside. I wonder if she knows. I take my nail polish and get out of there as quick as I can.

I make sure not to glimpse my reflection in the mall windows as I beeline for the exit. More and more I hate to look in the mirror. It's getting worse every day. The first little bits of hair are pushing their way up from my face, and my voice dropped so early it's almost a lost cause. I'm way too tall and my shoulders are getting broad.

The mall doors slide open and the outside air hits my face, cool and wet. Spring in the Pacific Northwest: come for the moist, stay for the damp. I pick up the pace and trot through the parking structure. There's a space in back of the mall, out of the way and behind a corner. The kind of place you get an instinct for finding if you grow up a certain way, the way that teaches you how to hide. I've used this spot before.

With a last glance around to check if I'm in the clear I duck out of the parking structure and head down the back side of the mall, toward the ramp that heads up to the elevated roadway running through the city's heart. The space between the mall and the ramp is deserted and strewn with ancient litter. There's a little wall segment sticking out from the side of the mall, an architectural brain fart that serves no function I can see, but is perfect for giving me a little privacy in the heart of one of the largest, most densely packed cities in the country.

The sky is low and gray. Traffic hisses above me. The cement is cold where I sit on it, and I am utterly alone. For the first time this week, I'm happy.

The nail polish is a nice deep red. I've been running mostly with blue recently, but I think it's time for a change. The cotton balls soak up remover and the blue polish rubs off my toes a bit at a time. It feels right. It feels *necessary*. Painting my toes is the one way I can take control. The one way I can fight back. The one way I can give voice to this idea inside me that gets heavier every year:

*I'm not supposed to be a boy.*

Sometimes I want to climb up on a table in the cafeteria and scream it out at the top of my lungs. There's been a horrible mistake. I'm trapped on the wrong side. I'm not a boy. I won't be a man. I'm a girl. I'm a girl.

*I AM A GIRL!*

The lie is suffocating. Every time I have to play along, I feel like I'm betraying myself. Sometimes when I see myself in a mirror I get a little jolt, a little splash of fear sluicing down my spine.

Maybe I'm only imagining things. Sometimes I hope I am. There are things that don't make sense. Like, for instance, my junk. It doesn't bother me, but I feel like it's "supposed" to bother me. Isn't that how it's supposed to go? These changes in my body—I don't like them, and I'm constantly getting surprised at all the different *ways* I don't like them, but the one thing I thought I could count on hating doesn't really bother me. I don't feel much about it one way or the other. And so the uncertainty is never far away, the lingering doubt (hope?) that maybe I'm making it up. Maybe I'm normal; this is all normal. Maybe it just means I'm scared to grow up. Or maybe I'm just a freaky little boy with freaky little thoughts that don't mean anything.

But then in health class when the teacher starts talking about reproductive systems, I get this feeling of cold invasion. My body knows what it's missing, and being reminded of it is the worst feeling in the world.

Obviously I can't tell anyone about this. If it got back to Dad, he'd kill me. He's obsessed with "making a good man" out of me. "You're a man now," he says as his justification for friggin' *everything*. He wants me to be strong and boisterous and popular. It's bad enough I'm quiet and like to be alone, bad enough I don't like sports even after he forced me to join the football team, bad enough I couldn't care less about cars. If he found out I might be a girl…well, I don't really want to think about what might happen.

The dirty little secret about growing up as a boy is if you're not any good at it, they will torture you daily until you have the good graces to kill yourself. The posturing and the dominance games are almost inescapable. It's hard to walk from one end of school to the other without getting shoulder-checked in the halls. Locker rooms are a forgotten circle of Hell. God forbid anyone ever catch you sketching flowers in class, or reading a book that's "for girls." Maybe for people who really *are* boys, that stuff works. Maybe it fits for them.

But I don't get to fit. Not anywhere.

The one thing I must never do is try to fit in with the girls. I don't know what would happen if I tried, but I have a screaming animal instinct that tells me not to even consider it.

When I turn eighteen, if I haven't killed myself yet, I'm going to move out of the house and go on hormones. Maybe save up for surgery. But for now, what I have is nail polish. I've finished wiping the chipped remains of last week's polish off my toes, and have a clean canvas again. The air is cold. I lay my feet on my backpack as I lean against the wall and close my eyes. For now, at least, I am safe.

A hard, flat bang smacks against the sky and echoes back down.

It's the first time I've heard an explosion in real life, and so I don't understand what it is at first. I get to my feet and peek around the wall, and there across the road a black-and-red cloud is blooming from the top floors of an office tower. Another explosion rips through the building, blasts the top three floors to glass shrapnel, and like a stunned yokel I just sit there and stare. Little bits of charred rubble begin to patter down around me, and I'm starting to think I should take cover when a painfully bright blue flash from the upper floors makes the whole world go dim for an instant. A blue laser punches out of one side of the burning floors and sweeps the sky like a lighthouse.

Oh. Great. A superhero fight. Just friggin' *wonderful*.

Yeah, yeah, superheroes are super cool and all that, but it's insanely dangerous to be near them when they're fighting. They can't always keep the bad guys from hitting bystanders. The concrete is cold against my back and shoulders when I duck back behind the wall and try to press myself into the corner. An actual metahuman brawl, right across the street from me. What are the odds? If I keep my head down and stay in cover I should be okay. Maybe I should make a run for the door, get under a roof. No, too dangerous. I'll stay here. The Legion is usually pretty good about taking this kind of thing outside the city when they can.

Another *crump* of impact, and then a flapping, fluttering noise. Something soft and heavy slams into the ground on the other side of this wall.

No. No. No. Go away. Crap.

On my hands and knees, I peek around the painted cinderblocks again. There's a man lying there, crumpled up and broken. He wears a blue bodyglove, and a charred and tattered white cape. Of course I recognize him. He's probably the most famous person on the planet: Dreadnought. Mightier than a battleship, faster than a jet, and so on. He's not supposed to be lying in an alley. It's wrong and terrifying in ways that go straight through me.

"Hey," I call out to him. "Dreadnought. Are you okay?"

He only moans in response. Every bit of profanity I know leaks out of me in one long, hissing chain. I crane my neck to look back at the tower's top floors. Whatever could do this to a man like him is nothing I want to meet.

"Dreadnought! Can you hear me? You have to get up!"

Dreadnought puts an arm under his body, tries to raise himself up. His arm shakes with the effort and he collapses with a cry of pain.

Chanting curse words like a prayer, I crawl out from my little hiding spot and grab him under the armpits. He's so heavy. Up close, I can see the things about him the cameras always miss. How deep the hollows under his eyes are, how heavily lined his face is. As he turns over, I go weak with shock. There's a hole in his chest about the size of a golf ball, his suit charred and melted at the edges. It looks like it goes all the way through.

Dreadnought tries to speak. It's just a slurring noise. He sounds different than he does on TV. His voice is higher and weaker than I expected. He tries again. "Get out. Leave me."

There's a giddy fear bubbling up beneath me. I manage to stop cussing long enough to say, "There will be firefighters here soon. They'll help you." I drag Dreadnought away from the mall, toward the ramp. We'll hide under the road until the emergency crews arrive, and then I'll find some paramedics and bring them back here.

"Kid, I'm done," he rasps. "Save yourself."

He's heavy and limp but I manage to get him up over the concrete lip and drag him under the ramp. He grinds his teeth against the pain, but when I've finally got him all the way into the deep shadows he seems to relax a bit. In the distance, I hear sirens.

A pale blue glow blooms across the back side of the mall. My hair begins to float on a static charge. A flat wave of blue light flits across ground where Dreadnought landed—once, twice. There is a snapping, hissing sound, and something else, an almost musical series of tones.

My lungs are locked with fear. Beside me, I feel Dreadnought go statue-still. Finally, the light fades and the sound disappears.

"What the hell was that?" I whisper.

"She said her name was Utopia. She had some kind of… weapon." Dreadnought arches and clenches in agony. I scuttle out of our hiding space and dash to my backpack. If there's one good thing to come out of being conscripted into the football team, it's that I was carrying a water bottle today. For a panicked moment I think I left it at school, but when I push aside my ratty sketchbook and some French comics, I find it. Dreadnought is breathing heavily when I return, and I trickle water into his mouth. He drinks, but swallowing is difficult for him.

"What's your name, son?" he asks.

"I'm Danny."

Dreadnought's eyes focus on me like he's really seeing me for the first time. "Christ, you're just a boy."

I don't know why I can't lean into the familiar lie the way I do with everyone else. It just feels wrong to lie to Dreadnought, and it hurts that he thinks I'm a dude. "I'm *not* a boy!" I hiss at him.

"Don't be in such a hurry. You'll be a man—" Dreadnought breaks off in a fit of hacking coughs. "You'll be a man soon enough." More coughs wrack his body. He seems to come to a decision. "Guess that's it, then. It's on you now, Danny. The world needs Dreadnought. I'm sorrier than you'll ever know."

Dreadnought reaches up to his chest, and his fingers seem to sink right into his breastbone. He pulls a fizzing white ball of light out of his chest, and holds it out for me.

"Take it."

My head feels like it's filled with cotton. I reach out with a shaking hand and touch the—

—a billion, trillion suns roaring silently in the night

—becoming light, scalding everywhere

—spilling out inside of me as

—a lattice of light and heat, blinding glare against the black

—but *more* than that

—twisted up out of potential and into *being*

—the pain is everywhere, filling me

Everything. I see everything. From the biggest galaxy to the smallest atom. I understand it all. And I can *change*—

—the part of the Universe that is me

—wrap it around

—folds in on itself

—unravels, reweaves

—tightens up into a new

—bones bending, my ligaments melted

—begins to fade

—What was clear is

—no! No, please!

—I'm not done yet!

—grab and heave

—shove back the darkness

—fight

—almost, *pull*—

I slam back into myself with a gasp. My hips ache. My chest burns. My skin feels tight and wrong. My throat, my guts, my legs. Everything feels different. I'm lying on the filthy ground next to Dreadnought, and the world is spinning. I sit up, and when I move my clothes seem to pull on me in ways they haven't done before.

Dreadnought lies perfectly still. I pat his cheek, but he doesn't respond.

"Dreadnought. Dreadnought! Wake up!"

I stop, and listen to myself.

I have a girl's voice.

# CHAPTER TWO

A buzzing thrill shoots through me, all the way down to my toes. I bolt away from Dreadnought, scuttling back on hands and heels. I stop and take a look at my hand. It seems smaller now. My fingers taper gently in a way that's new to me.

"Dreadnought," I say in this voice I don't want to believe I have. "Something's happened. What's going on?"

I look down at my body, and yeah, that is *not* the chest I woke up with. When I go to reach down into my pants, my hand kind of jumps back on its own, nervous and scared. After I find the nerve to feel what's between my legs—or rather, what's *not*—I explode in tears. Everything is wrong, but so perfectly right. I wrap my arms around my legs and rock back and forth. The last little doubts are gone, and the fear leaves with them.

I'm free. I'm finally free.

Nearly as abruptly as they came, the tears leave and I feel empty and calm. I crawl back over to Dreadnought, and when I do so I have a moment of vertigo. His eyes are open, and he's staring up at nothing.

"Thank you. I—thank you." I reach over and close his eyes. A surge of almost painful affection and gratitude sweeps through me. Somehow, I will find a way to honor his memory. Nothing to do now but wait for the cops to show up, and try to explain what happened.

It's not the cops who show up first. The cowgirl finds me sitting with my head in my hands on the concrete lip that separates the space under the ramp from the empty area behind the mall. I hear footsteps and look up.

She's wearing a wide-brimmed gray hat, and a red bandanna around the lower half of her face. What I can see of her face makes me think she might be Latina. Under a long brown riding jacket, her torso is wrapped in custom Kevlar, and her mottled gray cargo pants are crimped in at the knees by hard plastic kneepads.

And oh yeah, she's got a pair of the biggest revolvers I've ever seen sitting casually in her hands. Big, modern-looking pieces with matte-black finish and molded plastic grips.

"You okay?" she asks, and I realize she's no older than me. Vigilantes are not—to put it mildly—*unheard* of in New Port City, but I've never heard of one my own age.

"Who the hell are you?"

"The name's Calamity. Is, uh, is that…?"

"Dreadnought? Yeah, that's him. You two worked together?"

"No, I'm a mite bit particular about who I ride with," says Calamity. She holsters her guns in a belt hanging low on her hips. "Is…?"

I shake my head. "He's dead."

"Jesus, Mary, and Joseph."

"Yeah." *You don't know the half of it.*

"Did he say anything before he died?" She approaches, bends over to get a better look at the corpse.

"He said it was someone called Utopia, and that she had some kind of new weapon," I say. "Do you—wait, you're not *with* her, are you?"

Calamity scrunches her nose. "Hell no! I was practicing my roof running when I saw the explosion and decided to come on over."

"All right, so then…who is she? I've never heard of a supervillain named Utopia."

Calamity shrugs. "Me neither, and I've heard of most of the players who could do this. She's either really new or someone from the little leagues who got lucky." Calamity's eyes fix on me, and she asks, "What's your name, anyhow?"

"I'm Danny."

Calamity is silent for a long time. "Well, Danny." She reaches up and taps a curly wire leading to an earbud taped into her ear. "The cops say they'll be here in a few moments, so we'd best be leaving."

"Why?"

"If the police find you here, they'll want you to testify against a *supervillain*." Calamity shrugs. "I'll not claim expertise on how things work from where you're from, but in *my* experience of the world, that is a poor choice of behavior. Might be you decide to keep your mouth shut. Might be Utopia doesn't take the chance. Best be leaving."

When she puts it that way, I'm throwing all my crap into my bag and running next to her as she sprints for the parking garage's rear. Around us, I can see the occasional shopper huddling behind a car, waiting to see if it's safe to come out yet. We zip across the street, down an alley; she vaults a chain-link fence like a gymnast on a high bar, and I'm up and over it too before I realize I should have had more trouble keeping up. Around another corner and down another alley, we slow to a stop. It's quiet here, and the sirens seem distant.

Calamity looks at me, her brow knitted in confusion. "You uh…you on the track team or something?"

I realize I'm not winded. "I'm a wide receiver," I say, which is true, but also not really an explanation for why I could mistake a dead sprint for a light jog.

"Whatever you say, Danny. I think we'd best part ways here. I've got some things to run down. Might be seeing you soon." Calamity turns, and from a standing leap catches the lowest rung of a fire escape ladder.

"Hey, wait!" I blurt.

"What?" she asks as she slithers up onto the escape's lowest landing.

My cheeks get warm. "Do you have a mirror with you?"

She turns back to me and spreads her jacket wide so I can see the flash grenades hanging from a harness she wears around her chest. "Do I *look* like I carry a compact around with me?"

"Oh."

There's a smile in her eyes over the bandanna. "Put your shoes on, kid. You'll cut your feet." Calamity climbs the fire escape like a squirrel, and slips over the roof's edge and out of sight.

Now I'm alone again, with this new body.

I sit down on a stack of abandoned milk crates and begin to shake. I'm dizzy. Is this what shock feels like? I stare at my hands, and my legs. It's hard to tell but I think my shoulders are narrower. My pants are pinching me pretty hard around my hips. I feel my face and the scratchy peach fuzz is all gone. David is going to freak when he sees this. I laugh, and the sound is beautiful. I'm a girl. A *real* girl, at last.

The sirens are everywhere now. A fire engine roars past the alley's mouth. I should be going. I slip my feet into my shoes—they're so huge!—and head for the nearest train station.

As I'm climbing the stairs to the elevated train stop a green line train pulls out from station. Someone whistles from atop the train as it passes me. I look up, and Calamity tips her hat to me. She turns into the wind, her coat streaming behind her as the train makes speed.

• • •

The train rocks gently as we shoot along a straightaway. The windows are fogged in the early evening gloom, and I sit at the very front of the car so I can keep my back to everyone else. I can't stop smiling, even when somebody looks up from their phone and announces to everyone in the carriage that Dreadnought is dead. Some people are crying softly, others talking in hushed voices. This train has the air of a funeral, but I can barely keep from giggling. A quiet part of me in the back of my head says I should be ashamed.

Dreadnought is *dead*. People are in *mourning*. But I can't be sad. As sick as it is, I'm excited. He gave me the greatest gift imaginable, even though I don't deserve it. He fixed me. Made me a girl. I don't understand how. As far as I know, none of the men who wore the mantle of Dreadnought ever had powers like that.

Now that I've had time to think about it, a possible explanation has occurred to me. One I almost don't dare hope to be true. It almost feels presumptuous to think about. My mind skitters around it, looks in from the edges.

Here's what I know, courtesy of way too many late nights fangirling about superheroes on Wikipedia: In February of 1944, an American pilot whose name has been deliberately lost to history encountered an unidentifiable glowing light in the midst of a fierce battle over Germany. Thinking it was a new German weapon, he attempted to follow it, but it vanished into a cloud. He went in after it, and his plane simply…disappeared. A week later he returned to Allied Command in England and changed the course of history.

Forty years before that strange encounter over Germany, the British had built a warship that revolutionized naval warfare. *HMS Dreadnought* was faster, stronger, and tougher than anything else afloat. Overnight, it made every other battleship in the world obsolete. That's what the first man to wear the mantle did to metahumans. Nobody had ever flown as fast or as high as he could. Nobody had ever been able to throw a punch like he could. Nobody was able to soak up the kind of punishment he could. So they called him Dreadnought and he was fearless.

In two months of fighting, he'd killed or captured half of Nazi Germany's metahuman operatives, Hitler's famous Übermenschen. Infamous villains like Kristallnacht and Doctor von Sieg didn't even slow him down. The survivors went underground and stayed there almost the rest of the war, right up until the big showdown in Leipzig in April of '45.

After the war was over, when the alliance between the Western powers and the Soviets began to break down, everyone in Washington assumed the twin superiorities of American nuclear power and American supermen would be enough to force the Soviets to capitulate to any demand the Allies wished to make. That lovely notion, along with a dozen city blocks of downtown Berlin, was demolished during Red Steel's debut bout against Dreadnought.

And then the arms race was on.

Dreadnought wasn't just unprecedented, he was the harbinger of a new wave of metahumans more potent than anything that had come before. For a short while it seemed like a major new player took the stage every month or so. All efforts to find the source of this new glut of powerful metahumans failed. Atomic radiation, ancient curses, exotic chemistry, eldritch magic—the variety of origin stories was as broad as the variety of people they happened to. Despite an aggressive search, no common cause was ever identified.

In the decade after the war, we started getting our first supercriminals. In '61, Mistress Malice made her bid for world domination, and suddenly we had super*villains* as well. The first Dreadnought's death at her hands stunned the world, and flags flew at half-mast all over the planet. For an eerie six months it looked like she would win, her floating citadel appearing without warning over major cities to collect tribute and declarations of surrender before disappearing just as quickly. Again and again, teams of heroes broke themselves upon the teeth of her fortress' defenses.

The second Dreadnought's appearance sent electric waves of hope across the globe, and that famous picture of him, a lone, tiny figure confronting her invincible fortress over the White House became *the* image of the twentieth century. For three days and three nights they fought a running battle across the width of North America. In the last great gasp of radio journalism, the whole world stayed glued to their sets to listen to the live reports as Dreadnought and Mistress Malice savaged each other. Cities burned and forests died. Mountains shattered and rivers boiled. Finally, at the edge of endurance, at the limit of hope, Mistress Malice fell. With the help of Red Steel, the new Dreadnought managed to sink her fortress into the Pacific and undo her ambitions. She was vaporized when the reactor blew.

The second Dreadnought's controversial decision to team up with Red Steel to take down Mistress Malice signaled the beginning of a troubled relationship with the US government, for Dreadnought personally and for the superhero community in general. The turmoil of the civil rights movement and Vietnam split the happy relationship most American capes had enjoyed with their government, and over the course of the '70s, the first cape teams formed up as independent entities.

After the second Dreadnought was killed in action during the Kaiju Crisis of '85, his successor saw the end of the Cold War and had his hands full dealing with the dozens of Soviet Bloc heroes who were suddenly on the market as high-end mercenaries. The Miami Horror and Black Christmas proved that Earth still needed heroes, but it seemed that for the first time in almost sixty years the world was more or less a safe place. Men like Dreadnought would keep it that way.

Until today, when he gave me *something* as he lay dying. Something I don't understand, that changed my body and made me perfect. Because of what he did, whatever it was, I'll be able to live the way I was meant to. As a girl. Finally. I'm grateful; hell, I'm practically vibrating with excitement. It seems almost greedy to hope for more.

But who *wouldn't* want to be able to fly?

I have to do something to pay him back, to honor his memory. Maybe what he gave me will let me do that. Maybe I'm going to be the next—

My stop comes up, and with a jolt I realize I haven't thought at all about what I'm going to tell Dad.

# CHAPTER THREE

It's full dark now, and I'm still hidden here behind the tree near our driveway. How the hell do you explain something like this? *Well you see, Father, I was out buying nail polish to wear in secret because I've been half the colors of the rainbow for years now, when the greatest hero of the age fell out of the sky, gave me his power, and died. Somehow this turned me into a girl. Anyhow, I'm off to buy some bras and panties, ta-ta! Come, Mother, and show me the wonders of the tampon aisle!*

But maybe that's getting ahead of myself. Here's the real problem: are they even going to recognize me?

My phone buzzes. A text from Mom: Danny, we talked about this. Where are you? Come home immediately. Your father is upset.

I send a text to my best friend, David: I screwed up and missed my curfew. My parents are pissed.

His reply comes almost instantly: Shit. Are you still out?

Yeah.

Okay, it'll be all right, but you need to go home. It'll get worse the longer you're out.

I'm scared, I type.

It'll be okay. Text me later if you need to.

He's right, of course. David's always there for me. But this time I feel like it'll be different. What with the girl thing and all. How can I explain that in a text message? I bite my lip, bounce on my toes. Eventually I give up trying to type out a coherent reply and walk slowly up to our front door. My keys shake in my hand as I turn the lock. I slip the door closed behind me and try to set my feet down quietly. It's an old house, with wooden floors and a fireplace that doesn't work anymore. If I can just make it to the steep, narrow staircase, maybe I can slip sneak past them and get up to my room before they notice I'm back. And then...and then.

Master of the cunning plan, am I.

Mistress. I mean *mistress* of the cunning plan. I start giggling halfway through the living room, and that does it. Cover blown.

Mom comes around the corner. Mom's a smallish woman with deep worry lines. She's wiping her hands on her apron, and there's that tightness around her eyes I've learned to take as a warning. "Danny, where have—who are you?"

"Um...hi."

Mom's face goes to stone. "I'm sorry, but you need to leave; Danny shouldn't have—"

"Mom, wait!" She looks like someone slapped her. I keep going before she can stop me. "I'm Danny."

Mom opens her mouth, blinks, closes her mouth. It was hard to get a clear look at my reflections in the windows I passed on the way home, but I saw enough to know I still resemble my old self. Same short blond hair, same basic face, but softened by the puberty I *should* have had, not the one I got. "What?"

"Something happened. I, uh—"

"Roger. Roger, get in here," says Mom, not looking away from me. She's twisting her apron in her hands. Her fingers have gone white.

Well. This is going swimmingly.

My father enters. He's got a receding hairline and a voice made for shouting. Which is real convenient, because he shouts. A lot. "Who the hell are you?" he snaps. "Get out."

"Hi, Dad."

"Wh—I don't have a daughter."

"Um, you do now. I'm Danny." My posture folds inward. My arms cross across my stomach, and I can't look him in the eye. I hate how I always wilt like this, but, well, it's easier this way. Sometimes even this isn't enough. Sometimes it pisses him off that I'm a coward. But it's not like there's an alternative.

"Danny put you up to this? You tell him he's grounded until—"

"I *am* Danny, Dad." I put as much defiance as I dare in my tone, which I admit isn't much. I'm not looking him in the eye, because I never do that when he's angry. It's not safe. "Something happened today. Didn't you hear the news?"

"I don't know what kind of joke you think you're playing, young lady," Dad says, his voice rising. "But you're trespassing and you need to leave! Now!"

"Dad, I *live* here. I'm Danny." My voice is faltering. I'm collapsing in on myself. He'll start yelling now, and then there will be nothing to do but wait him out. Of course it's going this way. I can't imagine why I thought it would go any other way.

"No! I've had enough of this bullshit!" His voice seems to shake the room. "You get out, and you tell my delinquent son—"

"Roger," says Mom. Her voice is shaking a little, but she steps to my side, and I love her more now than I ever have before. "This is Danny. Look at...well, *look*."

My father's eyes get wide. His face goes the color of spoiled milk. "What did you do?" he asks, quietly enough to scare me.

"I didn't do anything! It just happened. Dreadnought was fighting someone, and there was this flash of light, and then...I was this." My cheeks are burning. It's not really a lie, right? I brace up and get ready for it.

For once, Mount Screamer doesn't detonate. "Danny? Oh hell, what happened to you?"

"I don't know. There was a superhero fight. And I was nearby, and then...this."

"Don't you worry." He draws himself up, as tall and proud as he can, like he's about to be magnanimous. "We're going to make this right. I love you. You're my son."

I take a half step back. "Well...not anymore."

"We'll go to doctors. We'll get this looked at," he says. Dad doesn't sound like he's all here anymore. He's not really looking at me. He's looking past me, toward some kind of pathetic optimism where he doesn't have to deal with who I really am. "Hell, we'll talk to the Legion if we need to. If it was done, it can be *un*done."

"I don't think that's how it works, Dad. I'm a girl now. Maybe"—I lick my lips—"maybe we should just accept that."

He seems to come back to the here and now with a jolt. He sets his jaw. "Don't say that. We're going to get through this, okay? I will find a way to fix this. You have my word."

"Uh, sure. Thanks."

And then he sweeps me into one of those rough, manly hugs he's so big on. A healthy masculinity, he calls it, over and over again. I am suddenly filled with contempt. It takes an effort of will not to peel him off me, and I shiver with disgust. I don't care what he says. I don't care what he wants. I don't care what he thinks. I am a girl. I am free.

And I am never.

EVER.

Going back.

• • •

My door locks behind me with a comforting click, and I let out my breath. That was frustrating, and scary as hell, but it's over. Dad spent twenty minutes thinking out loud—brainstorming, he said—about all the ways he's going to try and take this away from me. I'm sorry, I mean *all the ways he wants to help me.* Jackass. There'll be a lot of doctors and a lot of tests, and so on. Good luck, buddy. You're going to need it.

I slide the butter knife out of my sweatshirt sleeve and sit down on my narrow bed. I slipped it up here to test a theory. With just a few fingers at either end, I try to bend the metal. It resists me, and for a moment disappointment wells up in my chest. But then I get a sense of something, like if I pushed in just *this way*, then—

With a quiet whine of tortured metal the knife bends in half, easy as folding a piece of paper.

Holy shit.

I feel cold and shaky. The knife slips out of my fingers. I'd hoped. I'd really sincerely hoped, but I didn't—

Holy *shit*.

Go ahead, Dad. Hit me like you mean it. What do you think you can do? Force me to take testosterone shots? I pick the knife back up, and tie it in a knot. Nobody is going to force me to do anything ever again.

The giggles come back. I hug myself. I struggle not to laugh too loudly. I can't jump because of the low slanted roof of my top-floor room, so I hop for joy—

—and forget how to come down. Now I do laugh out loud, and screw it if he hears me. I hang up here in the air, flailing, trying to get down. I feel like I'm stuck here, like there's this net *behind* the world that I've become tangled in. I could almost grab onto it, if I only knew how. I close my eyes and feel around with my arms. I flop over in midair and end up floating upside down.

Someone's coming.

"Danny," Mom says from the other side of the door. "Are you okay?"

"Uh. Fine." My hair is brushing the floorboards, and I've got a slight spin that is slowly, slowly rotating me.

"Danny, I want you to know that you can talk to me. About anything. Okay?"

Which is not even close to true, but she can't know how wrong she is. "Okay, Mom. I…I just want some time alone, okay?"

"Okay. I love you, sweetie."

"Love you, too."

Now. To figure out how to get down.

• • •

I wake up, and immediately look down to make sure my body is still the proper shape.

"Oh, thank God."

I slip a T-shirt over my head, and fight on a pair of jeans. My hips are wide enough to give my old pants problems. The legs are too long and I roll them a few inches up.

As I'm getting dressed, my eyes fall on the poster of Valkyrja that's hanging on my wall. She's another member of the Legion Pacifica, the regional superhero team. Maybe I'll get to meet her. At the thought of it, a deep flush rises in my cheeks. Maybe that would be a bad idea. I'd probably fangirl all over her. She wouldn't be impressed.

When I come downstairs, Dad looks at me with disappointment, like he was hoping it was all a dream. I fix myself breakfast and sit down.

"Mom. Can you take me shopping today?" I ask over my bowl of cereal.

Mom glances at Dad. "Um, maybe."

"What do you need to go shopping for?" asks Dad. Fear tickles the underside of my heart.

This is delicate. I pick my words carefully. "None of my clothes fit."

"Danny, we're going to fix this pretty quick. We don't need to be spending a lot of money on clothes that we'd only have to give away."

"Can I get new shoes, at least? These things are like boats. I'm going to be tripping all the time." I've got to figure out something that will get Mom and me out of the house with the intention of spending money. Once I get her away from him, she'll be a lot more reasonable. "I mean, just to wear until we fix me. They don't have to be expensive."

Dad sighs, and nods.

"Sure, Danny," says Mom. A fizzing light of joy goes off in my chest, but I keep most of it off my face.

• • •

Mom takes me to the discount shoe store downtown, one of those places with the neon-orange carpet and the salespeople who are a little too friendly to feel safe around. The door gives an electric chime as we enter the shop, which summons them like sharks to bloody water.

"Hi there! Is there anything I can help you with today!" says a man in a neon-tangerine polo shirt. He's got a huge friendly smile that goes only as far as his eyelids.

"Where are the girls' sneakers?" asks Mom.

"Aisle three! Do you need help looking for something!"

"That's okay," I say quickly. The trick with these guys is not to make eye contact. Like restless ghosts, they want to drag you down to Hell with them.

We slip down aisle three, and Mom measures my foot with one of those metal ruler things with the slide. Then she measures my foot again when we realize she'd accidentally used the men's scale. There's a whole wall of generic gray sneakers to choose from. I notice the colors for these are much calmer than I'm used to seeing in sneakers. Pastels and grays and so on. Boys' shoes want to look like they're made of knockoff hypertech. Boys' shoes are friggin' ugly.

While Mom is searching for a pair of shoes in my size that are on sale, I slip around the aisle and head down the other side. Something caught my eye on the way in. These are the more distinctly feminine shoes. I find a pair in my size and clutch them to my chest, blushing. Flats, glossy black with straps. Super cute. I've always wanted some.

Mom is pretty smart. If I show these to her, she might start putting things together. I don't know if that's good or bad.

Screw it. I really want these shoes.

"Danny, I want you to try these on," she says when I come around the corner again.

My voice is quiet when I say, "I want these. They're on sale."

"Oh, those are nice," says Mom, and then an instant later I see her realize what Dad will think of them. A moment after that, she looks at me, puzzling. I'm sitting on the knife edge of hope, waiting for what she'll say next. "But...oh. Yes, you can have those."

My smile is huge, as wide as it goes. I hug her, and she hugs me back and I love her so, so much. "Thanks, Mom."

After a long moment, we break apart and I decide to press my luck.

"Now how about some underwear?"

• • •

There are cops all over the back side of the mall when we get there. It feels a little creepy being back here. Everyone's walking around like they just lost a relative. As ecstatic as I am about what's happened, someone had to die for it to be possible. I don't like thinking about that, because it reminds me that I'm a horrible person. It's disconcerting to realize Dad is right about how selfish I am. We have to go around two sides of the city block that the parking garage is on to get in.

"I can't believe Dreadnought is dead," says Mom. "You were near that?"

"It was really scary," I say.

She grabs my hand and squeezes it tight. "What were you doing back there?" she says as she locks up the car.

I want to tell her everything. And I mean everything, from the powers to how I wanted to be a girl this whole time. But no. It doesn't feel safe.

"I was exploring." It's an amazingly lame excuse, but Mom doesn't push.

The mall downtown is built over several city blocks, with extensive skyways between the main buildings. We cross the road through a glass-and-steel tunnel on the third floor and come out near where we need to be. The lingerie shop in the mall is packed front to back with floor-to-ceiling photos of impossibly beautiful women posing dramatically in their underwear. And I mean literally impossible. These women have all been airbrushed and retouched until they are something that basically does not exist in nature. Even actual models don't really look that way—it's a full-time job for them to do the kind of dieting and exercise needed to be a top-tier model, and then on top of that they have staff to help them. Dermatologists, dietitians, personal trainers, makeup specialists, talented photographers, and even digital artists all work together make it possible. Our health teacher made sure to show us a really long documentary on the subject, about how every little human imperfection, from pimples to scars to pockets of fat, is digitally erased by artists before these photos are shown to the public. With an almost guilty jolt, I realize I look a lot like these pictures. Maybe not so…developed, but pretty close. There's a weird moment of dissonance as I process that.

A clerk walks up to us. They must pay better here; she doesn't have that desperation that fills you with pity and fear. Her eyes are red and a little puffy like she's been crying. A lot of people's eyes have been like that today. Everyone loved Dreadnought. "Can I help you two?"

"My daughter needs a bra," says Mom. Another little burst of joy flits through me hearing her say that. Her *daughter.*

The clerk takes my measurements, looping a tape measure around my chest, and then higher around my breasts. "You should have been in here a while ago," she says.

"Uh, there were complications."

She raises her eyebrows, but only says, "Oh, of course. I'll get you a few different styles to try out in the changing rooms."

The changing room happens to feature the first full-length mirror I've had access to since I changed. I snuck into the bathroom to stare at my face for a solid hour late last night, but finally seeing all of myself, seeing the shape of my body, gives me goosebumps. For more than a few moments, I only stand and stare. I'm a girl. Finally.

I'm just so happy. I can't believe it. I keep expecting to wake up, to see the end of this delirious, wonderful dream. But I am awake, and I'm free.

I pick the three bras I like the best, and Mom makes me put the push-up bra back. When I come back to her, she's got a distant look in her eyes. She's looking in my direction, but I'm not sure she sees me.

"Mom, are you okay?"

She smiles. "I was just remembering when my mother took me to buy my first bra. I didn't think I'd ever be doing the same thing."

"I like that we're doing this," I say. It's the closest I can come to saying we were *meant* to be doing this.

Mom smiles, but it doesn't reach her eyes. She looks away.

We get up to the register and the clerk rings us up. The price is shockingly high.

"Holy crap! We can't afford that!"

"I've got a little money put away," Mom says quietly. I don't have to be told this isn't something to repeat. "We can splurge on this."

"Thank you," I say softly.

We pick up some panties from the cheaper department store at the other end of the mall and head home. I wear the sneakers into the house and carry the flats, the bras, and the panties in the shoe store bag, which is less likely to catch Dad's eye and be a problem. I claim to have a lot of homework and lock myself in my room again.

I put on my shiny black shoes and practice hovering in midair. It's easy now. I can spin on all three axes, and stop precisely in whatever orientation I choose. Tomorrow is Monday. I can't wait.

School is going to be *amazing*.

# CHAPTER FOUR

"Where do you think you're going?" asks Dad, just as I'm about out the door.

"School?" A girl can hope, anyhow.

"I don't think so," says Dad. "You're sick, and you're not going to school until you're well again."

"I feel fine," I mumble.

"You have a doctor's appointment at eleven. You can send a text to David and ask him to email you your assignments. No phone calls. He doesn't need to hear what's happened to your voice."

Slowly, I shut the door and trudge back up to my room.

• • •

The doctors peek in the door again. Dad took me to our family doctor, Doctor Cho, and when he finally gave in and admitted it wasn't very likely I had a twin sister we'd been keeping secret this whole time just to fool him, he immediately retreated and called for reinforcements. Since then, every doctor in the office has been in to look at me. Blood pressure, heartbeat, height, and weight. Urine sample, stool sample, saliva sample. They tried to get a blood sample, but the needle wouldn't punch through my skin at first. For a scary moment I thought they were going to figure it out, but then I imagined the lattice again, imagined the net loosening, letting something through. The needle went into my arm with a pinch, and they got their blood sample. I was poked, prodded, weighed three more times.

Finally, they leave me sitting on an exam bed, dressed in nothing but a paper gown. The walls are papered in medical information posters. I learn the early warning signs of heart disease, and how to examine a pair of testicles for cancer. (Won't ever need to do that! Ha!) There's a list of 1-800 hotlines, and a diagram of what to do when someone has a seizure. The place reeks of antiseptic and nonlatex gloves. I should have brought my sketchbook. Every once in a while, someone will poke their head in, stare at me for a few seconds, and then back out. They're like curious gophers.

"Can you tell Doctor Cho I'd like to speak with him?" I ask.

"Sure," says one. She keeps staring at me for a long moment.

"Soon?"

"Right." She backs away and shuts the door. I can hear heated conversations on the other side.

A century later, Doctor Cho returns. He's got three other doctors with him. "So, have you figured it out?" I ask.

"Not yet, but—" he begins.

"Welp, you tried," I say, hopping off the examination table. "Don't blame yourself, I'm sure anyone would be stumped, you can just go tell Dad it's hopeless." I start pulling my socks on.

"I don't think it is," says Doctor Cho.

"What?" I look up sharply.

"We need to get you to an endocrinologist. I think that, given the circumstances, we can skip the psychological counseling necessary to begin treatment for gender identity disorder."

"*What?*"

"There are these rules called the Harry Benjamin standards of care that mandate at least three months of counseling to clear you for hormone replacement therapy, but since you were male until two days ago, we might be able to start you on testosterone shots right away. I'd need to get an opinion from a specialist, though."

He doesn't even know the Harry Benjamin standards have been out of date for years now. Hell, they're not even *called* that anymore.

Part of me wants to laugh, and another part wants to cry, and a third part wants to scream. They butt up against each other and form a kind of tripod of misery, a stable equilibrium of horror and despair. NOW they want to treat me. NOW they want to change my gender. NOW it's all hands on deck to consider the pressing possibility that something might be wrong with my body.

I'm surprised by how level my voice is when I say, "Oh. Okay."

• • •

Dad is tapping his fingers on the wheel during the long drive home, jiggling his knee, fiddling with the radio. Finally, at a red light, he says, "We can start the testosterone right away, probably. If this endocrinologist he's sending us to won't do it, we'll just find another. But don't worry, we're not going to leave it at that. We're going to figure out a way to get back your…you know."

"My dick?"

"Don't be flippant with me, son," he says, staring straight ahead. He doesn't normally call me son. "I know this is a hard time, but you've got to keep a cool head."

"Maybe it's not coming back." For values of *maybe* that approach *absolutely*. That brief moment of panic in Doctor Cho's office is behind me now. I need to remember that nobody can force me to do anything. Not anymore. Not ever again.

"Don't say that! It'll be fine. We'll get you back the way you need to be."

"Surgery is pretty expensive, Dad."

"We have insurance, don't worry about that," says Dad, and I almost pity him.

I'm really pretty sure our insurance doesn't cover reverse boob jobs and penis grafts. And even if those were covered, these hips ain't going anywhere. I've done research at the library, in moments of curiosity or despair. Transitioning from male to female, mostly, but I got curious and looked to see how the reverse works. Short version: it's just as difficult, but in different ways. Even if I started on testosterone shots tonight, they wouldn't make my shoulders wider or my hips narrower. They might make me a smidgen taller if the caps at the end of my bones haven't fused yet. I'm fifteen, which in this body means I'm even further through puberty than I was as a boy, but I probably still have a few inches I could grow. Puberty leaves a mark human science hasn't figured out how to erase yet, not that it's a real high priority or anything. Unless the transformation I was subjected to when I took the mantle could somehow be reversed by the same process that caused it, my body is going to have undeniable evidence of femininity until the day I die, no matter what we do.

And that's if I allow the needles to pierce my skin. Which, ha, fat chance.

I'm careful not to smile. He'll get used to it. He'll have to.

• • •

**Minovsky_Particle has signed on.**

**CombatW0mbat:** are u okay? Was everything cool with your dad?

**Minovsky_Particle:** yeah. He was upset, but it wasn't too bad.

**CombatW0mbat:** cool. Did you cut class today?

**Minovsky_Particle:** no. just sick. I guess.

**CombatW0mbat:** u guess?

**Minovsky_Particle:** Yeah. I got a weird thing with my skin. Spent all day in the hospital.

**CombatW0mbat:** is it contagious?

**Minovsky_Particle:** Horrifyingly so. Half the west coast will be dead within hours.

**CombatW0mbat:** lol gak

**Minovsky_Particle:** Dad is flipping out about it. Had me at the doctors all day. I feel fine, tho

**CombatW0mbat:** sux. you gonna be out tomorrow?

**Minovsky_Particle:** prolly. What did we have for homework today?

**CombatW0mbat:** chap 6 in history, chap 4 in math, odds, and finish reading mockingbird. dunno what you had in french and chem.

**Minovsky_Particle:** thx
**CombatW0mbat:** but srsly your okay? Things are cool?
**Minovsky_Particle:** Oh yes. They're not angry anymore, and I think Ill
    be better soon. Can't wait to come back to school! :)
**CombatW0mbat:** your a fucking weirdo lol
**Minovsky_Particle:** bored. Wanna hang out! ^_^
**CombatW0mbat:** wanna play a couple rounds after dinner?

I hesitate before replying. I'd love to play some games, but he can't
hear my voice. Yes, I want to tell David—I've been thinking about
how he and everyone else at school will react off and on all day—
but I want people to find out on my terms.

**CombatW0mbat:** u there?
**Minovsky_Particle:** yeah sure, we can play. My mic is busted tho.
    can't talk.
**CombatW0mbat:** better thn nothing!

• • •

A week later, Dreadnought's funeral is on TV. We all gather in the
living room, Mom and Dad on the couch, me sitting off to the side
on a cushion the way I like to. It's good to sit down here because
I'm close enough that I feel like we're all together like a family, but
I'm out of easy line of sight. It's safer that way.

The Legion Pacifica is decked out in mourning colors as they
carry the casket from the hearse to the grave. The President gives a
speech, and then introduces one of Dreadnought's teammates, an
enormous man named Magma, who gives the eulogy.

As he speaks, the guilt comes back, stronger than ever.
Dreadnought is dead, and I just watched him die. Maybe it was
my fault. Maybe if I were smarter or better or had done something
different, he'd have survived. But no, I took his powers and went
home with a big grin on my face. I'm a selfish, horrible person.

I'm a horrible person and I feel guilty as hell, but I can't pretend the days since it happened haven't been the happiest of my life. Every day I wake up and get excited again about what I see in the mirror. Every day I quietly read aloud, just to hear the sound of my new voice. When I see myself, I see *myself*. My body is everything I ever wished for, everything I told myself I'd never have. Maybe I'm not good enough. Maybe I don't deserve it. But I have it now. There's no going back. As they lay him in the ground, I silently promise Dreadnought that someday, somehow, I will find a way to honor his memory. To earn what he did for me.

• • •

I can see the structure behind reality. Okay, not *see,* precisely. But it's there. An infinite lattice of matter and energy, of thought and form. It spreads across the universe—it *is* the universe. I imagine it like a fine mesh net, searingly bright with coiled potential, and all the things in life little more than tangles in the light. The lattice gets twisted up into the shape of water and trees and people and music. As I imagine grasping it with my mind, my feet leave the ground.

Flying takes concentration, but I think I'm getting better at it. With my legs crossed and my textbook in my lap, I hover above my bed and read my homework assignments. It's difficult. When I start getting into the assignment, I tend to wobble and sink. When I'm steady in the air, I'll find that I've gotten to the end of the page and can't remember a single thing I've read. But I'm getting better. For a few paragraphs at a time I can read, understand, and stay up in the air, too. I'm better than I was last night. Tomorrow I'll be better still. When I've got enough practice to concentrate and fly at the same time, I'll—

A *tap-tap-tapp*ing at the window. I drop from the air, feeling guilty. A man in silver and green power armor is hovering just outside my window, beckoning me to come outside.

Or, you know, maybe the Legion Pacifica will come pay me a visit before I'm ready. That could happen, too.

The Legion is the cape outfit for New Port City and parts beyond. Their territory is everything west of the Rockies, north of California and Nevada, and south of Canada. They're the most prestigious team on the West Coast, and possibly the country. With Dreadnought as their anchor, they haven't faced a serious home-turf fight in ten years, and spend most of their time assisting the eternally jumbled and fractured Californian capes or working with the continent-wide Northern Union team to handle the really big stuff, like the asteroid that almost hit us last year. With Dreadnought's death, that might have to change.

I slide across my bed and open the window. The armored figure is floating on whining jets that vent from his back and feet. Of course I recognize him, he's Carapace. My stomach flops over.

"We need to talk," says Carapace in a filtered, almost mechanical voice.

"Oh," I say. "Um. Sure. Let me...let me get a sweater and I'll come out."

Carapace nods, and leans back. His jets flare and he squirts up and away from my house. Holy crap, the Legion wants to talk to me! Yeah, it makes sense, but *holy crap, the Legion wants to talk to me!*

My fingers are clumsy as I pull open my dresser and pull out a sweatshirt. I put it on, take it off, and put it on right side out. I decide to float to the window so he won't see my knees shaking. The night air is cold and damp against my skin, and I wobble a little in the air as I leave my house behind. This is the first time I've flown in the open air. I was hoping to do this in private. Carapace is hovering twenty or thirty yards away, and maybe two dozen yards above the ground. It's an overcast night, but the clouds are thin enough that the moon's light punches through and reflects off the silver highlights of the plate-armored woman floating next to him. It's Valkyrja, and the moment I recognize her my cheeks start burning. Did he see the poster I have of her on my wall? Did *she?*

The bushes in our cramped back yard tickle my feet and I realize my concentration has drifted and I'm sinking. The lattice is clear in my mind when I reach for it, and I shoot back up into the air, arrest my momentum, and approach them under controlled flight.

"Uh, hi," I say to two of the most important people in the world. Wow. I am a dork.

"Hello. I am Carapace, and this is Valkyrja," says Carapace, as if they would need to introduce themselves anywhere in North America. "And you...are Daniel Tozer." Nobody outside the Legion has seen his face. His helmet gives him a metal glare that's hard to face straight-on.

"Danielle," I mutter.

"But your legal name is *Daniel* Tozer," he says, like this is very important to be clear on and he's a little confused. "You were present when Dreadnought was murdered."

"What Carapace means to say," says Valkyrja in a low, husky voice, "is we know that receiving the mantle can be an abrupt and difficult transition." Up close I can see the pale blue nimbus that surrounds her wings. It's well known—okay no, it's well known to her fans, at least—that she doesn't fly by flapping them, but by some kind of magic contained within them. Her blonde hair spills out from under her helmet and down her shoulders. "It is no easy thing for any mortal to come into such power and retain herself. Nor for a child to do the same."

Carapace looks at her for a long moment before turning back to me. "Yes. As a minor coming into powers within our jurisdiction, we are prepared to offer you guidance and support," he says. "This is contingent upon good behavior, of course." There's something in his tone that's hard to read through the mechanical filtering, but it sort of sounds like he thinks good behavior will be a problem for me.

"You want me to...to join the—"

"No," he says. "We do not accept minors into the Legion at this time."

"You would be a provisional member," says Valkyrja as if he hadn't spoken. "You would be welcome in our halls and at our tables, but we would assign you no duties, nor grant you a stipend." She looks at Carapace and raises her eyebrow. "That is a fair description of the program you designed for young champions, is it not?"

"…yes," says Carapace. He continues, sounding like he's reading a script he'd rather not. "We encourage all young metahumans to take advantage of the opportunities we provide."

"Um. I wasn't—my body didn't always look this way. Do you think you can figure out why the mantle changed me?" I want to know. Not so I can turn back, but just so I'll know. There's so much about my own body I don't understand.

"Very likely," says Valkyrja.

"I'd like that a lot, please."

"Can you manage the flight across the city?" asks Valkyrja. "There are things we would discuss with you, and one of our associates will need to examine you."

"I think so."

"Then lead on, child. We fly to Legion Tower."

I dart back down into my room to lock my door and turn out the lights; with any luck my parents will think I turned in early. A few minutes later, I'm ten stories high, zipping across the city toward the glittering night skyline. I've been up high before in tall buildings and airplanes, but nothing really prepares you for being a hundred feet in the air with nothing between you and the ground but a long scream. The barrel rolls come naturally, and soon I'm laughing.

Things are getting better all the time.

# CHAPTER FIVE

Legion Tower is a landmark in New Port. Fifty floors high, a full ten to twenty floors taller than most of the buildings around it, it stands at the northern end of the downtown core of towers along the southeast shoreline of Puget Sound. The bottom floors are rented out as office space, but nobody really knows what they do with the top thirty. The tower is a throwback to the days of stone and steel, with its almost cathedralesque styling and art deco arches soaring to meet each other at the tower's apex. At the top a huge balcony protrudes from the building's east side, mirroring the one on the west. The balconies are large enough to land military helicopters, but the main thing to notice is their lack of guardrails. They're not meant for casual loitering. They're entryways for people who can fly. We zip around and between skyscrapers downtown and approach Legion Tower from the south, bank around, and come up on the east landing pad. As the lip of the balcony comes up fast I realize my speed is much higher than I thought. It's okay to land with your face, right?

The impact is jarring all the way down to the root of my spine. I go end over end for a good twenty feet, and skid to a stop spread-eagled on my back. A week ago, something like this would have splattered me all over the landing pad. Tonight, it rips the knee of my jeans, and that's about it.

"I'm okay," I say, getting to my feet. Valkyrja sets down gently next to me, and Carapace drops to the ground with a clank a little ways off. In front of a pair of double glass doors, a woman in a lab coat waits for us. Her dark hair is pulled back in a braid reaching most of the way down her back, and her steel-rimmed glasses are perfectly circular. Her cigarette tip flares, and then she says, "Welcome to Legion Tower. I'm Doc Impossible. You ever had a physical, kid?"

I've had two in the past week. "It's my new hobby."

Doc Impossible smiles, and blows a stream of smoke back over her shoulder. "We're going to get along fine. I'll see you two at the briefing," she says to Carapace and Valkyrja. They head one way and Doc Impossible beckons me to follow her in another.

She leads me to an elevator, which drops us deep into the building. Maybe I expected the elevator to be…I dunno, special? It doesn't feel like I'm really here. The elevator opens on a floor that appears to only have one small antechamber before another door, a massive sliding thing that clicks and thunks elaborately before it opens and closes. Doc Impossible stabs out her cigarette in an ashtray next to the door, fishes in her jacket's inner pocket for a piece of gum, and pops it in her mouth. She doesn't chew it; she just crimps it in her back teeth and holds it there. We pass through an airlock, where a field of golden light sweeps over us, up and down, forward and back. The panel above the door to the exit lights up with an anime-style happy face, and dings.

"Welcome to my lab," says Doc Impossible as the airlock's magnetic bolts thunk open, and a door like a vault opens in front of us. "We might be here a while. Lavatory's over there, but make sure you stand still for decon once you're done."

Doc Impossible's lab takes up this entire floor. The place is wall-to-wall hypertech, the superscience that brings us wonders from a thousand possible futures, devices that are decades or centuries beyond what baseline tech can manage. Nobody really knows what makes hypertech possible. What's obvious is that some people, most of whom don't show any indication whatsoever of being metahuman, seem to have a knack for the development and manufacture of technology far in advance of what's normally considered the state of the art. The only reason we're not all living in space stations orbiting a neutron star or something like that is because hypertech has—well, it has *problems.* The biggest is probably that it's amazingly hard to replicate, to the point where the government has officially given up trying to get mass production working. (Nobody believes them when they say that, though. The Pentagon uses as much hypertech as they can get their hands on, but it's all custom-made gear that's hard to replace.) At first, some hypertech developers tried to explain their work, but it never clicked with the mainstream. Experiments failed when universities tried to replicate them, functioning devices sometimes contradicted known laws of physics, et cetera, et cetera, and so now they're mainly a community unto themselves, studiously ignored by mainstream science, which tends to mutter and grumble every time the "speculative technology" is mentioned.

Every hypertech artifact has to be more or less handcrafted, often out of components which themselves require days or weeks of work. Reliability is a huge issue, too, since it's all buggier than a Louisiana swamp, and if you didn't make it yourself you probably won't know how to fix it. Safety can be an issue, as well. All those metahumans who get their powers in lab accidents? Guess what *kind* of lab they were working in. And not all lab accidents are happy ones. People have died in really horrible ways.

But that doesn't make it any less amazing to step into the future. Everywhere I look there is glass and steel, with displays and readouts projected against floor-to-ceiling windows. The floor glows softly white. You'd think it would feel sterile and maybe a little cold, but everything is colorful, inviting. The readouts are projected in vibrant colors, so this wall might be five shades of blue, but the room next to it is done up all in green. The air is just the right temperature, and somehow feels soft. Somewhere, there are speakers filtering ambient electronica through the air, gentle rising and falling tunes to comfort you even as you forget they're there.

"Holy crap."

"You like it? Took me ages to figure out what to do with all this space," says Doc Impossible. She's got her hands deep in her lab coat pockets as we walk down a hallway that is daffodil yellow on one side and watery blue on the other. We come to an intersection and encounter a robot that looks like a crash test dummy with a camera for a head, walking a pug. "Hey, make sure he gets it all out this time, okay?" says Doc Impossible. The robot nods at her and heads the way we came, the pug trotting alongside it.

"You built a robot to walk your dog?"

"No, I built it to test a new colloquial speech voice interface. Putting it on poop patrol was just a bonus. This way."

We take a turn down a hallway and pass a room where the windows have no projections. Inside are two rows of steel pedestals topped with cylindrical glass tanks. Each tank is filled with human brains floating in a soupy liquid, all run through with wires and tubes. Some of them have big chunks replaced with what looks like a bundle of spindly circuitry.

"What are those?" I ask.

"Donor brains. Carapace and I are working on a new kind of neurological prosthetic." Her face lights up as she speaks. "It's really cool stuff, actually; we're learning how to program nanomachines to turn neurons into synthetic replacements without interrupting the continuity of consciousness for the patient. Early applications will probably be things like new therapies for Alzheimer's or MS, but the possibilities are—"

A chirping noise sounds from a phone deep in one of her jacket pockets, and at the same time the lights under one of the brain tubes switch from white to yellow.

"Oh, damn!" says Doc Impossible. She throws open the lab door and sweeps inside. In half a moment she's got the casing to the yellow-lit tank's pedestal open and is kneeling, elbow deep inside the machine. "I told him! I fucking told him!"

I poke my head in the lab.

"What's going on?

"These damn Cerita links keep cutting out! The process requires a very steady, very *clean* power supply. I'd use a hypertech solution but Carapace talked me into using some off-the-shelf components. We're trying to—shit. Hold on. There." She looks up. "Hand me that voltmeter. It's the fat yellow phone-looking thing with the wires coming out of it."

There's a device like that sitting on a table just inside the door. I pick it up and hand it to her.

"Thank you," she says, tapping up some program on the machine's screen. "Anyhow, we're trying to generalize the technology to baseline tech so that someday it can run without hypertech. I think we should have just gotten the damn thing working first before we got ambitious. This brain right here, we're trying to convert it to one hundred percent synthetic and still retain its continuity profile. If we could do that, we could make a true neural prosthetic for almost any kind traumatic brain injury. Hell, maybe even immortality is—"

Something Doc Impossible said finally clicks over in my head. *Continuity of consciousness*, she said. A horrifying possibility occurs to me. "Wait, you mean these are *alive*?"

"Of course not," says Doc Impossible sharply. She looks up at me, her brow drawn in. "That would be horrible. These are all from dead people. The test data is still good, though."

"Oh. Um, sorry."

Her lips press thin, but then she shrugs. "Just because we're doing superscience doesn't mean we run without an ethics review board, kid." Doc Impossible closes the hatch and the lights under the brain-tank turn white again.

The medical examination lab is done up in soothing blues, and once we're inside Doc Impossible taps a button projected onto the glass. The room's walls become frosted and nearly opaque for privacy. There's an examination bed, some counters cluttered with papers and supplies, and a lot of exotic and high-tech equipment I don't think I've ever seen before.

"Okay, kid—ah, do you have something you want me to call you?"

"Danny."

"Okay, Danny. I've got eight doctorates and two of them are

medical, so it's nothing I haven't seen before, but I'm gonna need you to get naked here in a moment."

"Right. Uh. Why?"

"I told you: I've got to give you a physical."

"Why?"

"Ah. You see, this has never happened before. Three other people carried the mantle before you, and none of them—"

"Gotcha."

Doc Impossible turns her back, and so with trembling fingers and warming cheeks, I start pulling my shirt off.

"When you're indecent, step under that big tube over there." She gestures vaguely to one side.

I drop my clothes in a pile, and my underwear on top of that. There is a whoosh of air from around the lower edges of the wall, and suddenly the room is ten degrees warmer, and much more comfortable to be naked in. I step under the tube she indicated, a big thing of thick, curved glass that slides down from the ceiling to seal against the floor with a hiss. My ears pop. A bulky ring of steel studded with all sorts of what look to be projectors is set around the top. Doc Impossible is looking at a whole interface projected on the wall, including a simulated keyboard hologram floating in mid air. She taps a few buttons and the tube goes opaque.

"Thanks," I say.

"Don't worry about it," she says, her voice piped in through speakers I can't see. "This will take a few moments. Try to stand still, please."

A clunk, a thunk, and a deep, heavy thrum. The ring of sensors drops down to the floor, and I can see the wall going transparent wherever the sensors are looking in. The sensor ring pulses out thick bars of light. It travels up and down, washes every part of me in light. It feels like being in a flatbed scanner. An aperture opens in the chamber's ceiling, and a thin hose drops down.

"Please drink several deep swallows of this," says Doc Impossible.

"What is it?" I ask, and then start sucking on the tube hesitantly.

"Cherry soda," she says. I take a deep swallow. It's just the right level of cold and fizzy. "And also enough radioactive contrast dye to light you up like Chernobyl."

"*What?*"

"You're wearing the mantle of Dreadnought, Danny. You really think a little thing like cesium is going to hurt you? Now hold still for a moment, I want to watch what it does."

The sensor ring drops down again and scans my stomach intensively for a few moments. "Okay, now drink from the tube again."

Root beer this time.

"What's in that? Cyanide?"

"Naw. Strychnine."

"What could you *possibly* learn from that?"

"By itself? Not much. But it is *also* irradiated, and strychnine permeates the body's tissues very quickly. In your case that happens to be *all* it will do. I presume you want to be done with this before the sun gets up."

The tube retracts, and a small plastic baggie on a hook is lowered in its place. Inside the baggie is something that looks like a pill, except it's about half the size of a tube of chapstick. It's got rounded edges and seems to be coated in soft rubber. There is a small green LED on one side that is flashing on and off.

"What's this?"

"A suppository."

"No."

"Shove that up your butt."

"No."

"It's for science."

"No."

"Please?"

"You are going to buy me pizza."

"Deal."

"A *lot* of pizza."

• • •

The sensor ring locks into place above me, and the tube hisses open. Doc Impossible is facing away from me, sitting in a chair and consulting what look like full body X-rays of me projected in 3D against the glass.

"Good news. You're definitely not going to die of radiation poisoning. Because that would have happened already."

She pops her tab of gum out, tosses it in the trash, and slips another into her mouth.

"You're really tied to that nicotine, aren't you?" I say as I step into my pants.

"Yep," she says.

"That stuff will kill you, you know."

"Danny, I'm in the super science racket, and I'm not nonpartisan—uh, that means someone who doesn't take a side in our little fraternity of extraordinarily empowered social rejects." She circles a finger in the air to indicate the whole of Legion Tower. "If you pick a side, you're going to make enemies. If a lab accident doesn't get me, one of them will. I won't have *time* to get cancer."

I pull my shirt over my head. "Or maybe it just means you'll get like, *super* tumors, and they'll petition to be recognized as independent people."

Doc Impossible laughs, and flicks a glance over her shoulder to check if I'm dressed. "Yeah, and then they'll be my *mortal enemies*, but they're also the only ones who know who killed my father—"

"—yeah, and then they start going out at night—"

"—and doing their own experiments! So they—"

"—so they get all huge and *rargh!*" And I start pantomiming out some eldritch horror leaping out from my chest, claws hooked, teeth bared. Doc's out of her chair doing the same thing, and we're halfway through theorizing how the National Guard will get called in when the door opens and there's Carapace.

Doc Impossible and I freeze mid-pantomime-and-snarl.

"Have you prepared your briefing yet?" he asks.

"Ya mind?" says Impossible with narrowed eyes. "We're bonding."

"Just get your report ready on the…situation."

"Yeah, fine. Whatever," says Doc. She makes a shooing motion with her hands. After a long, awkward moment of staring at me, Carapace turns and clanks away. The door slides shut.

"Did I…do something?" I ask. Oh God, what if I messed this up already?

Doc Impossible seems to sag a little. "No. It's just… Dreadnought was really important to him. And, to tell you the truth, Carapace wasn't super excited to learn who'd gotten the mantle. I'm sorry. You really deserve more time to get used to this before you have to deal with that kind of thing. Capes in private are…"

"Weird?"

"That doesn't even begin to describe it." She gestures to a chair. "Have a seat. You know Darkfist?"

"Yeah, he's big news in Empire, right?" I say as I slide a chair over and sit in it.

"Yep. He's just a billionaire with a utility belt." Doc sits in her own chair. "His 'superpower' is being rich, okay? Not a single real power to his name. He doesn't even use hypertech."

That doesn't sound right at all. "Are you sure? The things I've heard—"

"Are the things that criminals tell each other to make themselves feel better about getting beaten up by a rich boy in fancy cosplay. I've met the dude, and I promise you he's as baseline as they come. What do you think convinces someone with that kind of money to patrol the streets at night, going hand to hand with thugs who have automatic weapons? Are you starting to see? He's someone we *choose* to hang out with."

"But…I do have superpowers," I say. "And I kinda want to help people."

"And that's normal! It totally is, and good for you! But did you see how Carapace was still wearing his armor? He *lives* here. This is his home. But he's still walking around ready to slug it out with a platoon of tanks. The whole whitecape thing isn't a real great way to spend a life. The normal thing to do with powers is to use them to get a job. You've seen aerial couriers downtown, right?"

"Of course." Every major city has a few people who can fly who make their living zipping time-sensitive materials from one end of the city to the other. Once you get ten feet in the air, there's no such thing as a traffic jam. Until now, I'd never really stopped to think about why they'd be doing that instead of fighting crime. It seems normal; they're just able to fly around town, right? It's like being really good with a bike, but a little cooler, is all.

"Right. Courier work is real popular with anybody who has a mobility power. High pay, short hours, and dead easy work that lets you spend most of your week doing whatever you want to do without worrying about money. A lot of fire departments will pay more than you'd think for people whose powers would help them with search-and-rescue work. Hell, one in a hundred of those guys doesn't even need to breathe. They don't do much to draw attention to themselves, but they're there. That's what a normal person who wants to help people with their power does: they join a government, or a nonprofit, or even just a company that's not evil."

"But those are just special abilities, right? Not real superpowers?"

"Eeehhh." Doc Impossible spreads her fingers out and waggles her hands from side to side. "That line between *special abilities* and superpowers is something the nonpartisans came up with. A lot of the nonpartisans even have abilities that, if used to their full extent, would be superpowers no matter how much they torture the definition. They don't want to be associated with us. Someone hears you have a superpower, and suddenly they don't want to date you, or hire you, or rent an apartment to you. Because everyone assumes superpowers mean you have super *enemies*, and who wants to be out at dinner with someone when a psychopath in a black cape shows up and starts melting people with a death ray? So all of the sudden it's, 'No, sir, I don't have a superpower, I just have a special ability.' It helps cut down on the jealousy, too."

There's a flutter of unease in my chest when she says this, because yeah, I went through some phases where I was *very* jealous of people with superpowers. But, strangely, *not* of people with "special abilities." Doc Impossible seems to read the thoughts flitting across my face and nods. "Yeah, you see how that works?" she says. "Look, I don't want to scare you away from being a whitecape if that's who you want to be. There's nothing like it in the world, and when it's good, it feels like you're a god. I wish I could spare you all the gruesome details until after you've gotten comfortable with your powers, but you're going to be making some decisions soon, sooner than I think you should have to. You deserve to do it with your eyes open."

"What kind of decisions?"

Doc Impossible sighs and leans back in her chair. "Dreadnought was very important to the status quo. It would mean a lot to us, and to the city, if you were willing to take his place once you're old enough. We've been real lucky that all the other people who have worn the mantle wanted to be whitecapes, but there's nothing that says you have to. You have zero obligations here, do you understand? This isn't like political power—you didn't fight for this; it was dropped in your lap. So all those great responsibilities that come with great power, those are only yours if you want them to be. It's not fair to demand more of you, and worse, it's not safe. This is a hard life. Someone as strong as you, if suffering from mental and emotional trauma, could quickly become dangerous. So a lot of people are going to want you to be a whitecape, but only you can decide if that's right for you."

"Maybe I could become a blackcape," I say with a smile.

Doc Impossible looks at me the way you'd look at someone across an open grave. "Don't *ever* joke about that, Danny."

"Sorry," I say quickly.

"It's okay, it's just…we've all lost people to them. They're the scum of the Earth, and don't let any graycape tell you differently.

In fact, don't hang out with graycapes; they're just capes who aren't *always* horrible."

"Right. I guess…well, being a cape—a whitecape, I mean— sounds like it would be pretty cool. It's not like I've never been scared before, so why not do it? Why not join when I'm old enough?"

Doc Impossible rolls her chair closer to me, and puts her hands on my knees. Her face is as open and sincere as I've ever seen on anyone. "First, please understand that I don't mean to talk down to you. Okay?"

"Okay."

"You're fifteen. Right now, you see the fights, and the excitement, and the power. And all of that is sexy as hell. I know, believe me, I know. But trust me, the world is not always going to look the same to you as it does now."

"I know—"

"*Listen to me!*" Her fingers dig into my knees a little more than I'd expect of merely human hands, and I lean away from her sudden vehemence. "Someday, you might get tired of needing to know where the nearest safe house is at all times. Someday, you might be sick of needing to take vacations in disguise. You might want to buy a house and be able to invite casual friends over and not lie to them about who you are. You might want to be able to make plans that don't involve being on call for combat duty for the rest of your life. You might fall in love with someone who *can't protect themselves* from the kind of people you're going to piss off if you put on a cape. You have a family now? They're going to have to go into a witness protection program if you start caping. They might to have to go underground if your identity is compromised. Do you understand? It means living under siege. We're not all roommates in this tower because we can't stand to be apart from each other. We live here because it's safe here. We go anywhere else in the world, except maybe to another team's HQ, and we have to be ready to throw down at a moment's notice. Once you choose this, it is really hard to walk it back. If your identity gets blown, it's basically impossible. They want you to make a decision that is going to change the rest of your life. It will narrow your world, and narrow your choices. You will do things nobody else can even dream of, but you'll never be able to do almost everything normal people take for granted. There is a reason, Danny, a really good reason that most of us are nonpartisan." Doc Impossible drops into silence. Her eyes plead for me to understand.

"I think I get it."

"Good. Good." She lets go of my knees and scoots back from me. Now that she's done speaking, she suddenly seems tired. Doc Impossible takes a moment to collect herself, and then puts on a smile. "Now, I found a few things in your physical you might be interested to know."

"Oh?"

"To start with, you're as fit as an entire Olympics team. Fitter, actually, than any individual athlete could hope to be. Nobody has enough hours in the day to train every part of themselves to the level you're at. You've got the cardiovascular system of a marathon runner, the flexibility of a gymnast, and the muscle tone of a swimmer. Your muscle density is off the charts; you weigh about a hundred and eighty pounds. Your strength and speed are beyond all human limits, of course, but even without them you're a better physical specimen than basically anyone else alive."

I smile. "Cool!"

"And here's the bad news: if you want kids, you're going to have to let me convert some of your blood into sperm and have someone else provide the egg and womb. You don't have a uterus. You'll never get pregnant."

I'm falling. I'm falling down, down into a deep pit. And at the bottom, there are flames. I'm up on my feet before I know what I'm doing. I kick back at the chair and it rockets across the room, gets embedded into a wall behind me. An enormous spiderweb of cracks slams out across the entire wall panel, which flickers and throws random, contorted image across its shattered segments. "Dammit!"

"What the hell, kid?" says Doc Impossible, rising.

"Sorry! Sorry! I…" I sigh. The bubbling cauldron of frustration is still there, even if it's not boiling over. "I guess I just thought that I was finally a real girl."

"Hey! None of that!" She takes me by the shoulders. "You think it's a uterus that makes a woman? Bullshit. You feel like you're a girl, you live it, it's part of you? Then you're a girl. That's the end of it, no quibbling. You're as real a girl as anyone. And you *really* need to learn to express your anger better."

"I'm sorry. Really. And, thanks." I close my eyes and take a breath. "How did you know that was bad news?"

Doc Impossible smiles gently. "This whole time, you haven't even once asked about being changed back. It's pretty obvious you're transgender, Danny." She taps my forehead. "If you were a boy up here, I think you would have mentioned it by now. The other Dreadnoughts reported that when they took the mantle, it changed their bodies into what they'd always wanted it to be. Some got a little taller, one grew back some lost toes, that sort of thing. But they were all cis—that is to say, they weren't trans—so their bodies didn't change to match their gender identities because they were already matching. *You*, on the other hand, became a very pretty young woman who, upon extremely close examination, can be seen to have a history of masculine dimorphism. *Real* close. Like chromosome-level close."

"Why not…you know, change it all?"

Doc Impossible shrugs. "I don't know. You're a sample size of one, so it's hard to draw any firm conclusions. If I had to say, I'd guess that the mantle can only do so much with what it has available to work with when the change happens. For instance, your testicles have migrated up into your abdomen and have been reconfigured to secrete estrogen and progesterone, but they don't have any eggs, and are anatomically recognizable as testes."

"Oh." Then it hits me. This "ideal" new body—the magazine cover perfection, the shampoo commercial hair, even the fashionable shape of my thighs—it's more than a different look. It's a window inside my head. "Oh. Gross."

"There's nothing wrong with being trans, Danny."

"No. I mean, why I look this way. Mom took me to a fancy bra store the other day, and there were posters everywhere of these women that, well, nobody looks like that in real life, right?"

"Except you, and a few genetic lottery winners."

"Yeah. So my ideal self—"

Doc Impossible chuckles. "Is a photoshopped underwear model, I see."

"I guess it sounds a little stupid to be upset over being pretty—"

"Yes! Yes it does. You think you're immune to advertisements? That'd be a hell of a superpower, but even if Dreadnought were immune to mind control—and he wasn't—you've spent your entire life swimming in the stuff." Doc Impossible turns back to the test results—at least the wall I broke wasn't one she was working on—and starts sliding files and images into a new folder with a few flicks of her fingers. "Don't beat yourself up over it. They'll find some way to make you unhappy with your body sooner or later, so until then, enjoy it. Keep it in perspective. I'm gonna be a few moments here, okay? There's a cup of what looks like orange juice in that fridge over there. Drink it and head on over to the lavatory marked with the nuclear radiation symbol, just outside the door and across the hall. You're going to want to purge those irradiated fluids from your body before you go home and contaminate your family."

The fridge is one of those minibar deals you get in hotels sometimes, or so I've been told. The drink actually does taste like orange juice, and it's a good thing the radiation toilet was so close because, well…

Look, that stuff cleared out my entire digestive tract in a few minutes. How do you *think* it went? Medicine, especially the hypertech kind, is gross.

"I don't think I want to use the toilet again for a week," I say, as I return to the medical lab on wobbly legs.

"It's all out of you? Good. Let's get you suited up."

"You *just* explained why I shouldn't be wearing a cape yet."

"You're a teenager with friggin' superpowers. You think we don't know you're going to experiment? We'd rather you do it in throwaway colors, a suit that won't signify a cape persona, but will protect your identity from anyone who sees you. Come on, you're going to love this."

She takes me to a different part of the lab, where the machinery is all hypertech 3D printers and clusters of robot arms like giant metal spiders curled up dead. I'm wearing a charcoal gray bodysuit, still warm and smelly from the fabricator. It's snug but flexible. Matching boots and gloves, with a separate cape that goes down to the back of my knees. The cape is longer in back, but also wraps around my chest like, well, like a mantle that covers my chest down past my collarbones. I experiment flexing my arms a little, trying not to be too obvious that I'm seeing how the cape would sit with my arms stretched out in front of me in the classic flight pose. It's actually pretty thin material, but slick and sort of heavy. It shouldn't bunch up, or get in the way of throwing a punch. I'm not super thrilled about the cowl. It feels constricting around my neck—not that it's hard to breathe or move, but it's there, and kinda bugging me. It's open at the top to let my hair grow out, and I'm touched that she included this traditionally female-gendered touch to a suit that otherwise seems to be patterned after Dreadnought's classic uniform.

"You like it?" asks Doc.

"Yeah. Yeah, it's cool. But…"

"The colors, I know." The suit doesn't have any markings or emblems, and the grays aren't solid but mottled with a kind of soft-focus camouflage pattern. "It's what we mean by throwaway colors. They'll make you basically invisible in the night sky, and it signals to other capes that you're not looking for a fight."

"What if someone decides they want a fight anyhow?"

"Don't give it to them," she says firmly. "Run here. They won't follow you inside the tower. You're always welcome here, Danny, okay?"

"Okay. Thanks."

"Cool." She turns and spits her nicotine gum into another little trashcan, pops a replacement in her mouth. Those things are supposed to last for longer than that, right? "Now, let's go get you introduced to the team proper."

"Ah. Okay. Right." A flare of giddy nervousness lights up my chest. I'm going to meet the entire Legion Pacifica. Like, tonight.

# CHAPTER SIX

The briefing room is surreal because it's exactly how I imagined it would be. The elevators here are mundane, and the hallways are normal, but then you turn the corner, and past some sliding doors there's a fifteen-foot-high holographic projection of the Earth, with glowing dotted lines tracking the orbital trajectories of at least five space stations and color-coded markers for important surface contacts. Off to the side, near a wall of floor-to-ceiling windows looking out over New Port's skyline, there's a conference table with smaller projections floating above it. All the chairs are softly lit by unobtrusive spotlights, and the table is gleaming glossy wood with holographic haptic sensor interfaces embedded in it at each seat.

Standing near the table is the most oddly dressed group of people you're ever likely to meet, the holy-crap-no-kidding Legion Pacifica. These people are so famous I recognize them by their silhouettes. Valkyrja is chatting with Magma, an enormous slab of muscle in the shape of a man, with his dark brown skin and bushy black beard, and his eyes glowing visibly even from over here. He normally fights wearing a kind of circus strongman getup, but in here he's content to wear a suit with his shirt collar unbuttoned and no tie. There's Graywytch; her dark robe's hood is up and she's facing away from me, but she's instantly recognizable by the raven that's always on her shoulder. She's standing apart with Carapace, their heads tilted toward each other in quiet conversation. Chlorophyll is half man, half plant, and wearing a tight T-shirt over his lithe green chest. He's reading a paperback book, which is such a normal thing to do that it's weird.

The glass doors slide shut behind Doc Impossible and me, and then we have a good half-minute walk across the briefing room to get to the conference table. A half minute is a long time to get self-conscious about wearing a friggin' glorified wetsuit indoors. Please, please, please tell me this cowl covers enough of my cheeks to hide the blushing.

"Yep, she's got superpowers all right," says Doc Impossible by way of greeting as we arrive. "I told you the physical was a boring idea."

"We needed to know what happened," says Carapace, stepping away from Graywytch. "In any case, we'd like to hear your report formally."

"We'd also like to meet the young lady," says Magma in a surprisingly rich and urbane voice. In most of the video I've seen of him he's roaring like fire and brimstone and smacking blackcapes into the ground.

"Sure," says Doc Impossible. She gestures for me to step forward, and I do, feeling like I'm someone else watching from the far distance. In the elevator, Doc Impossible asked me how I wanted to be introduced like it was no big deal. She's good like that. "Ladies and gentlemen, may I introduce Danielle Tozer, carrier of the mantle."

"*Daniel* Tozer," says Graywytch. She's looking at me like I'm an interloper. Her face is pale, heavy black eyeshadow standing out against almost white skin. Her dark hair hangs lank against her forehead. The raven on her shoulder tilts its head sideways and eyeballs me.

"Myra, can you at least try to be pleasant?" says Doc Impossible.

"You can call me Danny, if it's easier," I say, almost on reflex. Crap. Why did I say that? Impossible was standing up for me and it felt good to hear someone use my girl name, my *real* name, and then I just—ugh. I am such an idiot.

That all passes through my head between one heartbeat and the next.

"Pleased to meet you, Danny," says Magma, stepping forward

and offering me his hand. Mine disappears into his when we shake. "I'm Magma."

"I know," I say, again on reflex. Jesus Christ, what is *wrong* with me? But he smiles and nods, and I feel a little better.

Valkyrja steps forward and bows to me.

"Uh, hi. We already met," my mouth says before I can stop it. Someone, please. Stop me before I kill my dignity again.

"Not formally. Well met, young champion." Okay, I'm going to be honest: I've had a crush on Valkyrja since about the time I discovered boobs are a thing that exist, but this whole ye-olde-tymey talk is way clunky in everyday conversation and it's kind of weirding me out.

And with that, I suddenly feel okay. Because I'm not the only freak in here. I smile and bow back to Valkyrja, and she nods solemnly.

Chlorophyll shakes my hand. His skin is cool and a little moist. "Hello. I'm Chlorophyll. It's always nice to meet another queer with powers." My stomach lurches. Oh yeah. I'm gay now. It'd never occurred to me. Now I'm wondering how obvious my crush on Valkyrja is. "It's nice to see some trans representation in the community."

"Ah, so, uh…" I kind of trail off lamely. For some stupid reason, I'd thought Doc's examination would be the end of it, and my transition wouldn't be up for discussion anymore.

"We *all* know," says Graywytch, who hasn't made a move toward introducing herself. I mean, not that she needs to, but still. "Your little 'transition' was caught on video." The way she says that puts me on guard.

"What?" I snap a look over at Doc Impossible.

"That's how we found you—but don't worry," she says. "We got to the video before anyone else did. Our copy is the only copy in the world."

"Can you delete it?" I ask. "That was private."

"It happened in public," says Graywytch.

"I didn't get to choose where," I mutter. Dad's in my head

telling me I shouldn't be such a pussy and should speak up when I'm talking. I wish he'd shut up.

"Uh, we'll look into that, Danny," says Doc Impossible with a glance at Carapace. "But for now we need it for the investigation. I promise you, the video isn't going anywhere."

"Why don't we take our seats?" says Magma, gesturing toward the conference table.

The chairs are the really expensive kind, with a whole rack of knobs and levers on the side and soft leather covering deep, inviting cushions.

"Dan—Danny, we need to discuss some things with you," says Carapace after we're all seated.

"Okay."

"First, you'll see on that tablet in front of you that there are two books we'd like you to read. One is an ethics manual for handling Dreadnought's—uh, your new powers." That nervousness from earlier is coming back. It's kind of amazing how clearly it's being transmitted, even though his voice is mechanically filtered and he's wearing power armor. I pick up the tablet—it's an off-brand knockoff, which is disappointing, somehow—and see two files prominently displayed on the home screen. "The other is a guide for young metahumans, which you may wish to read."

"Okay. You said I was going to get a provisional membership?"

Carapace looks at Graywytch, and she leans in. "That is still in consideration."

"You'll have to agree to abide by certain rules," says Carapace. "Nothing onerous, but we're serious about them."

"Okay. So what are they?"

"First, you must keep your powers secret as much as possible. This is to protect yourself, and the people around you." I nod. That seems reasonable, especially after what Doc Impossible told me in the lab. He continues, "If you are going to experiment with your powers, you will do it while wearing your suit. Get into the habit of not using your powers when you're in civilian clothes. You never know when you're on camera. Fly only at night, with at least one hundred feet between you and the ground except for takeoffs and landings."

"Okay."

"And of course, don't commit any crimes. Don't harass anyone. Don't destroy private or public property. Avoid television crews and reporters. Don't interfere with the emergency services. Don't accept any payments for the use of your powers. If you have serious financial need, we can cover it within reason, so don't feel pressured to make money. This is all in that guide, along with detailed explanations should you wish to know the reasoning behind the rules. Most importantly, no caping. That means no investigations, no foiling bank robberies, no looking for trouble, all right? You don't have the training or the experience for that, and if you rush in without thinking you might make things worse than they were before you arrived."

I open the handbook file and scroll down to the big list of rules. There's a lot of Don'ts in it. "Okay," I say as I flick through it.

"Excellent," says Magma. "Now, on a more serious topic." He glances over at Carapace.

Carapace is silent for a moment, and then says, "We need to talk about Dreadnought's murder."

My stomach flips. Of course. It's still not something I like to think about; the best thing that ever happened to me came out of someone else—someone important, someone almost universally loved—getting killed.

"Right. So, uh. What do you want to know?"

Above the table, a trio of flat holograms appears, three video screens showing grainy security cam footage of the fall of Dreadnought. The recording is jerky, the frame advancing only once or twice a second.

"The video enlightens us not as to the method of his demise," says Valkyrja. She says *video* like it's the name of an eldritch anomaly. "His murderer, Utopia, is but a minor power, and young. We have little information on her. Nor do we know the masked girl with pistols twin."

"Oh, that's Calamity," I say. "She's a vigilante."

"You know her?" asks Doc Impossible.

"No. We only talked the one time."

"Start from the beginning," says Carapace. "What were you doing behind the mall?"

"I was, uh, painting my toenails."

"Oh!" says Carapace, shifting in his seat. "And this was even before your…empowerment."

"Well, yeah. I've always been a girl." I shrug. "That's the way I could express it."

Graywytch snorts, like at a bad joke. My little flicker of unease about her grows.

Carapace clears his throat, a sound like steel wool being dragged over cast iron. "Let's move on to when Dreadnought fell next to you."

"Why didn't you run?" asks Magma. "You had no obligation to act."

"Because he was hurt?" I say, confused. Isn't it obvious why I did it? But my answer seems to confirm something for Magma, and he glances over at Valkyrja. She nods slightly.

"Did he bid you to flee?"

"Yes."

"Yet you did not."

"Yes." My voice seems to be getting quieter with each answer. I hope these are the right answers. I'm screwing it all up. Just like I should have known I would.

"Why?"

"I wanted to help him."

"You have a champion's heart, Danielle Tozer," says Valkyrja, and I try not to sag too obviously with relief. A moment later a sunny glow blooms in my chest. Valkyrja gave me a compliment. Awesome.

"Did he say anything to you?" asks Carapace.

"Yes. He said it was Utopia, and she had some kind of weapon. He had a hole right through his chest—"

"We've seen the body," says Carapace.

"Right." My cheeks get warm all over again. Of course they have. Dad's right. I am an idiot. "Sorry."

More questions. We start going through that day step by step. Was I able to see anything about Utopia? Did Dreadnought have any particular last words he wanted to pass along? I tell them about hearing Dreadnought fall, about trying to move him under cover, and giving him water. As the video advances, they pause it and ask me questions about particular points. Little things, things that don't make sense to me, like did I smell anything unusual. Then it happens. Dreadnought is hidden behind some concrete, and I am barely in view. There's a flash of light, and then I collapse. My body glows for a moment, a much longer moment than I remember.

"I didn't realize it took so long," I say.

"That's something that struck me as unusual," says Doc Impossible. "Granted, we only have a single other mantle transfer on film, and a sample size of two isn't much to go on, but your transformation took a *lot* longer than your predecessor's did. I think it has something to do with how dramatic the changes were for you compared to him."

She starts the video again. On the holographic screen, I'm coming to, and a moment later jerk back from him in alarm. My throat clenches up watching this. Again, I am profoundly thankful to him, for this beautiful, wonderful, amazing gift he gave me.

We get to the part in the video where Calamity makes her appearance. While I'm staring down at myself in shock, she's creeping along the mall's side. She's got her pistols out and her mask up when she comes into frame. I'm sitting there, waiting for the police to show with my head in my hands, oblivious to the world. I see for the first time that when she stepped around the corner she had both of her guns pointed at my head.

"We looked at all the other security footage from the mall that day," says Carapace. "She doesn't appear in as much of it as we expected. She knows where all the blind spots are, it seems. What can you tell us about her?"

I try to reach back to that day, but honestly, the memories are hazier than I expected. The big neon exclamation point on that part of my life is getting my new body. Everything else seems fuzzy and unimportant next to that. "Um, she's my age, I think. Extremely athletic. She hadn't heard of Utopia, and was surprised someone she hadn't heard of could kill Dreadnought."

"Why did you leave with her?" asks Chlorophyll.

"She said if the cops showed up they'd make me testify against Utopia. I was scared what would happen if I did that."

"And you believed her?" asks Graywytch.

"She…seemed to know what she was talking about," I mutter lamely.

"Your credulity delayed our investigation," says Graywytch. "This is the first we're hearing about a new weapon."

"It matters not," says Valkyrja. "A minor delay will not keep her from us."

"It may cost lives," says Graywytch.

"Danny isn't responsible for what Utopia does," says Doc Impossible.

"What a friendly and convenient world you live in, Doctor."

"Everyone makes mistakes," says Magma. "There's no reason to dwell on this one."

"Agreed. Unless there are any more questions, let's move on," says Carapace. "We're going to need to start thinking about what your supranym will be."

"Uh, aren't I Dreadnought?"

"Not yet," Doc Impossible says at the same time as Carapace says, "No, that's not for you." They look at each other sharply.

"I can't see why she wouldn't be, *if* she chose to be a cape," says Doc Impossible.

"I don't think that's appropriate," Carapace says.

"Why not?" says Magma. "All her predecessors took the name along with the mantle."

"But isn't this…?" Carapace leans forward, hand out like he's trying to reach some common ground. "It's different, right?"

"How?" asks Valkyrja, with ice like a Viking's nightmare in her tone.

"Well...the circumstances of his empowerment are...unusual."

"Her," I say, and everyone looks at me, like they'd forgotten I was here already.

"That's in dispute," says Graywytch primly. "You were raised to be a man. Your privilege blinds you, and makes you dangerous."

"I'm just as much a girl as you are."

"Oh really?" She leans forward, steeples her fingers. "Do you even know how to put in a tampon?"

"Go to hell," snaps Doc Impossible.

"That's hardly called for," says Graywytch.

"This is fu—" Doc Impossible stops short, glances at me, and continues. "Nonsense, and you know it."

Absurdly, I want to remind her I go to high school. We cuss in high school.

"Your own medical examination proved he has a Y chromosome; he's even got a mutant pair of testicles!" says Graywytch, tapping a screen in front of her. "How is that not male?"

"Genetics aren't destiny," snaps Impossible.

"We're being sidetracked," says Chlorophyll. "Whether Danny is a boy or a girl isn't the issue. What we really need to be talking about is getting Danny ready to take Dreadnought's place, no matter what name we settle on."

"*We* settle on? It's her choice," says Magma.

"It is the way of things," says Valkyrja, nodding.

"There are extenuating circumstances that must be considered," says Carapace.

"Wait, hold on, she's fifteen!" says Doc Impossible. "We all agreed after Blackfish died that we only accept adults. We shouldn't even have this conversation for another three years."

"Sure, sure, but that's no reason not to be making plans," says Chlorophyll. "With the name, without the name, it doesn't matter. We need that powerset in our deck in case we encounter a Mistress Malice–level threat. Not to mention the funding we stand to lose without him. Dreadnought could justify a budget we won't be able to match without him." Oh. So that's what he wants. Thank you, Mr. Queer Solidarity.

"My fortune is vast. I will make good the shortfall, if and when necessity should compel me," says Valkyrja.

"That wouldn't be fair," says Chlorophyll. "You might as well announce you'll be voting twice from now on."

Valkyrja's wings pull in tight against her back, and she replies in clipped tones. "You already enjoy my coin. Does it sway your vote? This tower was but a dream before I—"

"That's apples and oranges, the tower is held in trust!"

"Danny, don't listen to him," says Doc Impossible. "We'll get along without you if we need—"

"No. Chlorophyll is right," says Graywytch, and a few people look at her in surprise. I'm getting the feeling these debates have expected factions, and she's crossing party lines. "The mantle is too powerful to be left to waste. Perhaps a more suitable host can be found."

All eyes drop on me like lead weights. My voice is small when I speak. "Doctor, would my transition stay in place if I gave up the mantle?"

"I…I don't know."

"Then I'm keeping it."

"As you should!" says Magma. He turns to Graywytch. "We've never set that precedent, and we're not going to start now."

"What makes him worthy?" she says. "Dreadnought was dying, he had no choice in the matter, no other options."

"That makes this different than how the last three people got the mantle in what way, exactly?" Magma opens his palms questioningly. "It's always been luck of the draw."

"Maybe that should change. You heard him yourself; he only wants to keep it to be sure of being able to continue perpetrating this masquerade of his."

"That's not what I said!" I say.

"It's what you *meant*," she says with poison syrup in her voice.

"Her meaning was quite plain to me," says Valkyrja. "You twist her words."

"Really, what is bothering you?" says Magma.

There's more, but I don't hear it. I'm falling away inside, to the place I sometimes go when it's too loud at home. This isn't how it was supposed to go. Isn't it enough to tell them I'm a girl? What does it really matter what my chromosomes are?

"Uh, maybe—maybe that's enough, Graywytch," Carapace is saying when I come back. He sounds uncomfortable, like if he could tug on the collar of his armor, he would do it. "Your...position is noted."

She stares at him, almost scary intense.

"You can take your provisional membership and shove it," I say, standing up. It's a bit sad these chairs have silent wheels because I would have really loved to scrape some chair legs over the ground just now. "But I'm keeping the suit. And I'm keeping the mantle."

"That is not your decision to make, young man," says Graywytch.

"Then come take it!" I shout at her. A few of them are taken aback. I don't think they're used to being threatened by kids, but I can see the realization sinking into them: they *can't* steal this from me. I'm sure fighting them would be way harder than I expect, but I have the powers of *freaking Dreadnought*, and even if they won, nobody knows how the mantle transfer works. "That's what I thought."

My guts are twisted in knots. My face is burning. I feel like a sodden, icy blanket is trying to press me into the floor. But dammit, I'm going to walk out of here with my back straight and my shoulders square.

Doc Impossible says something to Graywytch that sounds like it rhymes with *sure a ducking bunt* and there's an explosion of yelling back at the table. I don't stop to listen.

# CHAPTER SEVEN

The wind pulls at my cape as I stand at the edge of the landing balcony at the top of Legion Tower. Below me, city lights are like fireflies trapped in canyons of black ice. My heart is slamming in my chest and I'm shaking with rage. I can admit it to myself now: I wanted to join them more than anything. It was a desire I barely let myself daydream about. It felt presumptuous, arrogant.

But now it just seems naive. Nobody is who they look like on TV.

They want Dreadnought, all right. But they don't want a tranny.

Nobody does.

The door opens, and I hear footsteps cross the landing to me. "Danny, I'm so sorry," says Doc Impossible.

"Save it."

"I didn't—that was as much a surprise to me as it was to you."

"I don't know those people." I turn and glare, and it's a good thing I can't kill with a look or she'd be a smoking crater. "You do."

"Graywytch sprung that on me." Doc Impossible fiddles with her cigarette, an anxious *flick, flick, flick* between drags. "I knew she was old school, but I didn't think she'd go all MichFest on you."

"So you just sent her my medical file?" I shout at her. "Isn't that supposed to be private? You don't even know if she hates trans people or not and you tell her what chromosomes I have?"

Doc Impossible looks sick. "I'm sorry. That was a mistake. I—"

"*Why?* Why did you do that?"

"We needed to be sure the mantle hadn't been damaged. That

it wasn't malfunctioning. Showing them it was working the same way it always had—by making you your ideal self—seemed the best way to do that. And to explain that, it seemed necessary to tell them you were trans."

"Thanks a lot. Really. That makes it feel *so* much better."

"I'm sorry. I am. Really. I brought you your street clothes and phone. I put the handbooks on it, and my phone number, too." She holds a satchel out for me. I sigh and take it.

"Thanks. I don't think I'm going to be coming back here."

"Look, at least keep the provisional membership. It doesn't cost you anything, and Valkyrja and Magma really like you. I do too." An hour ago, hearing that Valkyrja liked me and wanted me on her team would probably have sent me to the moon. Right now, it feels like one of those stubby little trophies they give to the losing team in grade school soccer. "And Carapace is a good guy; he'll come around when he gets to know you."

"Carapace will come around when I agree not to pollute the memory of his friend." I make sure the satchel is strapped securely closed and slip it around my chest. "Wouldn't do to let an icky trans chick stand shoulder-to-shoulder with the great ones."

"He just needs time."

"And I needed to know I could trust you. All of you."

I step off the balcony's edge and fall.

• • •

I fly. It's easier to get home than it was to reach Legion Tower. After I stash my clothes in my room I consider trying to sleep, but my head is whirling. It feels like it's been weeks since I left. The clock says it's been about eighty minutes.

My cape snaps as I leave again, boosting for altitude. Below me the lights of my street drop away like candles off a cliff. The rage comes back, hot and thick, and I'm screaming. I'm screaming like I never have before. My voice echoes in the night air, reflects my fury back at me. It is a girl's rage, and it is *right*. It is *necessary*.

The clouds are low and glowing orange with reflected city lights. I punch through them, up into the hard clear night beyond. The temperature is dropping quickly, and I nose over, fly for open water. I reach for more power, more speed, and the mantle answers me. My power surges—and it is *my* power—until the wind tears at me with feeble fingers, until it seems the world itself is scared of me, begging me to stop. I will never stop. I will never give this up. I will never be what they want me to be.

The rumbling pressure builds at my forehead, pushes down around my shoulders, hangs for a moment, and then explodes in a cloud of vapor. I pass through to the other side of the sound barrier, to a world of silence and pressure. My screams slip away from me, gone before they reach my ears. It seems to bottle the fury. Bottle it, compress it, make it burn hotter and brighter.

Fifteen years trapped. Seven of those, aware of my prison and screaming inside.

The shelter of boyhood ended, and they called me a young man. For no reason at all, they looked at the things that felt right to me, and they *took* them. Even down to the way I carry my books and cross my legs. They took it. They took everything. Puberty came, and my body turned on me, too. Watching every part of myself I liked rot away one day at a time, the horrified impostor staring back at me. Watching the other girls, the ones they let *be* girls, head in the other direction. Every day, torn away further from myself, chained down tighter. Suffocated. Strangled.

They'll make a man of me. Show me how to be a man. Teach me to man up by beating me down.

THEY NEVER ASK IF I WANT TO BE A MAN.

And now I'm finally free. I'm finally myself, inside and out.

So they spit on me. They're embarrassed by me. They hate me.

FOR A MISTAKE THAT *THEY* MADE.

They want me to cooperate in my own destruction. They want me to tell them it's not true. They want me to help them believe the lie.

NEVER AGAIN.

I tip over, and shoot back down through the clouds. Five seconds later the ocean slams into me like a cement wall. The water is cold, and grips me tighter and tighter still as I go down. The black is absolute. The water wants to crush me like a soda can, but it can't. The pressure breaks itself against me. My ribs should shatter. My lungs should collapse. I hold. Effortlessly.

The sea floor rises to greet me, and though I can't see anything, I know it's there. I can trace the tangles in the lattice spreading out beneath me, a rolling smooth floor all the way out to the continental shelf. The mud is soft against my boots when I touch down. I can hear for miles. Whales call. Dolphins click. Schools of fish swirl and bloom.

Down here, in the heavy cold, there is peace. This scalding outrage cools and hardens to something stronger than diamond, and infinitely more precious. Resolve.

The water bursts and leaps after me when I leave it, a white geyser a hundred feet tall. I push for speed. Higher and faster, until the seawater that's left on me freezes and cracks away. Up, past the clouds and the birds, past the jets and the atmosphere. I let go of the speed and coast, floating so high the planet curves away from me in all directions. Earth is gauzy blue at the edges. There are lightning storms in Canada, and wildfires in Mexico. All of humanity is pinpricks of light beneath me. The silence up here is perfect. I can see forever.

And I see.

I see a world that is terrified of me. Terrified of someone who would reject manhood. Terrified of a girl who knows who she is and what she's capable of. They are small, and they are weak, and they will not hurt me ever again.

My name is Danielle Tozer. I am a girl.

No one is strong enough to take that from me anymore.

# CHAPTER EIGHT

**Minovsky_Particle has signed on.**
**Minovsky_Particle:** David, are you there?
**CombatW0mbat:** yeah. still sick?
**Minovsky_Particle:** Nope. I'm coming to school tomorrow.

• • •

Leaving through the front door is an invitation to a fight. Dad says I can't go back to school until they've figured out how to "fix" me, but it's been a week since it happened and I'm falling behind in my classes. It takes a long time to get in to see an endocrinologist, and the truth is even if we started testosterone injections tomorrow, it would take months for the effects to show. If Dad has his way, I'll be repeating sophomore year. After last night at Legion Tower I'm finished being a good little girl who does what she's told, so I'm going to school and showing people who I am. They can deal with it, or not. I don't care anymore. Whatever happens, David will have my back. It's been too long since we hung out already.

I slip out my bedroom window, close it behind me, and drop silently to the ground. The gate in our cramped back yard—really more like a pad of cement where we've got a small table—opens onto an alleyway, and I follow that down to the street and then toward the bus stop. I pass up my normal stop and wait at the next one. It's not like Dad could really stop me anymore, but it just seems better to avoid the fight until I've already done it. A *fait accompli*, it's called, an accomplished fact. Do it fast without their permission, and then there's nothing they can do to change it back. More and more, I'm starting to think that's the way to live. He's going to scream at me for sure over this, probably as bad as he ever has, but that doesn't matter anymore. I've got superpowers.

A few kids are already at this stop. I stand apart from the group, and try to smile in a normal, friendly way when a few of them look over with questions on their faces. There's the bus. A family of nervous centipedes is crawling around my guts. I clench a fist to steady myself. I can do this. I'm invincible.

The other kids file onto the bus, and I'm last in. There is something terribly fascinating about the floor between the seats, or at least there must be, because that's all I'm staring at until I find an open seat and sit down. But nobody says anything. Nobody points and laughs. As far as I can tell, I'm just the new girl to them.

The new girl. Yes.

We pull away from the curb and I watch the world slip by through the windows. Everything looks brighter, and better. I'm smiling like it's my job. I send a text to David: meet me at the normal spot.

Awesome, he texts back. Can't wait to see you.

• • •

The bus pulls in at my school, and we file off and toward our classes. The centipedes in my stomach have joined the circus and are doing a trapeze act. There's the spot where David and I always meet up, against the front wall of the school, right under the tarnished metal letters that spell out KENNEDY HIGH SCHOOL. It's a nice spring day, the sky pale and crisp. A dozen different ways this could play out are running through my mind, no matter how much I try not to think of them. The hard part is going to be holding back from blurting out that I have superpowers right away. We need to get somewhere private first, so I can prove it. Screw what the Legion says; clearly they *don't* understand what's good for me after all.

It's almost time to go inside. I'm checking my phone for the third time when I hear him say, "Hey, are you waiting for someone?"

David is taller than I remembered—no, I'm shorter. He's got short brown hair, glasses, a soft stomach, and big arms. When I smile at him, he blushes. He also can't stop scanning his eyes up and down my body. Well, I suppose that was inevitable. No biggie, as long as he knocks it off soon.

"Hi, David."

"Do I know you?" he says. I can see the gears turning. He's recognized me, but he's not letting himself believe it. "Are you waiting for Danny too?"

"I *am* Danny. This is why my dad was keeping me home."

David laughs. "No way, no. You're like his cousin or something, right?"

"My cousins live in Empire City, and they're all boys." As far as I know, anyhow. I suppose one or more of them could be trans, too. "There was…an accident, I guess you could call it?"

"You got turned into a girl?" he says. No, he yelps it.

The bell rings, and some people are looking over at us.

"Come on," I say, grabbing him by the arm and steering him toward a side door. "I don't want a crowd just yet."

"H—how the hell did this happen?" he whispers.

"A supervillain did it," I say, dropping his arm. "Dad wants to find a way to turn me back." We push through the side door and head to our lockers. David gets more than a few dirty looks from bumping into people in the crowd as his eyes are fixed on me.

"Um." David sort of gropes around for words, finally settling on, "Does he have to?"

A laugh is almost out of me when I notice he's staring at me, I mean really gawping. We go way back, and it's a big adjustment, so I brush it off. "No, and he can't make me. I'm going to stay a girl."

He blushes. "Oh, uh. All right. That's…yeah, great."

We get to our lockers, and I spin the combination into my lock. They're cramped half lockers, little better than what we had in middle school. I shove my bag in, take the books I'll need until lunch, and I clasp them in front of my chest, in the distinctly feminine hold that was slapped out of me as a child. It feels right. It feels necessary.

David hasn't opened his locker. He's just standing there, staring at me. Or rather, at my chest.

It is suddenly obvious to me why some girls hold their books this way. Oh Jesus.

"You're going to get a tardy slip," I say, and turn to head for homeroom, my cheeks blooming.

"You're really hot!" he blurts.

My shoulders hitch up, and I turn back. "Uh, thanks?"

His face is scarlet now. He laughs nervously, and I get to homeroom as fast as I can without flying. It's normal though, right? I mean, as normal as any of this can get. I look a certain way, and he's just getting used to that. David likes flirting. He'll get it out of his system, and then it'll be fine.

· · ·

"Townsend, Beverly." Mr. Macker is real formal about roll call. Last name, first. Sound off, soldier.

"Here," says Beverly.

"And Danny's still out, so—"

"I'm here," I say, raising my hand.

Every head swivels towards me. Inside my shoes, I'm clenching and unclenching my toes, but my face is solid, impassive. I'm invincible. I can do this. Last night I went from the bottom of the sea to orbit. I can handle high school.

"Young lady, I do not appreciate pranks in my class. What is your name?"

"Danielle Tozer. I've been in your homeroom all year long."

Mr. Macker scowls. It occurs to me that he might not recognize me; he's one of those teachers who spends all his time staring at his notes, ignoring his students as much as he can. "Your commitment to this prank is impressive, however—"

"*Danny?*" says Lisa, who sits next to me. Her face is pale.

"Hi, Lisa."

Someone cusses loudly, and that seems to break the spell. Everyone is standing up to get a better look at me. My cheeks are warm, but I stare straight forward, and try to keep a neutral smile on my face. This had to happen sooner or later; just like with David, I only need to ride it out.

"All right, that's enough!" shouts Mr. Macker, and eventually he wrests back control of the class. He's gripping his lectern quite hard. "Danny, if that's who you really are, I'm going to need a note from your parents explaining this."

There's a general ripple of laughter. Of *course* that's what he wants. Notes from parents make everything better. Why, if a girl can show up and report for class without a note to explain what she's doing, next we'll have anarchy. Where does it stop? *Soon they'll be dancing!*

"Sure thing, Mr. Macker," I say. I feel like I'm on top of the world, and just for a moment contemplate literally going back up there between classes.

But then it happens again in first period and it's not as fun. Second period is the same thing, and now it's actually getting annoying. What started as something that was almost an affirmation (*everyone is noticing I'm a girl!*) has now become tedious (*and now they won't get over it!*). When a runner from the office comes to fetch me out of third period, I'm almost grateful. I sit next to David in this class and he hasn't stopped staring at me. Getting yanked is a relief. This feeling lasts for about as long as it takes me to get to the office and see Mom waiting for me there.

Well.

Crap.

In a way, it would almost be easier if it were Dad. He would be deadly calm while we were still in the office, and then once we were in the car—BOOM. The detonation would be fast, and hard, and he'd scream himself hoarse at me. I'd know how to brace up for it, how to avoid making it worse.

But Mom isn't like him. What she does is almost worse. The moment I stick my head in the door, she's rising from one of the cheap chairs in a little waiting space in front of the big main desk where the school secretary sits.

"Danny, we have to go," she says.

"I have class."

"I'll pick your homework up from your teachers." She's already moving toward the door, moving to push me back out of the office. "We need to leave."

Everything about her is calm, serene almost, but there's something off. Nobody but me would notice how different she is right now. If she were Dad, I like to think I'd just shout back, that after last night, after the promise I made myself at the top of the atmosphere, that he wouldn't have that power over me anymore. But I'm not ready to deal with Mom.

She steps close and speaks quietly. "We talked about this. You're not going to school until your treatment begins."

"I don't need treatments," I say, but somehow we're already in the hallway. She's got me in her orbit and I'm just following her along.

• • •

She pulls out of the parking lot a lot faster than she normally does. It takes a few blocks in our beat-up old sedan before she slows to a more normal pace.

"Danny, you shouldn't have done this," she says, in that savage whisper she uses sometimes. "If your father finds out, he'll be very upset."

If? She's going to lie to him. She'll pressure me to keep quiet, too.

After a moment I realize we're headed the wrong way to go home.

"Where are we going?"

"The mall. You need some new clothes." With a start, I realize she's bribing me, and worse, this isn't the first time. It's a ritual with us. But now something in me has changed, made it seem wrong all of a sudden. I open my mouth to say something, and then stop. The sunlight catches her cheek, and for the first time I see the whole person. Maybe it's because your mother is always Mom to you, or maybe it's because I was in denial, but finally it hits me: Mom is just as much his captive as I am. She's not just the quieter parent, the more reasonable one. She's the trustee trapped between the warden and the other prisoner.

Immediately upon the heels of this understanding is another: I must not say this out loud. To say it out loud is to name it, and to name it is to give it irresistible power. That power will mean it can no longer be ignored. The polite fictions and convenient blind spots won't work anymore. Something will have to change. And I know, with a certainty that fills me with dread, this is something she will not do. If I say the name of this thing he's done to her, she will fight me. She will join him, because she'll have to. Because she'll have to destroy me or else admit I was right…

And then.

Dot.

Dot.

Dot.

And then somehow, it gets worse.

"Mom, I can't stay locked up forever."

"You're not going to. This is just for now." Her voice is soft and reasonable, but she doesn't deny they're hiding me.

"It's not going to go away."

"We'll deal with that when it comes to it," she says, and I know this means we won't deal with it until it can't be avoided any longer. Which, given how practiced we are as a family in avoiding things, could mean more or less forever.

"Everyone at school already knows."

Her knuckles are white on the steering wheel. "He won't ask them," she says, almost to herself.

Feeling sick, and alone, and very, very young, I let her drive me to the mall. There's a thrift store there, and she buys me some jeans. It goes without saying I am never to wear them around the house.

# CHAPTER NINE

**Minovsky_Particle has signed on.**

**CombatW0mbat:** dude where did u go?

**Minovsky_Particle:** mom came and picked me up. She doesn't want me coming to school.

**CombatW0mbat:** Oh man, that sucks. is your dad pissed?

**Minovsky_Particle:** what the hell does that mean?

**CombatW0mbat:** nothing. just hope your not grounded or anything.

**Minovsky_Particle:** ok. No, I'm not grounded. Yet.

**CombatW0mbat:** this whole thing is just so weird. Everyone has been asking me about it.

**Minovsky_Particle:** oh?

**CombatW0mbat:** you turned into a frikkin GIRL Danny! People are freaked out.

**Minovsky_Particle:** I guess they'll just have to get used to it

**CombatW0mbat:** as cute as you are, that shouldn't be a problem.

**Minovsky_Particle:** lol uh, thanks

**CombatW0mbat:** when are they going to let you come back?

**Minovsky_Particle:** i don't know

• • •

The next day I decide to go back to school again. Mom might try to pull me out, might be really mad this time, but I can't let that stop me. They have to know I won't be shut away anymore. I won't live in shame anymore. Truth is, I'm scared to think what will happen when Dad inevitably finds out. Yesterday I felt invincible, but Mom's quiet little freakout has me rattled. It'll be bad, I know it will. But I'm stronger now. I'll be okay. Sooner or later, he's going to have to accept the fact that I'm not his son. I'm his daughter. He'll yell and scream and pitch a fit that might last for days or weeks. I don't look forward to it. But I have to believe this can work. And really, how bad could it get? He hasn't hit me since he stopped spanking me as a little kid, and if he tries now, he'll probably break his hand. I can endure whatever comes of this, I know I can.

First, though, I have to get out of the house. Dad always has to leave early to beat rush hour on his way to the crappy retail tax preparation job he's had since the economy wiped us out, but Mom's vigilant even in his absence. I make a show of eating breakfast through the times when the school bus should arrive, and when Mom lets her guard down I slip out my window again. Taking a city bus is longer, but in some ways more comfortable since there aren't other students around. Flying would be faster, but if the kids at school learned I could fly now, too, that would make the crowds and the staring even worse. It might even get some people thinking about why I suddenly have a "special ability" just a few days after they put Dreadnought in the ground.

I get to school in time to be late for second period. Class ends, and as we file into the hall there are a lot of eyes staring, but I keep my face blank and pretend I don't notice. Over the squeak of linoleum and the cascading voices of dozens of conversations, I hear my name more than once. Every time I get nervous I remind myself that I can look down on these people like ants any time I want to. Literally, I can look down on them. Because I can fly, and they can't. That's the important thing to remember. I'm invincible.

At the end of second period, we have a fifteen-minute break, and I head for the bathrooms. My hand is actually on the door to the boys' room before I realize my mistake, and with a giddy kind of smile turn around and head for the girls' room.

The air seems to snap tight when the door shuts behind me. There are nine or ten other girls in here, and they all seem to look up at me at once, some breaking off in midconversation. My cheeks get warm, which happens way too often these days. I flick my eyes to the ground and go to stand at the back of the line to get a stall. (There are no urinals in here, so it almost doesn't seem like a bathroom to me.) To my great relief, most of the other girls almost immediately lose interest in me. Two leave quickly, another keeps staring, but nobody hassles me. When it's my turn, I shut the stall door and let out a quiet breath. This will get easier, I'm sure.

I hope.

When I'm done the bathroom is almost empty, just a few other girls still waiting to use the toilets. I'm washing my hands, trying to be quick but thorough, when I sense someone at the sink next to me staring.

"Yes?" I say, looking over.

It's a girl I sort of recognize. Long dark hair, dark eyes. She's looking at me intently, and is chewing on a kind of rubber pendant on a necklace. She probably doesn't like me.

"Nothing," she says, pendant dropping from her mouth to hang on its string. She looks down at her own hands, begins scrubbing them intently. "Never mind."

"No, really. What?" I say, a little more forcefully than I'd intended.

"It's just…well, I suppose this is all a big change for you."

"Only because other people make it a big change," I say as I wipe my hands.

"Right. Sorry. I didn't mean to stare." She grabs a fistful of paper towels and wipes her hands quickly, then holds one out to shake. "I'm Sarah."

"Danny," I say, shaking her hand.

The warning bell rings and we head for class. She goes the other direction from me, but turns back to say, "Welcome to being a girl. Don't mind the boys. You'll get used to them."

What the hell does she mean by that?

• • •

I think a memo must have gone around because my teachers stop demanding I prove who I am in every class. Whether Mom likes it or not, her coming to the office yesterday, asking for me by name, and then obviously recognizing me and accepting who I am in front of the school secretary has made it more or less official in the school's eyes. That's what I hope, anyhow. Fourth period goes by, and I let myself begin to believe the novelty of my transformation is starting to wear off, because most of the other students I've already had a class with today don't stare at me anymore.

The lunch bell rings and I hustle to put my books in my locker and meet David for lunch.

"So you're not getting yanked today?" he asks.

"Looks like, yeah," I say as I click my lock shut. "God, I do *not* look forward to the next test."

We join the herd moving toward the cafeteria and split up to the different meal kiosks. There's a lot of cruddy things about this school, but their food program is really nice. We've got plenty of selections, and because there are about a half dozen choices each day, we get to avoid the sort of huge lunch line that eats up half the break period that a lot of kids have to suffer through. I get a slice of pizza and am reaching for a second when I realize this is what a boy would eat. I mean, I've seen girls load up their plate like a boy, but now that I'm here I realize there is a big difference in the gender breakdown of different kiosks. The pizza line is almost all boys. Suddenly, I'm worried about getting fat, which is something that hasn't happened to me before. Nobody cares if a boy is a little chubby, but that's not true for girls. Crap.

But *can* I get fat in this body? It's my physical ideal, right? Does that mean forever? Crap.

I settle on one slice of pizza, and a side salad instead of a second slice. Now, let's see if I'm hungry for the rest of the day. David meets me at the exit from the food kiosk area to the seating area, and we head to our usual table in the back corner, where it's drafty and the light is always broken and flickering, and people leave us alone. It's so good to be back after a full week trapped at home. It feels a little surreal to think of it, and stranger still how normal it feels to be back here, finally, as the self I always wanted to be. Can I please never wake up from this dream?

I'm about halfway through my slice of pizza when I realize David is staring at my boobs again, and has been for our entire meal, and with that realization I enter a whole new realm of mortification. Don't get me wrong—I was in the bathroom looking at these things for like an *hour* when I first got them, but holy crap is it different when it's him doing it. And not just glancing, but staring with, like, intention.

"David!" I hiss. "My face is up here!"

He looks almost like I've startled him out of a reverie. Oh God. He was imagining me naked, wasn't he?

"Uh, sorry," he says, and his face is quickly turning scarlet. "I didn't, you know—it's not like I'm gay or anything."

"*What?*"

"Oh, I mean—"

"First of all, *I'm a girl.*"

"Okay, Jesus, sorry." He munches on a french fry sullenly. "You on your period or something?"

I slap my hand flat on the table, a bit harder than is strictly within the bounds of normal human behavior. It makes an impressive bang, and both our trays jump. "Not. Funny."

We're getting looks from the nearest tables. He sees this, and hunches over, embarrassed. "Christ, I said I was sorry! You don't have to be such a drama queen about it."

For just the briefest moment, I imagine what the look on his face would be if I introduced him to the stratosphere. Believe it or not, that helps. Maybe it's not healthy, but it helps. Compared to him, I'm a god. Goddess. Whatever. The point is, I shouldn't let this little boy get to me.

I snort. "And you wonder why you're single."

"Oh, oh, I see! I can't make a joke, but you can be hypersensitive about everything, and make fun of me for not having a girlfriend."

"You were being a jerk."

"And you're being a stuck-up bitch. I'll see you when you're over yourself." He gets up in a huff.

As I watch him leave, I take deep breaths and clench my fists. The hell is his problem, anyhow? We never had fights like this before. I go to take another bite of salad, and find that I've broken my plastic fork. Wonderful.

As my anger cools, I realize I've been feeling things a lot more recently. My highs are higher. My lows are lower. Before, it seemed like half the time I didn't have feelings as much as I had a script of how I thought I was supposed to feel, and I just followed the script. Maybe for people who are actually male that's not what it feels like, but for me, testosterone muffled everything. Now it's like the estrogen in my blood has taken the cotton out of my head, and I'm feeling things clearly for the first time. Maybe it's not fair to say my feelings are stronger now, but they have more resolution. Before I was living in muddy pastels, and now things are all lit up in neon. I like it. Even when it hurts, I like it a lot. David will calm down, and he'll get over my shocking insistence upon having boobs in public, and then things will go back to normal, except they will be better.

I know they will.

# CHAPTER TEN

David doesn't get over it, at least not today. He's sullen and won't talk to me in the halls, and in class he never once looks my way. We used to get warnings all the time for our whispered conversations, but now it's like a brick wall between us. *Dude, get over it already so I can tell you about my superpowers,* I want to shout at him. *Can't we just go back to hanging out?*

I'm relieved when the final bell rings and we head our separate ways to catch the bus home. I've got a whole lot of homework to catch up on. Even getting my assignments sent home hasn't kept me up with my classes. It sucks because I'd totally planned to have superpower practice tonight, but it looks like I might not have time.

When I arrive home, Mom is waiting for me with her lips pressed thin.

"Danny, we talked about this."

"No, you talked *at* me," I say as I pull my books out and get ready to start on French. "But I decided I didn't agree."

"Danny!" Her voice is sharp, and I look up in surprise. Mom is not the one who yells. "We are holding on by a *thread* here, do you know that?"

"Everything would be fine if you'd just let it be!"

"You know that's not true!" She glances at the front of the house, like she's scared he's going to come home early. "Your father is at his wit's end trying to help you."

"He's in denial. I'm a girl. That's not going to change."

"You don't know that. We might find—"

"It won't change because *I don't want it to*." Mom steps back a little. "I thought you understood that."

"Why would you think that?" she asks.

"Because you bought me those things. Because..." My throat clenches up and my eyes prickle with tears. Because we had such a nice day out together. Because I felt closer to you that weekend than I ever have before. Because I thought you loved me, and could see I was happy now. I have all the things I need to say, but none of the strength to say them.

"Maybe that was a mistake," she says quietly. "I shouldn't have encouraged you."

I close my French book, and gather my things to take them upstairs. I can't be out here, and I'm not sure I can study right now. Life on estrogen: the highs are higher, and the lows...well, the lows really suck.

"I'm going to have to tell him when he gets home," she says to me as I climb the stairs.

"Go right ahead." He can't hurt me. He'd hurt himself trying. "I have homework I need to do."

• • •

A few hours later, Mount Screamer erupts. Dad practically pounds my door out of the frame before I open it, and then it's an hour and a half of some of the worst I've ever had from him. At first I think I'm going to stand up to him, that my new strength and resolve will let me laugh off his bellowing, scorn his fury, and deliver an unending stream of witty, insightful arguments that will force him to see where he might be wrong. That's not even close to how it goes. After a few wavering counterarguments, my resolve collapses. He drags me back down to the living room because that's where he likes to do this kind of thing. He's screaming so loud, so close, I have to fight the urge to wipe my face. He pins me to the couch with the sheer volume of his rage.

Once, at one of those hearing tests they give us every few

years, they found out my left ear was worse than my right. I told them I didn't know why that would be, but the truth was I knew immediately. It's because when he's like this, I always look away to the right and he screams at the left side of my face. Now, with my improved hearing, heightened to the upper limit of human senses, he is louder and more painful than he has been in years.

He tells me I'm stupid. That I'm not thinking big picture. That nobody will respect me while I look like a freak. That he only wants what is best for me but I'm screwing it all up. He says I've damaged my reputation, that nobody will take me seriously now. He demands to know why I don't have the good sense to be ashamed of what happened to me, but doesn't wait for an answer before saying I've embarrassed them all. He says I'm pathetic, that I'm delusional, that I'm sick. He suggests I might be a pervert, and that he—generous, caring, and steadfast as he is—might have to fight to keep me off the sex offender list for using the girls' bathroom. He tells me I'm disloyal, that I'm a bad son, that I'm selfish and disgusting. He tells me I'm weak, and gross, and that I have no moral fiber. He says he's never been so ashamed of me, and then he goes on to emphasize how low that is, given all the other times I've shamed him. He says all of this at a volume to shake the rafters. When I start to cry he calls me a sniveling pussy and says he's glad his father is dead so he never had to see what a failure I am. I suck it up fast, force the tears back as quick as I can, because I know the longer I cry the worse it will get.

Mom doesn't even watch, but that's no surprise. I stopped expecting her to help me years ago.

The worst part is, I can't help but believe him. He always has a way of making me believe him. I really am disgusting and pathetic. I can crack the sound barrier, but I can't stand up to this man. If I were worthy of my powers, I wouldn't even flinch. But I'm not. I don't deserve them. I don't deserve anything. I'm crumpling like a cardboard box in the rain. The promise I made myself feels like a sick joke. There's no way I can just *decide* not to let anyone push me around. God, I was so stupid. I'm always stupid. I always mess it up. I'm a worthless, stupid, disgusting little freak.

I start crying again because I realize I still hate myself.

. . .

Later, I'm curled in bed and trying to keep my sobbing quiet. From past experience I know that if I cry too loudly, he will slam on my door until I open it so he can start in on me again. The lows are lower. This hurts more than it ever has before. I'm not upset, I am *shattered*. It's important not to cry too loudly, but it's so hard: the muscles controlling my voice are all so much stronger now. I hear him climbing the stairs and I try to hold my breath, just freeze in bed until he goes away.

He calls me a coward through the door, and goes back downstairs.

After a long moment I crawl over to my door and make sure it's locked. I turn off my light and head to my closet. I've buried the supersuit back there, way in the back, behind a chest of drawers. I don't deserve to have this, but I need it. With shaking hands, I undress and put the suit on.

Once I'm safely away, I let my breath out, and the sobs come back. I fly on, get up nice and high. Because I have an urge to hide, I head toward a bank of clouds. I find a nice thick one, and slip inside. It's cold and wet in here, but it's better than being anywhere someone might see or hear me. Finally I let it out. I float curled up in the cloud bank and I sob for what feels like hours. My tears leak into my cowl and smear all across my cheeks, by turns wet and gritty. This hurts *so* much. Why does it still hurt so much? Shouldn't I be used to it now? Shouldn't I be tough enough not to care anymore? I'm so weak. I'm so stupid. Of course this was going to happen. Of *course*. I deserved this. For being so stupid. For having hope. It's my fault, it's always my fault.

. . .

I'm empty and floating. The cloud has moved on, but I've stayed where I am, curled up in the air, looking across the Sound toward the city. Geese honk as they fly past a little ways off from me. It should be safe enough to stay here a while. Normally, after something like this happens I go to my room, go to sleep quickly, and my parents let me. They won't expect to see or hear from me at home for hours, and I seriously consider never going back. In the vacant calm that comes right after a hard crash, I realize I could just...fly. Fly away and never come back. The cold doesn't bother me—hell, being in *orbit* doesn't bother me—so I don't even need a place to sleep if I can find a comfortable spot in the woods. For food, I could figure something out. Maybe I could get an aerial courier job and get paid under the table.

A passenger jet roars past on approach to the airport. It's only a few hundred yards away, and I realize I've drifted into crowded airspace. I angle away and begin putting distance between me and the landing approach zone.

There's a loud crumpling noise, and something like tearing metal. I look back and the plane's right engine is in the midst of disintegrating. Flames shoot out the back, and a solid trail of noxious black smoke streams from the engine. As I watch, there is a short whine and then a loud bang as the engine detonates. I'm pretty sure airline engine casings are designed to contain explosions from the engine, but if that's the case, this one must be faulty. The whole rear of the wing gets sprayed with shrapnel, and a long piece of the control flap rips away and goes spinning down into the darkness. The plane groans in agony, tips over to the right, and begins to fall.

"No!" I shout, and without really thinking about it I'm boosting for speed with everything I've got. I cross five hundred yards in a matter of moments. In those moments the plane has tipped up almost all the way on its side. Its nose is coming down sharply. There's maybe a half mile of altitude to work with here, and the enormous jet is picking up speed as it dives for the black water below us. I get up under and next to the burning wing, meaning to push it back up and help the pilots level out. I throw my shoulder into it—

I bounce off.

With an icy lurch I realize I've never pushed anything in midair. I have no idea how. I hit the wing again; I bounce away again. Again. It's not working, and the only thing in my head is that I don't know what I'm doing.

The flames are burning hotter now, a trail of smoke growing to a streak of fire. These people have about forty seconds to live.

My hands scrabble at the aluminum, fingers sliding over metal. I get a grip on the engine pylon, try to pull it up, and it slips from my grasp. My heart slams in my chest and the water is so close *why am I so stupid these people are going to die and it's all my fault—*

No. Stop. How did I figure out how to fly? I shut my eyes and picture the lattice. There, that's the plane. I get my shoulder against it again, and imagine pushing, not against the plane, but against the lattice. It's not a matter of shoving it. It's a matter of thrust. With another tortured groan, the jet begins to move with me. The wing is lifting under the steady pressure I'm applying, but so slowly. I open my eyes, and almost scream. The water is closer than I'd thought possible. I push harder, and the wing shoots up. Too much, too fast. The wing over corrects, and the jet wobbles up onto its other side. With a desperate heave I yank it back down, force it into proper alignment. The other engine screams and the water rushes up to greet us.

We are still falling. Still nose-down.

Three hundred yards and falling.

I pop down from the wing, keeping it lifted on my fingertips while I pivot in place and look at the tail. The control surfaces on the tail are still responding to the pilots. The elevators are *all* the way up, begging for altitude, and the rudder keeps flicking over to the left to compensate for the missing engine. The nose is coming up, but not fast enough.

Two hundred yards and falling.

It's not enough. We'll never make it. I was too late. Because I'm worthless and horrible and can't do anything right. Because—

*Stop it, goddammit!*

They'll belly flop at a hundred miles an hour if I don't do something, and do it now.

I take a chance. I abandon the wing. At maximum acceleration, I cover the distance from the wing to the nose in less than half a second. In that half second, they drop another thirty yards. I slam into the jet's nose, right under the forward wheel well, and heave upward with everything I've got.

The nose rises. I open my eyes, and I can't stop the wail of fear that escapes me. I can see individual waves now, and *we're still falling.*

One hundred yards and falling.

Seventy yards and falling.

Fifty yards and falling.

Forty yards.

Forty yards.

Fifty yards and climbing.

I scream and whoop and holler for joy. I steal a look back under my armpit and see that the flames on the wing have gone out. We're going to make it. Ahead, I see the runway, another two miles distant and off to the right. I drop away from the plane for a moment, and it continues to rise. The pilots seem to want more space between them and the waters of the Sound before they make the final turn for the runway. When I'm sure the plane won't fall from the sky if I leave the nose, I flit up to the cockpit and tap on the window. It takes a moment for them to notice me, because honestly, who looks out the windshield of plane and expects to see a girl there, even in a city like New Port?

The pilots break into huge grins when they see me. I point at myself, then point back at the wing, then down at the nose, and then shrug theatrically, hoping they understand the question. They trade words and then one of them points forcefully back at the wing. I nod at them, point to myself, and then back at the wing. They nod back, so I pull away from the cockpit and drop back, letting the plane pass under me. I dip under the wing again and take my place back by the engine. I take the load slowly, and as I take more, the wing seems to get heavier as the pilots drop whatever tricks they used to handle the unequal thrust so they can focus on lining back up for the final approach. It's a little unsteady, the weight coming and going, until I realize I should probably replicate thrust more than lift. The jet's skin screeches when I dig my left hand into the pylon that the engine's charred husk is mounted on. I find a solid-feeling bit of aluminum to hold on to and begin to push forward. The metal groans, and there's a thumping from inside the wing. For a moment I ease up on the pressure, worried I'm damaging the wing even further, but it seems stable enough, and without me pushing the wing is beginning to wobble a bit already. A little more gently this time, I push forward against the engine pylon again.

We're climbing now, up past three hundred yards and slowly beginning to level out. I hear the control surfaces shift, the pitch of the remaining engine changes, and the plane begins to tilt over to the right again, but deliberately this time. The wing shifts and flexes against me. We pass over the shore, and the city lights begin to pass under us. There are little popping twangs all up and down the wing. The nose stays level and begins swinging over to the right, bringing us in line for the final approach. The left wing begins to rise, and the load on the right wing shifts again. It starts as a series of pops like gunshots, one right after another.

The wing jerks against me, and then with a groaning shudder the rest of it simply folds up and twists off.

It pulls up and away from me, twirls once, and slams into the tail before falling away in a shower of torn aluminum. The plane immediately flops over on its back. There's just enough time for me to experience a bolt of embarrassment before the other wing whips up and around to slam into me. It's like getting hit by a city bus, a flat explosion of shock and pain across my face, neck, shoulder, and chest that sends me spinning away. I right myself and for a heart-stopping instant I can't see the airliner anywhere—it's just not in the sky with me. I look down and it's headed for the ground like a javelin.

I dive as hard as I can, arms pinned to my side, clawing for every bit of speed I can get. There's no real time to think, just images and instinct. The buildings below us are like matchboxes, and growing fast. I buttonhook back up under the chin and slam into the forward landing gear like a pile driver. Metal shrieks, and then I'm inside the plane up to my shoulders. The whole jet seems to shudder as I kick the nose up back into the sky. Aluminum knives try to slice me up and I pull myself from the nose.

The airliner is pointed the right way now, but we're still falling and those matchboxes are full-sized dollhouses now. It won't be a javelin, it will pancake. Below us people are starting to run. We're close enough that I can see their horror.

Flying backward is something I haven't practiced much, but I can't afford the time it would take to turn around. I jerk myself backward, arms out, feeling blindly for the place where the plane's body widens out to meet the wing roots. That will be the strongest place, the only place this will work. This jet is landing on a runway if I have to *carry* the damn thing.

The instant I feel the bulge thud past my shoulder blades, I spread my arms and push *UP.*

Oh God.

It's too heavy.

# CHAPTER ELEVEN

Metal crumples around my shoulders. I fight and kick and push as hard as I can upward. We're dropping like a rock, and barely slowing.

Fifty yards.

The aluminum skin gives way with a shriek and I crunch six inches up into the guts of the plane, my legs dangling free. A huge support strut is pressing into my back.

Thirty yards.

I've stopped breathing, I've stopped blinking. Everything goes to pushing.

Ten yards.

In my head, I can see the lattice—

—there's the tangle of the jet, and the trailing, unraveling threads of its momentum—

—grab it, grab it *all*—

—I can *pull*—

—but I'll have to pull it *through* myself—

—I pull.

Pain rips through every muscle in my back. I cry out in scarlet agony. Pain is everywhere. It fills me, packs every part of me tight. My legs spasm, and my fingers go slack. Something loud and wet snaps in my chest, and a lance of fire pierces me. It doesn't stop. It gets worse. I can feel my body breaking, tearing, ripping.

But we should have hit by now.

I force an eye open, and I see the ground rushing past me, and falling away. The final threads of our downward momentum pass through the fingers of my mind, transformed by channeling them through my body to momentum that carries us up and forward. We sail over the signal lights at the end of the runway, and begin sinking toward ground again. Finally, finally, the suffocating pain begins to recede back to something I can think through. There's a sharp grinding somewhere along my flank, and my body is alive with sprains and tears.

I grit my teeth and push up and forward as hard as I can. The metal around me groans and buckles. Without so much momentum forcing us down, I can delay us long enough to slip over the runway's edge. The landing gear to the left of me unfolds and locks in position, but the nose and right side wheels stay folded up. The plane begins to wobble and tip, balanced imperfectly on a single point, the uneven thrust from the single engine trying to spin the whole thing off of me.

The runway is zipping beneath us at highway speeds. Just a few more yards.

My feet hit the ground with a jarring impact I feel hard in my pelvis. We bounce once, twice, and then I'm running, great bounding strides that cover a dozen yards at a time, but the steps start to catch up with me, and just before I slip I set my legs and skid along the ground on my boots. My knees lock and almost instantly my feet start digging furrows in the concrete. A spray of gravel explodes up, fast and hard enough to dimple and dent all the metal skin around me. It's like getting sandblasted in the face by a machine gun. The airliner's nose pitches up into the air, and the tail slams into the ground. We skid for another seventy yards. My legs clench and tremble, sharp little bolts of jagged ice cutting through the broader ache of everything below my thighs.

Finally, we come to a sliding stop. With one last great heave of effort, I let the plane down gently on its right side and scramble out from underneath the fuselage on my hands and knees. I am unspeakably weary. My stomach suggests it might throw up. The pain is *everywhere*. When I try to get to my feet, I stumble and have to try again.

One last effort. I can do this. I fly, wobbly at first, and land on the stubby remains of the right wing. The emergency door comes off quick in my hands, and I huck it away into the darkness. A terrified man is looking out at me.

"Leave your bags and get out on the wing," I say. "You're going to want to slide off the front; the broken side is too jagged."

I leave him, and half leap, half fly to the rear emergency door. It's already opening, but the inflatable chute is jammed against the ground with several thousand pounds of air pressure. I pull and drag and shove it until it straightens out enough that people can start using it to jump the eight feet or so safely to the ground. The front slide is having the same problems, so I fix it too. Then I fly around to the forward exit on the plane's left side, the one that's sort of pointed up at the sky, and rip the door off.

A confused flight attendant with a seriously impressive black eye turns to look at me as I enter.

"Get them out!" I say, and push past her toward the cockpit. When I yank the door open, one of the pilots looks up from examining a wound on the other's head.

"Is there any chance of fire?" I ask.

"I don't know, it depends on—Christ, you're just a kid!"

"*What* does it depend on?" I snap.

"On fuel leaks and ignition sources. We think the starboard tanks should be empty, but who knows?"

"Is he okay?"

"No."

I nod and step in. He moves back to make room, and I undo his copilot's seatbelt. An adult isn't a real heavy lift for me anymore, but there's nothing as floppy and awkward as an unconscious human body, so I have a little more trouble than I expected getting him out. Instead of taking up a spot in the line forming to jump down the yellow slide, I hop out the left side, slip back up and over the plane, and set him down on ground near where the first evacuated passengers are starting to mill around.

"If anyone has medical training, please help the pilot here!" I shout.

Then I dart back over to the ruined wing stub, searching the concrete around it for any signs of a leak. I don't see any, and it doesn't seem like anything here is sparking or glowing, either.

With a sigh of relief that comes all the way up from the root of my spine, I step away from the plane. It's over. Around me, passengers and flight attendants are catching people as they make the short hop out of the plane. Sirens wail as the airport's fire company pounds down the runway toward us. I am just so freaking tired. I stick around, more out of a dazed sense that I need to be on hand if somehow something else goes wrong than any particular reason.

Someone tugs at my cape. I turn around. It's a kid, maybe just three or four years younger than me. "Thanks," he says. "No prob—"

He grabs me around the middle and hugs like he's scared he'll fall off. "I thought I was going to die!" he cries into my chest. Something in my side sends a spike of pain through me, but I force it down. After a moment, I hug him back, and he begins sobbing.

I look up, and people are starting to gather around. Dozens of them. Bruised, some bleeding, a few clutching arms or limping. But alive. I saved them. I saved them all.

Someone starts clapping and in the next instant everyone is. Some whistles and cheers and then I'm getting pounded on the back, my hair is getting rubbed.

And crap, I start crying, too. Just little clenched lip sobs, but they're there.

"What's your name?" someone shouts.

"D—I don't have one, yet."

People start shouting suggestions, and mostly they're really stupid, but I laugh. It's okay. Everything is okay.

I gently peel the kid off of me and smile at him. He's got a grin as wide as the world on his face, looks almost as happy as I feel. Everything is wonderful, and for once I am happy to be me.

"Uh, gimme some room, I gotta take off."

"Don't go!" someone shouts.

"I have homework," I say, and it shouldn't be funny, but people laugh. Gently, slowly, I push myself into the air. There's another burst of applause, and I turn and wave to them as I gain altitude, then pivot away and head for the night. I don't feel so tired anymore. Everything is loose and airy. Bizarrely, I think about how maybe this was a little too close to caping for me to do in throwaway colors, and I consider putting some serious sonic boom distance between me and the scene. But...

Oh, what the hell.

I turn back, do a slow orbit of the crash scene, and when enough people are pointing up at me, I give them a fast flyby and a barrel roll. They whoop and cheer and I take off into the black.

# CHAPTER TWELVE

The first thing I notice when I wake up is pain, but I feel good. My side is complaining loudly, and when I feel around, I notice that my whole flank is a little swollen and there's a spot near the bottom of my ribs that *really* does not like being pushed on. Purple bruises mottle the skin all up and down my side. I don't really understand how I did what I did last night. I wish the other Dreadnoughts were here. There's so much I need to ask them. That thing with the lattice worked, but I hurt myself. Last night made it obvious I don't understand my limits at all, or how I can get around them. Once I'm healed up, I'm going to need to do a lot of experimenting.

Gingerly, I get dressed—socks are fun, what with the bending over and all—but eventually I get presentable while I wait for my ancient laptop to boot up. It was a gift from Grandpa just before he died, and it will be with me as long is it functions because we're not the kind of people who buy new computers anymore.

Three geological eons later, I'm checking the local news. The lead story is: *UNKNOWN SUPERHERO SAVES PASSENGER JET*.

Oh, so very much yes.

There's a photo of me hugging that kid, kinda blurry and dark with someone's shoulder in frame, but there we are. There I am. As much as I hate that stupid cowl, I'm really glad I wore it last night. I read the story to see what they figured out after I left. Early signs are that the engine sucked in a goose, and there was some problem with it that meant it didn't handle that kind of a situation like it was supposed to, but blew up instead. Three hundred and eleven people. That's how many I saved. Holy crap. A few are in the hospital, but it seems like everyone is going to be okay. The wing hit a warehouse, but there wasn't anybody working in it at the time. Damage to the runway will take time to repair. Okay, so not a ten out of ten, but holy crap, three hundred and eleven people! I'm so proud, I don't know what to do with myself. I want to cheer, but I can't let anyone hear me. There's really nobody I can talk to about this, and suddenly that is the most frustrating thing in the world.

I guess I could go talk to the Legion, but—but hey, screw the Legion! I'm still pissed off at them for what happened last time I showed up there. No, this one was mine, and even if I can't tell anyone about it, everyone will hear about it. Then, when I'm ready, and I make my official debut as Dreadnought—

But when did *if* become a *when?*

Maybe I should slow down.

No. No, today is a day for feeling amazing. I won't do anything I can't take back, but right now, I'm done policing my thoughts and managing my expectations. I'm freaking fantastic, and I'm going to enjoy that as long as I can. This is the best feeling ever. I want more. I never want it to stop. Someday, I'm going to save the world.

My mood is so good, even Dad sneering at me on the way out the door when he sees me with my backpack at the breakfast table doesn't bring me down. Mentally, I kick myself for forgetting to leave the bag upstairs until I'm ready to go.

But all he says is, "You don't have the sense God gave a tapeworm, letting people see you this way. It's disgusting, parading around like that when they all know you're really a boy." I play it smart, though, and just stare into my cereal. "I tried to protect you," says Dad. "Tried to keep them from knowing. Of course, you've always been too stupid to help." Slow breaths. Don't let him in. "How'd I get stuck with a retard son, anyhow?"

Somehow I manage to get through breakfast without letting him bait me into saying something that will give him an excuse to blow up again. After I drop my bowl in the dishwasher I scoop up my bag and am out the door as quick as I can go.

This time, I catch my bus from my regular bus stop, and a few of the other kids even say hi. More, in fact, than would say hi before I changed. Quiet joy suffuses me. Things are getting better all the time.

· · ·

David isn't at our normal meetup spot at the beginning of school, but that's not unheard of. He's not around at break either, and I get a little nervous. I hope he's not avoiding me. Maybe he's just absent. We don't see each other until lunch. It's gray and drizzling out today, and the draft near our back corner table is particularly strong. David's still looking sullen when he sets his tray down, and I smother a little flare of exasperation. I'm not going to let him ruin my day, so even though I totally didn't do anything wrong, I smile and say, "Sorry I snapped at you yesterday."

That brightens him a bit. "Thanks."

"Did you hear about that plane last night?" Lunch today is a chicken salad with shredded cheese on top. Let's see if *this* leaves me hungry all day like my last school lunch did.

"The one that crashed?"

"The one that *almost* crashed," I say, a little too quickly.

"No, I saw the pictures, that was pretty crashed. Cool how nobody died, though."

"Yeah," I say, and I can't stop smiling. It is cool. David has been my friend since we were little kids. Maybe…maybe I can trust him. God, now that I'm having a conversation about it, it's all I can do not to scream out loud about how I'm the one who saved them. Not yet, though. I've got to pick my moment. "Did you hear about the cape that caught them?"

"I guess. Hey, do you mind if we talk about something kinda serious?"

"No, go ahead." Actually I sorta do, but it might be suspicious if I never shut up about the plane crash. I mean, the *not*-crash.

"You know, it really upsets me how girls are always so quick to jump up and down on me." I stop chewing for a moment, and a little choir of dread starts singing in the back of my mind. "Like how so?" I hear myself ask.

"Like, they're always sneering at me. It's not fair."

"Yeah, uh, that…that sucks, man." David strikes out a lot, so this isn't the first time he's talked about this, but it seems like I'm hearing him more clearly than I used to. I take a long sip from my cup of diet soda to cover this new disquiet. My memories of him batting off the advances from a girl named Shelly last year are still pretty vivid. She's about as chubby as he is, so he wasn't interested. But I don't want another fight, so I don't mention it.

"Oh good, I'm glad you still understand!" he says with visible relief. *Still understand*, he says. This conversation feels like I'm missing some really important context. "So, I was thinking. I've been your friend for, like, ever. You know I'm a nice guy, but I never get a fair chance. Well, this is my chance."

"Your chance?" Oh no.

"I mean, uh, you and me." Oh no no no. "We could, you know, date now." Oh no. Oh no. Oh no.

No.

After an empty moment I say, "You know I'm gay, right?"

"So that works then!"

"Um, no?"

But he doesn't even hear me, just talks right through me. "I've been lonely a long time. I guess I'm ready to settle." He says this like he's making an intimate, painful, and somehow brave confession. There's a seriousness in his face that is begging me to be impressed.

"Ready to settle?" Oh, how big of him. He's willing to settle. For the most beautiful girl in school who, OH YEAH, HAS FREAKING *SUPERPOWERS*.

"Well, what I mean is it's not ideal, I guess," says David quickly, perhaps dimly sensing danger. Oh, this should be good.

"Like, it might be awkward at first, but we could make this work. I mean, you look good enough that I don't even really care that you're kind of a dude inside."

For a long stretch, I don't know what to say. It feels like my mind is struggling to make some adjustment that will bring this into focus and explain why my best friend is suddenly treating me like I'm his to take, treating me like his terms are the only ones that matter.

I set down my fork. "I am not, and I never have been, a 'dude inside.' And just so you know, this"—and I flick my finger back and forth between us—"is never going to happen."

"Oh come on, gimme a chance!"

"I don't like boys, *any* boys. If I did like boys, I wouldn't like boys who talk to me like you just did."

"This is unbelievable," he mutters, and I don't know why, but that sets me off more than anything else he's said so far.

"Get up and walk away right now," I snarl. "Stay away, and maybe I won't tell everybody about that birthmark you showed me when we were eight."

"Whoa!" His eyes are wide with shock. He leans in and whispers, his voice tight with fury, "That's not cool!"

"Try me. See what happens."

David gets up and leaves, but as he goes, he says things to me that make me understand we will never be friends again. Not because I wouldn't forgive him; because he will always be too proud to let himself be forgiven.

# CHAPTER THIRTEEN

My final period is study hall, but I sign out from the classroom to take it in the library instead and then leave school early. It will probably get caught and counted as an absence, and there's a real chance I'll catch Saturday school for this, but I don't have much of a choice.

My supersuit is banged up from last night, mostly in the boots, which were almost scraped apart against the airport tarmac, and I need to see about getting some repairs. The heels are barely hanging on, and the soles have been rubbed away so much they look like sediment layers in rock formations. New ones might be pretty expensive, so my first crack at replacing them is going to see if I can get more from the Legion.

The problem is that I'm grounded more or less forever now, so if I'm going to be somewhere that's not school or home I have to do it in a way that my parents won't hear about it. Flying makes that easier, but I still want to finish this up before they expect me home.

I get lucky with a city bus and manage to get home in just a few minutes. After taking a quick look around to make sure nobody is nearby, I risk a super-speed dash down the alley and fly up to my bedroom window. Just a minute or two later, I've got the suit on and am leaving, going straight up just under the speed of sound. Today's drizzle, when encountered at such a speed, is like getting hit in the face with thousands of tiny grains of sand. Not painful, but annoying, so I get up over the cloud layer as quickly as possible. One nice thing I'm discovering about New Port is that it's always a beautiful day if you go high enough, and the clouds are usually nice and low. I nose over and boost for Legion Tower at a shade under 750 miles an hour, making the five-mile trip in a bit under thirty seconds.

Legion Tower has spotlights walking back and forth across the sky from its apex twenty-four hours a day, every day. From above, I realize that's so flying heroes can find it even when the clouds are thick over the city. When I see the spotlights tracing figure eights through the gauzy mist, I slow down and drop back down below the clouds to make my final approach. The art deco arches and gleaming metal lines of Legion Tower seem somehow less stern and imposing during the drab wet twilight. When I bank around and come at the landing balcony at a slow and easy glide, I get one of those moments of surreality that keep popping up. I'm dropping in unannounced on the Legion Pacifica, and that doesn't seem completely insane to me anymore.

When I set down I try not to be too obvious that my side is still tender and painful. Even though most of the other pains vanished as little more than a bit of morning stiffness, I still don't have full range of motion back. But, you know, I look real good for someone who had an airliner dropped on her.

The thick glass doors open as I approach, and an elevator is waiting for me. As I step inside, an intercom clicks on. It's Doc Impossible.

"Hi, Danny. We're on the common level—that's 37. Come on down."

"Um, when you say 'we,' who are you referring to?" No freaking way I'm going to talk to Graywytch today. Or hopefully ever again. In fact, maybe I can get replacement boots somewhere else.

"Me and Valkyrja," she says.

I hit the button for 37 so fast that if I were baseline I'd have broken my finger.

The elevator opens on the same floor where the disastrous meeting happened, what, only three days ago? But instead of heading left to the main briefing room with its giant floating globe and walls dominated by 3D projection screens, I head down the hall to the right, where I find an impressive kitchen, dining room, and a few different lounges. The countertops are thick slabs of polished granite, there's soft track lighting everywhere, and those same floor-to-ceiling windows offer an amazing view of downtown.

Doc Impossible and Valkyrja are seated on stools at a little island counter in the kitchen. Impossible has an ashtray she's working on filling between drinks from a black ceramic mug. Valkyrja isn't wearing her armor, which I guess makes sense around the house, but it still seems weird to see her in nothing more than a simple wool tunic and some leather breeches. The wings she keeps tightly folded against her back are a little trippy, too.

"'Sup, Danny?" says Doc Impossible.

"Well met, young champion," says Valkyrja.

"Uh, hi," I say, and then pull my cowl back because it feels indescribably weird to be having a conversation with people who know my real name while I wear a mask.

"You want some cocoa? Mugs are over there." Doc Impossible gestures to some cabinets along the kitchen wall. I fill one from a hot chocolate and cappuccino dispenser, and then I'm sitting and having hot chocolate with a pair of friggin' superheroes like it's something I do all the time.

"That was superb work with the jet, by the way," says Doc Impossible.

Valkyrja nods. "A mighty feat."

People don't pop from pride, which is the only reason why I don't. My cheeks are blushing so hard I imagine I can feel the blood in them, and I hide my enormous grin behind a sip of cocoa. The boots don't matter. The boots aren't why I'm here. Nobody else in the world can understand what I did last night, or how I feel about it, and I suddenly understand how desperately I need to talk about this. There's just so much here, so many feelings to untangle that I can't process it alone. "Thanks. You, uh, you're not mad I did it in throwaway colors?"

"Lives were at stake, kiddo. We don't frown on saving people, no matter what rules get bent."

"It was well done," says Valkyrja. "Perhaps your next rescue need not be under a temporary flag."

Doc Impossible sets down her mug. "She is *fifteen*, Val."

"As was I, when first I picked up a sword."

"This is the twenty-first century," snaps Doc. "We don't do that to children anymore."

"Um, do I get a vote?" I ask.

"It's not a vote, it's your choice. You get to make it unilaterally," says Doc Impossible. Then she looks at Valkyrja and says, "But I still think you're a little young to be getting pressured into it."

"There is no pressure. If the call comes to her, she will answer when she is ready." Valkyrja looks at me. "But you may be ready before your eighteenth name day."

A giddy, almost dizzy feeling floats through me. Do I *want* my own colors? Am I ready to be a real cape? I open my mouth, and what comes out is, "Um. I guess." Oh, so articulate! A little icy spike of embarrassment cuts through my good mood. Dad likes to say that unless I can speak well, I should shut up.

Valkyrja seems to sense how awkward I feel trying to answer that question. "Tell us of the rescue," she says. There's no hiding the grin now, so I take them through it, from floating in the air—although I say I was out practicing flying—to when I saw the engine explode. I tell them about how I pushed the nose up, and helped the plane start climbing again, and then how the wing broke, and I had to carry the entire airliner. I tell them about getting the nose back up a second time, and then how I wasn't strong enough to lift the plane so I—and here I get a little confused about how to explain it.

"Uh, I guess, it's like I could see the momentum and I sorta… tugged it in another direction?" I say. "Does that make sense?"

Doc Impossible and Valkyrja trade a look of confusion. "I confess it does not," says Valkyrja.

"Okay, uh, how to put this. I guess I can sorta see what's…

well, not 'see' exactly, but I have this sense of a lattice that seems behind and under reality. Did Dreadnought ever talk about his powers or say anything like this?"

"Not that I recall," says Doc Impossible. "He kept his powers pretty close to the vest to prevent his enemies from learning his limits."

"I believe he mentioned a mesh once." Valkyrja sets her mug down and looks at me with enough interest that I'm a little uncomfortable. Not like she's being rude or anything. In fact, it's still a little amazing to be talking to her, and more amazing that she cares what I have to say. It's just that I still have that poster of her up in my room, and suddenly that feels strange. "Is that what you refer to?"

"Um. Maybe? It's like, if you can imagine the world as a big net of light and heat, and everything in it a tangle, I can sort of sense that out, and I guess I can tug on the strings, too. It's painful, though. I hurt myself a little doing it, to be honest."

Doc Impossible sits up straighter. "Does it still hurt?"

"A bit, yeah."

She looks down at her mug for a moment and then says, "Would you mind if I examined you? Dreadnought never showed an ability to redirect momentum, and now you say you've done that, but you also injured yourself doing it. A big danger in meta-human medicine is we don't always understand our own bodies, and sometimes by the time we've figured them out it's too late to fix a serious problem. I would feel a lot better if I had a look inside of you to make sure nothing was wrong."

"Oh gee, I dunno. Does Graywytch really need to know about this?" The dripping sarcasm is out of my mouth before I have a chance to think about it, and when Doc Impossible tenses and her cheeks go a little pink, I almost regret it. Almost.

"I suppose I deserved that. Still, I'm concerned something we don't understand might be happening to you. You really need to get looked at, if not by me then by your own doctor."

Which, obviously, isn't going to be an option. *Hey doc, I've got this big, horrible bruise I can't tell you much about, please don't tell my parents I was here and no I won't tell you how I got it.* Yeah, that'll fly.

"Look, it's already a little better," I say. "It'll be fine in a week or so."

Valkyrja sets her hand on mine. "Go with her, Danny."

Awkwardly, because *of course* I'm awkward all of a sudden, I scoot my stool back. Doc Impossible follows, and oh God, I actually turn around and wave at Valkyrja like I'm leaving the building and please somebody kill me now.

• • •

The elevator ride is long, and starting to get a little strained.

Doc Impossible takes a drag on her cigarette. "She likes men."

Can one of my superpowers please be melting through the floor, disappearing forever, and having everyone who ever met me forget that I exist? Please? But I'm supposed to be an invincible badass now, so all I say is, "That's disappointing."

Doc Impossible blows a line of smoke over her shoulder. "Tell me about it."

The laughs take me by surprise. I don't want to be laughing with her, don't want to be warming up to her again. But it happens, and it feels good to laugh, and it feels good to know I'm not the only girl who feels her chest get tight when Valkyrja walks in the room.

"I'm happy for you," Doc says. "The first rescue is always the sweetest. I'm glad yours got to be a good one."

"A good one?"

"No fatalities. Sometimes rescue work is mostly about sifting through the corpses."

"Oh."

We get to her lab, and I wait for her to swap cigarettes for nicotine gum before we go through the airlock again. Into the tube I go.

The sensor ring drops and does a quick pass across my body.

The bruise is still there, and the center has turned a little black, but the outer edges are starting to fade to green and disappear. From outside the tube I hear a sharp bark of surprise, and then a stream of what might be (okay, what certainly is) profanity of notable creativity and enthusiasm.

"What? What is it?"

The intercom clicks on. "Danny, you broke three of your ribs."

"Oh." Somehow, I would have expected that to be a lot more painful.

"They've set themselves—which is amazing, by the way; most people's bodies don't do that—and on anyone else I'd say they'd be about one week into healing, but even that is a little slower than how Dreadnought normally healed."

"Oh."

"That's not the fu—freaky part," says Doc Impossible. "Your ribs were broken from the inside. I mean inside the bones themselves. They exploded. You've got scars consistent with bone shard perforations in your liver, stomach, spleen, and kidney."

Oh. That's new. "How did it happen?" Doc Impossible is quiet for a moment, and the sensor ring goes crazy, jumping up and down, twirling, spraying me with ten different colors of light before it settles again. "I don't know. Maybe this has something to do with how long your transformation took. What I can say is that if you were anybody else you'd be dead. Whatever you did, don't do it again until we understand it."

"How am I going to understand it if I don't try it again?"

Doc Impossible is quiet for a long moment and then says, "Fine. But no more airliners. Start with something small, like marbles small. Do it when nobody's life is on the line, and you stop the moment you feel discomfort. Deal?"

"Okay."

"Cool beans. Now, about your boots: they can actually heal themselves just like your suit can, but I can fab you up a new pair if you don't want to wait. Given what you put them through, it looks like they'd take a few days to get fixed up. Your suit has a few rips in it too. You want me to recycle them both?"

I hadn't even known my suit could do that. "Uh, yeah, cool. That'd be great."

"Okay." The tube starts to open, and Doc Impossible once again is hidden behind a screen that's dropped between us. "Look behind you."

Behind me is the wall I broke. The cracks are mostly gone, and the remainder are slowly disappearing one by one in little flashes of light. In front of that, there's a table that wasn't here last time. On the table are a neatly folded pair of jeans, a shirt, socks, panties, and a bra. They are still slightly warm to the touch, and have a faint odor of chemicals and plastic, but other than that they're normal clothes.

"I made you some civvies to wear in the meantime," she says.

The bra fits, which I now understand to be a minor miracle. I slip the panties on, and then the jeans. When I pick up the black shirt, it seems a little weird until I put it on and realize it's cut for a girl. I don't have any tops like that, and in fact have never worn one. My cracked reflection looks back at me from the window. It's the first time I've seen myself entirely in girls' clothes.

"They should fit, unless the printer's on the fritz again," says Doc Impossible from behind the screen.

"They fit," I say so quiet I barely hear myself. Then, louder: "Yeah, they're perfect."

"Cool." The screen between us rises up into the ceiling. "Anything else you want me to make you?"

For a moment, I don't realize what she's offering. She's got an encouraging, almost embarrassed smile, and I realize she's apologizing. Like it's just that easy. Like it could ever be simple. There's a brief, fiery moment where I want to throw it back in her face and spit on her, but the look on her face punctures my spite. Maybe it can be easy, just this once.

"Um. Maybe a skirt? I've got these cute flats at home but they look sort of weird with jeans."

"Sure thing!" says Doc Impossible, and she spins her chair back to the interface on the wall behind her. The wall to my right becomes white and opaque a moment before an entire menu of skirts fills it, like the world's biggest online shopping page. The main difference here is that every single one of those skirts is being worn by a model who looks exactly like me. Me in a dark pencil skirt with a white blouse. Me in a floor-length patterned skirt with a maroon sweater. Me in a blue dress with a purse dangling off my shoulder. A hundred versions of me, all happy and smiling and wearing clothes I've only daydreamed about. My throat clenches up, and that's the warning signal to tilt my head slightly back, disguise it by pretending to be really interested in the top row, and breathe shallowly until I'm sure the threat of tears has passed. Making sure you don't cry is a just skill like anything else, and I've had a lot of practice.

Thanks, Dad, you psychotic jackass.

After a long moment, I think I'm ready to speak again. "Can I have number 21?" I say, and I manage to keep my voice mostly steady.

Doc Impossible taps some commands into the wall. She's quiet, but smiling, and I wonder if she knows how much this means to me. "You can have more than one, you know. I've got enough stock for the matter fabber that I could part with a few outfits' worth."

That almost cracks the dam, but I'm able to hold back. Now I'm sure she knows, but she's polite enough to pretend she doesn't. When I can talk again, I say "14, 22, and 37."

"Cool," she says, and taps on her holographic keyboard some more. "Head on over to Bravo Lab—that's the green one. The matter fabber should be done printing in a few minutes, and I'll respec the walls to be a changing room."

Bravo Lab is about the same size as the medical exam room, and like she said, there's a slot in the wall where several pieces of clothing have been dropped. They have a kind of waxy residue on them, but that's evaporating even as I hold the first piece up to get a look at it. It's the blue dress, and my fingers are suddenly clumsy as I turn it over and look at it from all angles. The walls are opaque now, and a few moments later they flicker and become mirrors. I strip again and get into the dress, and it feels right. It feels necessary.

A few minutes later, I'm sitting curled in the corner with my new clothes bunched in my lap. Those old instincts to hide and clutch things furtively are still with me, it seems. That's what safety feels like. I rest my head against the wall and enjoy the feel of my new stockings against the skin of my legs. I feel relaxed and happy and free. So wonderfully, gloriously free.

# CHAPTER FOURTEEN

The new supersuit is exactly the same as the old one in all respects, but I still can't help but think it feels a little snug. Maybe it stretches out once I've worn it a little. The emulsion smell from Doc Impossible's matter fabricator is almost gone, at least. She gave me a small satchel to strap tight to myself that can carry all the clothes she gave me, so long as I pack them right. Valkyrja finds me on the western landing balcony, rechecking the packing for a third time because I'm so scared of something falling out. These are probably the only clothes that fit my gender that I'll be able to get my hands on until I turn eighteen and move out on my own. The thought of losing even one of them before I get a chance to wear it scares the heck out of me.

The glass doors slide open, and Valkyrja steps out. Her wings open, stretch once, and then come back to her sides, looser than before.

"Hi Valkyrja." I finish packing the blue canvas bag, strap it shut, and rise to meet her.

"Hello, Danielle. Before you depart, I would ask you a question."

I slip the bag's strap over my head, and fiddle with my cape so it won't be tangled up in the strap. "Go ahead."

"Do you know how to claim your colors?" she asks.

"Uh, I thought I would just ask for a different suit."

Valkyrja shakes her head. "The one you wear is the one you will fight in. Examine the inside of your left wrist. There you will find the toggle to change your colors."

Now that I know to look for it I notice there is a small blister there, a circle slightly raised from the material around it. I push on it, and it snaps down while another blister pops up next to it. The suit's gray camouflage begins to run and fade, and brighter colors push themselves up through the material until my suit is navy blue with a white cape, mantle, and cowl. The first Dreadnought was an officer in the US Army Air Force, and wearing naval-themed colors really pissed his superior officers off. One wonders if he enjoyed tweaking their noses. I pop the second blister down, and the first reappears as the colors swim back to the mottled gray camouflage of my throwaway colors.

"Why didn't anybody tell me about this?" A little prick of disappointment pokes me. Doc Impossible likes to talk about how she wants me to have all the information, but then she conveniently forgets to mention I could take Dreadnought's colors any time I want.

"It is in the handbooks we gave you, is it not?"

"Oh, uh." And now I feel like a jerk. Good job, dumbass. "I've had a lot of homework to catch up on."

"Indeed," says Valkyrja, and she either doesn't notice my embarrassment or pretends not to. "If you choose not to carry Dreadnought's banner, you can command your suit to display heraldry of your own design. There is a small lead on your suit, near the belt line." I look down and, after a few moments' searching, find it. The cord is kind of springy, and retracts back into the suit automatically when I let it go. "To access your suit's advanced functions, insert it into the port of USB on your telephone cellular."

I look up at her, suspicious. My *telephone cellular*, she says. "You're just screwing with me now, aren't you?"

"I don't know what you refer to." Valkyrja's smile is too wide not to be in on the joke. "Would you like my address for mail electronic?"

I trade email addresses with an honest-to-Odin valkyrie, and try not to giggle too loudly. But as she slides her own phone back into the small purse hanging from her belt there's a look on her face that makes me nervous. Compassionate, caring, but firm. Resolute, I'd call it.

"Danny, why did you lie to us?" she asks. She doesn't sound mad, and she doesn't sound curious. She sounds like she already knows the answer and wants me to confirm it.

My whole body tightens. "What? I didn't lie—"

"This body was born in 1979, but I am the sum of my mother and all my mother's mothers; my years number nine and twelve hundred. I have heard every lie tongues can speak. Scant few can deceive me, and you are not among them. You were *not* practicing flying. Yet you were there. Why were you there, and why did you not tell us of it?"

"I was just, you know, going for a fly," I hear myself say. The city spreads out beneath us, and I stare out at it rather than look at her. Even as I say it, I know she spots the lie.

Her voice is soft and kind. "Danny, do you feel safe at home?"

No.

There it is. I don't feel safe at home. I open my mouth to say something, and as I do I realize that like my mother, I can't give it its name. Not out loud. Not even to Valkyrja. Because if I admit it, if I call it what it is, then I can't hide from it anymore either. It becomes real in a way I am not ready for. Might never be ready for. There will be no illusions of safety, no peaceful times alone in my room.

There will only be times when he's *not* hurting me.

She puts her hand on my shoulder. "I can arrange for you to have quarters here. You need not return there."

"It's fine," I say. "I'm fine." I'm struggling not to hyperventilate.

"Sometimes it requires great strength and courage to ask for help."

My throat is tight, and I can't look at her. "Don't tell anyone."

"Danielle—"

But before she can do anything I'm stepping away, pulling the cowl over my head, and blasting up into the clouds. She could follow me, but she doesn't, and for that I am grateful. The clouds fall behind me a few moments before the sonic booms start rippling out behind me. I slow down and do a few orbits of the city. According to my phone, I still have twenty minutes before I'm expected home from school.

Flying feels good. The wind pulling at my hair and snapping my cape is soothing, in a way. Up here, the world is a wet, gray carpet broken through with patches of trees and water. There are no problems in the air, nothing I need to hide from or watch carefully. My heartbeat slows, and on my eighth trip around the New Port City metro area, I finally start feeling better.

It'll be fine. Dad had his blowup, and now he'll start to get over it. The more time he has to think about it and grow used to the idea, the better it will get. He'll start to understand this is permanent, and though he may not ever like it, and I probably still will need to leave the house on my eighteenth birthday, I don't think there is going to be another night like last night again any time soon. As long as I stay out of his way, and don't do anything really femme around him, things will be okay.

The justifications, the optimistic scenarios, come naturally to me.

Because it's a skill set.

And I've had practice.

· · ·

Dinner is quiet and strained, the way it normally is for a day or so after a big blowup, but aside from some grumbling and some snide remarks, we get through it fine. All the homework I didn't get to yesterday is still waiting for me, and TV is one of the things I'm not allowed to do anymore (I haven't been foolish enough to ask how long I am grounded for) so I hit the books straight away and stay with them until the sun goes down.

Conjugation in French is a special kind of horror, on par with the sort of things you'd need to do to call up the Old Ones when the stars are right. Reading comic books is a way more fun way to learn the language, but it's not really going to help me on tomorrow's test, so I'm doing my best to get through this exercise on gerunds when I hear a tap on my window. There's nobody there when I look, and I almost start to believe I didn't hear anything after all. The Legion has my phone number, so they're not going to do the knocking-on-windows thing again, right? Just to be sure, I get up and open the window. The moment it's open enough to clear a body, Calamity swings down from the roof and into my room in a single liquid motion. She looks around curiously, and then turns back to me. She tips her hat.

"Howdy, Dreadnought."

# CHAPTER FIFTEEN

For a moment, I'm frozen. How did—wait. I recognize her eyes now, and the way she holds her shoulders.

"Sarah?"

"No," blurts Calamity. "Don't rightly know who that is."

"No, you're totally Sarah. You just have a bandanna over your face and you're talking funny."

"All right, fine, shut up about it!" she whispers sharply. "You want the whole world to know?"

"You're the one calling me—" Her finger is on my lips.

Calamity looks over my shoulder at my bedroom door. "Best be having this conversation outside," she mutters. I gesture to the window like *after you.* She does a diving roll out the window. Her jacket flutters as she drops to the ground and lands like a cat. That kind of grace is far outside my reach for getting through the window itself, but I like to think being able to float down at whatever leisurely pace I want evens things out a bit. Her expression is hard to read behind the red bandanna, but I think she's impressed. She frickin' *better* be, anyway.

"I'm not Dreadnought," I say quietly.

"I beg to differ," she says, pointing up at the window and tracing my path of descent.

"Dreadnought was more than his mantle. Yeah, I got his powers when he died, but that doesn't automatically make me Dreadnought too."

Sarah, or Calamity, I guess, hooks her thumbs through her

gun belt. "Don't see why not. Seems that's how it's been working since Eden."

"Do you really have to talk like that?"

"Sure do; gotta sell the persona. Elsewise, I'm just a freak with a gun, and then where would I be?"

"New Port?" One thing our fair city does not lack for is freaks or guns.

"That mouth on you is gonna hold you back in life, hun," says Calamity, but I can hear the smile in her voice.

"So what did you want to talk about?" I ask as I peek around the side of the house to make sure nobody is in the yard.

"Well, as to the first reason, I needed to confirm I had the right girl. Seems I made the correct call there, so we can proceed directly to the second." She leans forward a little bit. "Wanna go caping?"

There's a little fluttery sensation in my chest. I've been think-ing about it, obviously. That rescue, man, that was amazing. Even after everything that happened today with David and Valkyrja, the high from saving those people is still with me as this quiet little trickle of joy in the background. So hells yeah, I want to go caping! But am I ready? Is it right? Is it a good idea? Maybe I got lucky. Maybe I'll screw things up. Maybe I'll find out I'm not cut out for this. Maybe I'll get someone hurt. Or killed.

"I'm not sure I'm supposed to," I say at last. "I'm still using throwaway colors."

Calamity's eyes narrow over her bandanna. "Throwaway colors."

"Yeah, like just a neutral outfit to say I'm not—"

"I *know* what they are. I am less certain as to why you'd fall for all that prissy whitecape crap."

"Oh. You're a…"

"You can say it," she says encouragingly. "Ain't a dirty word: *graycape*."

"So, does that mean you, like—"

"Have exceptionally strong moral fiber? Yes, it does."

I was going to say *kill people*, but somehow that seems impolite. "Then why not be a whitecape?"

"That's a luxury for the rich and the powerful. People working my side of the street don't have the option of avoiding difficult moral choices." Calamity's voice is sharp, almost aggressive. "Not a whole hell of a lot of us can fly, so we don't get to be *above it all*, like the fancy folk up at the Legion."

I think of Doc Impossible and Valkyrja. I think of Magma, and how he stood up for me at the meeting. Suddenly I'm feeling defensive, like Calamity is talking shit about my friends, even though I barely know them. "If you hate whitecapes so much, why are you coming to me? I'm not even any kind of cape yet, and even if I was, I like the Legion."

"Please. You're better than that."

"What's that supposed to mean? Some of them have been really nice to me!" I'm wearing the shirt Doc Impossible made for me.

"You mean to tell me you haven't noticed how insufferable they are? The little tin gods who abandon us when they get bored?"

"They seem to want to help people to me," I say. "They stopped that asteroid last year, and they went out of their way to protect my identity."

She rocks back on her heels a little bit, looks at me across her nose. "Shoot, maybe you *haven't* seen it. Might be they're on their best behavior around you. They'd want you on their team for sure."

"I don't know about *that*." Now all I can think about is Graywytch calling me a boy, and Carapace getting nervous about the idea of me being called Dreadnought, or how Chlorophyll was ready to throw me under the bus just as long as the team got what it wanted out of me. They all seemed awfully quick to want to avoid dealing with me, one way or the other. When I think about it that way, Calamity starts to make more sense.

"Why not? You're the new Dreadnought, ain't you?" she says. "Mightier than a battleship and faster than a jet, if I've heard correctly."

"They…well, I'm a minor. So I can't join yet. And…"

"And what?" she presses.

"Some of them seem uncomfortable about me being transgender." It comes out almost as a mutter, and I feel like such a tool. Almost as if by not speaking up strongly I'm betraying myself, but by saying anything at all I'm betraying them.

"There. You see?" Calamity nods sharply. "Whitecapes are happy to draw neat little lines that make neat little boxes and act like they're Justice with her scales, but the moment someone doesn't fit into their cute little grid, suddenly they don't quite care about what's fair or not, do they?"

"Some of them really stood up for me."

"Did they kick the other ones off the team?"

"No, of course not."

"Then they're aiding and abetting your enemy." She steps close, and for a brief moment drops the accent. "Don't be so fast to hop in bed with them. Trust me."

That seems a bit simple to me. I can't imagine Doc Impossible or Valkyrja putting up with that kind of crap on a long-term basis, and though I don't know Magma as well, he was on my side, too. Even knowing I'm trans, they still let me keep the provisional membership, and Doc Impossible gave me all these wonderful clothes.

But they've all been teammates for years, saved each other's lives a million times, I bet. Calamity might be right. It might be really stupid of me to expect any of them would turn on their own if it came down to a choice between me and one of their team. I really *don't* know them well. Can I afford that kind of risk?

"I dunno…" I say, which is the closest to a coherent thought on the subject I can muster up. It's like I can see both sides of the argument with perfect clarity, but I can't see what my own opinion should be.

"It ain't like you need to decide right now," says Calamity, maybe picking up on my uncertainty. "You wanna go caping or not? You can't tell me that after that plane rescue you're not itching for more action."

There's nothing confused about the enormous smile that breaks out across my face. "Yeah, no, that was excellent."

She reaches out and pulls on my sleeve. "Come on, it'll be fun. I won't even make fun of you for wearing prissy throwaway colors. Not too loudly, anyway."

The window to my room pours a little yellow square into the night. What do I have going for me here? Homework and sitting silently in my room all night so I won't invite another screaming session. When I think of it that way, it's not even really a decision.

"Wait here, I need to get my suit."

# CHAPTER SIXTEEN

It took a moment to get the hang of following Calamity from a few hundred feet up so I wouldn't be spotted. She has an expensive-looking motorcycle, with an aggressive riding posture that's got her leaning so far forward she's almost on her stomach, and fat road-grabbing tires. "What's a cowgirl without her horse?" she said to me as she straddled the machine's enormous engine. To my dismay, she obeys all the traffic laws except for the one about being sixteen and having a license. Her helmet hides her age, and she doesn't give cops reason to pull her over. It's as good a way of traversing the city as any for a flightless cape.

It's also maddening. I'm already used to jetting off at just under the speed of sound, and then cranking up past the sound barrier when I'm away from the city. Keeping my flight under the city speed limit, waiting for stoplights and even roughly following the roads has me antsy and impatient for us to get to wherever we're going tonight. Calamity takes a turn onto a freeway on-ramp and snaps her throttle open with a howling whine I can hear all the way up here. I almost cheer with relief, but then she hits the highway speed limit almost immediately and her acceleration dies. We crawl along at a groaningly slow sixty miles an hour, cross the Anderson Bridge onto Anderson Island, follow the highway across the island and then over the Anderson-McNeil Bridge.

Calamity pulls off the highway, and then it's another tortuously slow crawl through surface streets until we're at the edge of the really seedy part of McNeil Island, the middle of the three islands, two peninsulas, and curving line of mainland that make up New Port City. McNeil Island was a real solid working man's neighborhood during the mid-twentieth century, but then the Mayo Cove shipyards went out of business, and the other industrial yards followed suit a decade later. After that, the whole island did a swan dive into urban rot. There have been some efforts to rejuvenate it, and I hear it's better than what it was like in the '80s and early '90s. It's still not a place I'd want to park a bike like Calamity's, but she seems to know what she's doing. She circles a block once before she pulls into a narrow alleyway between two decrepit brick buildings, kills the engine, and backs the bike into some deep shadows.

When I land next to her, she's unfolding a thin black tarp and throwing it over the bike.

"Is that going to be safe here?"

"Safe as houses. Back in the shadows and under the tarp like that, it will be two steps from invisible. I've locked the wheels, and it's got a pair of GPS trackers on it."

When she's satisfied her bike will be safe, Calamity takes to the roofs in a flowing series of jumps, pull-ups, and climbing. She beckons for me to follow, says we're going to be staking out a block that's one of the worst parts of the whole island. I follow low and close enough to talk quietly, but far enough to stay out of her way as she dances across the rooftops.

Calamity is amazing. She runs full-speed across the roof of one building, leaps like a gazelle over an alley, and keeps going. Without breaking stride she hurdles air conditioner ducts, fire escapes, and skylights. Her feet are light and silent. She seems to barely touch the ground after she vaults off of one roof with her arms stretched out, flips her legs back over her head once, and touches down on the other side like a leaf skimming across the sidewalk.

"Why, exactly, are you not on every varsity team at school?" I ask her after about the tenth amazing, Olympics-class feat of gymnastics performed in the dark, on wet surfaces, over concrete.

"Nobody with anything useful to do has time for that," says Calamity just before she leaps off the roof of a three-story building, rotates twice in the air, and lands on the roof of the two-floor brick building across a wide alley. She's not even breathing hard.

"How the hell does your hat not fall off?"

"A girl needs a few secrets." Calamity slows to a walk, does a slow lap of the roof, and comes to a rest at the corner of the building. "We'll lay up here and wait for someone to do something stupid."

We're at the corner of an intersection with a broken streetlight on one side. Across from us is an all-night liquor store, and all the windows around here have bars on them. Calamity plops down at the building's edge, feet dangling off the roof like it's the most comfortable spot in the world. I realize now what a soft suburban-ite I am, since even with freaking superpowers I'm nervous to be hanging around here. The clouds are low and orange from reflected city lights, and a gentle mist is falling. There's plenty of light to see, but plenty of shadows to get lost in, too.

She pats the roof next to her. "Have a seat, partner."

After making sure I'm not about to sit in something unmentionable, I take a seat next to her. Or, I try to. Sitting down with a cape on is something that takes a little practice, and I end up falling off the roof, hanging in midair while I right myself, and then floating back up and settling down next to her.

Calamity's eyes twinkle. "You all right there, hun?"

"Yeah. I've just—well, this is new to me."

"I imagine so." She kicks her legs out, swinging them back and forth a little. "What's it like to fly?"

"It's fun," I say. Calamity ducks her head, as if to say *go on*. I take a moment to try and collect my thoughts. Flying is wholly unnatural to a human being, and yet, when I'm up there, it feels like the most natural thing in the world. It's hard to put into words. "There's this great feeling of speed, and weightlessness. Or, no, not weightlessness. I can feel my weight until I get into orbit—"

"You can get into *orbit*?"

"Uh, yeah, I guess I can. I have to work at it, though. I have to get up to one or two kilometers per second to get that high; I can only really go that fast when I'm at high altitude already, so, I can do it, but it takes some effort."

"I never thought I'd be jealous of a cape with real powers," says Calamity.

Is it weird to be flattered by jealousy? It's weird, isn't it? I'm weird.

"Your acrobatics are pretty amazing," I say, hoping she can't see me blush in the dark. "My powers kinda fell in my lap. You had to work for everything you can do."

Calamity shrugs. "Not as much as you'd think. Don't tell Uncle Sam, but I'm a super soldier."

"What?"

"Yeah, my hand-eye coordination is inhuman, my flexibility is beyond human norms, and my muscle density is fantastic. I can bench press three times my body weight without straining too hard." She shrugs. "I've never had a cold or a flu."

All this time she's been walking around at school like she's nothing special, and at any moment could toss one of the var- sity linebackers around like a bag of potatoes. Between me and Calamity, I'm starting to wonder how big a segment of the student body is secretly metahuman. Maybe we can form a club. "How did it happen?"

"Born with it. Hell, everyone on my dad's side of the family has it. Anyone who traces a direct line back to grandpa gets it."

"And where did *he* get it?"

"Uncle Sam. Back during World War II, the government got to playing around with exotic chemistry. They were trying to create something that could call out Hitler's Übermenschen. Uh, this was *before* Dreadnought showed up, obviously. Once they whipped up a batch of this super serum, they needed someone to try it out on, so they did whatever white men do when they have a dangerous, unpleasant job that wants doing—they looked around for some brown people and volunteered them. That was Granddad. They told him it was a new kind of vaccine. The serum worked, and after the war when he had kids we found out it was heritable, too."

"That's…wow. How come nobody's ever heard of this?" The government has done all sorts of sketchy things over the years, but human testing of a superweapon is screwed up even for the Pentagon.

"It's all still top secret. There were some glitches; all the test subjects died within six months except Granddad. But that's only for the people who were directly treated with the serum. If you get it through your parents, it only carries a fifty-percent risk of leukemia within ten years of exposure. When I was born, I had three brothers. Now I have one."

"Jesus Christ!"

"Ain't nothing to worry your mind about." She sets her arm on my shoulder. "I've been in remission for ten years, and I get a blood screen every other month."

The complications I've been dealing with seem petty and insignificant all of the sudden. I want to say something profound and insightful. What I come out with is, "That sucks."

"Eh, you get used to it. You won't be telling *nobody* about this, by the way." She says this with the kind of vehemence that lets me know that, superpowers or not, this isn't a subject I want to make her angry about. "*We* know the serum's effects are heritable. The Feds don't, and we aim to keep it that way. They've done enough to my family already."

"Of course."

"Good." Her body relaxes, and we look back out across the intersection. She brushes back her jacket, and flips a switch on a radio strapped to her belt that has a wire running up to her right ear. "Let's see what's on for tonight."

"Is that a police scanner?"

"Hell no. By the time we hear it on the police scanner, it's time to leave." She fiddles a little with her earbud, pulls it out, peels some tape off it, and sticks it back in. "No, at the moment it's tapped into a few private alarm companies." She fishes in her jacket and comes up with a small roll of electrical tape. She snips a short length off with the scissors on a multitool. "That's where we'll get our first sniff, and then I'll switch over to the police band to know when the bacon's getting ready to stick its nose in. When I tell you to get, you get, understand?" Calamity asks as she retapes the earbud into her ear. Pretty much no matter how hard she jumps around, that earbud won't come out now.

"Yes, ma'am." I sketch out a sloppy salute.

"I warned you about that mouth, partner." She punches me lightly in the arm.

So we sit and we wait for something to happen. My first hour of real caping turns out to be a lot quieter than I thought it would be. We sit and we chat and get to know one another. It's weird. We never hung out at school before, and in fact I was barely aware of her existence. But now, sitting on a roof at night in costume, we seem to know each other better than we ever did back in the real world. That's what this feels like, like I've left my life behind. Here, it's totally normal for a girl dressed like a cowboy to be parkouring all over the city, and for me to be floating along behind her. Here, it's not any kind of problem for me to be a girl. Here, no one has ever called me a boy.

Calamity tells me about the adventures she's had caping around the city, and I tell her about how I transitioned. When I tell her about David, and how he suddenly became a jerk overnight, she surprises me by nodding along. "He is not blessed with an overly positive reputation among the girls I know at school," she says.

"What do you mean?"

The accent drops. "I mean he's a frickin' creeper! You never noticed?"

"No?"

"Yeah. There ain't a skinny girl in our year he hasn't made a pass at. Ain't nothing wrong with flirting, but he don't even shower first. He does nothing to pretty himself up, and then he's always sulky when someone brushes him off. Maybe that kind of thing is hard to see when you're a boy—"

"I was never a boy," I say, sharper than I intend to. "I mean, I was always a girl. But now people can see it."

Calamity shrugs. "Fair enough," she says, like I corrected her about my hair color. "But he couldn't see you were a girl, either. So he didn't treat you like one."

For a while I'm silent, trying to decide if I really didn't see this side of him, or if I was only ignoring it because it wasn't my problem. He never seemed creepy to me before. Lots of things have changed. Eventually, I say, "I was hoping he'd get over it."

"Sounds like there's a 'but' in there."

I repeat to her what he said as we last parted, and she sucks in a breath. "You're kidding."

"No." It sucks, really, and I've been trying to avoid thinking about it. With everything that's been happening, it's been easy to jump from distraction to distraction all day and ignore what happened between us. But now it's kind of lying out there in the open, and I can't seem to look away again.

My best friend in the world called me a tranny and said he hoped someone would rape me.

I don't really know how to deal with that. Maybe nobody knows how to deal with that.

What David said to me settles over us like a sodden blanket. Sirens pass us in the distance, and I look up hopefully, thinking maybe something is going down that will distract us. Calamity shakes her head. "That's a paramedic. Nothing we can do."

This thing keeps happening, this thing where something amazing happens to me, and then before I can even really enjoy it, somebody comes along and kicks mud in my face. It starts slowly. A few words here, a sentence there. Calamity dips her head encouragingly, and I start to talk about it. Finally, I get to be who I want to be, and to stop pretending to be something I'm not. There's nothing wrong with being a boy, but that's not who I am, and I never have been. But instead of being happy for me for being able to live as a girl, they all want to make me miserable, like I did something wrong and need to be punished. I hate it so much, and as I talk about it, I am surprised by how much heat comes into my voice. I guess I didn't know how angry I am. My fingers start to crack and crumble the bricks I'm sitting on. One of the bricks shatters and sends a little spray of masonry shrapnel out into the street.

There's a stunned moment of silence, and then we're both fighting not to laugh too loud. We roll back onto the roof and clap our hands to our mouths. For reasons we can't explain, this is the funniest thing we have ever seen. We laugh until our ribs ache, sprawled out on the roof under the glowing orange sky. It's not really funny, and when we realize that, we laugh even harder.

Finally, the laughter leaves us, and we clamber back over to the edge of the building. We sit in a comfortable silence for a while, watching the street, waiting for something to happen. I don't really care if anything happens one way or the other, I think. I'm just glad to be out of the house, away from the real world and all the things that try to push me down into the mud.

Eventually, I get a little bored and pull out my phone from the pouch it sits in on my belt. When Calamity sees it she raises an eye. "That your everyday phone?"

"I only have one." After a moment of experimentation I find I can still use the touch screen through my gloves.

"Best be fixing that at your earliest convenience," says Calamity. "Dangerous to be caping with a phone that can be traced back to you."

"By the time someone is able to take my phone from me, I think I'm going to have bigger problems." I reach down to my side and fiddle around until I can find the little cord that spools out from my belt line.

"Or, they might pick your pocket. Or, it might fall out in battle. Best be taking this seriously. You should get a burner and use that instead."

"When my family is magically rich enough to afford that, I'll let you help me shop for one." Finally I get the cord pulled out again, and plug it into the mini-USB port on my phone.

"What are you doing, anyhow?"

"'Accessing the higher functions of my suit,' she called it."

My phone's screen goes dark, and an application begins to launch. (Very slowly, of course. This is a knockoff brand.)

"Who?"

"Valkyrja."

"Oh." Her eyes are wide.

"She's really nice in person." I smile at Calamity. "She talks almost as weird as you, though."

"One of these days you'll understand how deeply that wounds me," she says, and doesn't sound hurt at all. "So what exactly are those higher functions?"

"Other than changing color, I don't know yet."

"You mean there's *more* than that?"

"Looks like it." Several colored icons are popping up on my phone. I read off their labels. "Diagnostics, repair mode, color shifting, and something about radar and thermal masking modes."

"How the *hell*—"

I shrug. "It's hypertech. Doc Impossible made it for me. Oh hey, it's got Bluetooth."

"White girls get all the cool toys."

"Yes, that's why they gave this to me. Because I'm white."

Calamity drops her eyebrows at me and I feel silly already. "Are you seriously whining about a little bit of teasing?"

"No," I mutter.

"Good. Because that'd be fucking petty, and I'd hate to have to stop liking you."

"So you like me."

"I haven't shot you yet, so it does stand to reason." Something incredibly stupid is about to come out of my mouth, but I'm saved by Calamity straightening up and pointing across the street. "I'll be damned. Someone's robbing that liquor store."

# CHAPTER SEVENTEEN

Calamity scooches off the front of the building and drops two stories straight down with a flutter of her jacket. The sound of her fall is louder than her landing, and she rolls up to a crouch behind a car parked across the street from the liquor store. I drop down behind her, just fall off the building and wait to catch myself until I'm only a foot or so in the air. The harsh fluorescent light pouring out from the store's barred windows makes it easy to see inside. A man in a hooded sweatshirt is pointing a pistol with what looks like an extended clip at someone we can't see behind the counter.

Calamity draws an enormous revolver from her belt and a bolt of alarm snaps through me. I grab her by the shoulder. "You're not going to shoot him, are you?"

"Well, yeah. That's what guns are *for*." She shakes me off.

"You can't kill people! We're the good guys!"

Calamity flicks the cylinder open and draws out one of the bullets nested inside. She holds it up from the shadows for me to get a good look at it. The tip is strange. It looks orange, and almost seems translucent. "I'm loaded with jelly rounds. These things have no penetration whatsoever. It'll be like hitting him with a baseball bat."

"Oh. Okay."

"Are you sure?" asks Calamity with theatrical concern. "Because I could fall back on my impressive arsenal of harsh language if that's too violent for you."

"Just don't kill anyone," I mutter.

"Haven't yet. Don't intend to start tonight." She slips the

round back into the cylinder and snaps it shut. "Now, if it's all the same to you I'd like to snag this guy before he gets away."

From across the street we hear the electric *ding-dong* of someone passing through the door, followed by running footsteps. The robber is sprinting down the wet sidewalk now, and a terrified-looking clerk is rushing to slam and lock the door behind him.

"Damnation. There he goes," says Calamity, standing. "I'm gonna herd him into the next alley; cut him off!"

She doesn't wait for a reply before she breaks into a sprint and starts shadowing him parallel down the street. I pop up into the orange sky and trail him closely. This is something I've never done before, but I know I can get pretty close to him before he'll notice—I've already realized most people never look up.

Calamity waits until he's near the mouth of an alley, and then steps out from behind the cab of a parked panel van. Her magnum barks twice. A car window near him explodes, and he drops his gun. Calamity is back in cover before he knows what's going on. The robber snatches up his gun with his other hand, loops his cash bag over his shoulder, and ducks into the alley. It's narrow, crowded with empty milk crates and dumpsters. I wait until he's about halfway down the alley, and then spear down from the air. I anchor myself in the lattice…

When he hits me, it's like he ran full-tilt into a concrete post. My injured ribs give a faint cry of protest, but he gets the worst of it by far. I can feel his body bend around me, his flesh press and stretch, his bones flex. It is unspeakably gross, and for a terrified moment I'm scared he will burst upon me. He bounces off me and lands flat on his back. A heartbeat later, he heaves convulsively, his bruised chest gasping for air, and he curls up in pain.

"Hey, man, are you okay?" I take a step forward.

The robber rolls over, swings his gun up, sprays me down with hot lead. The burping roar of his submachine gun is astonishingly loud in this narrow brick canyon. The alley's gloom vanishes as a foot-long muzzle flash leaps out at me. A line of explosions ripples up my chest, neck, face. The shock of it drives me back a step. The noise, the thudding, stinging impacts, the unexpected heat and light—it's all so much, so fast. I should be dead. A burst like that at this range should zip me open and leave me as a cooling bag of meat on the ground.

But I've got superpowers, so it just smarts like hell. There's a moment of silence as we both try to process what just happened. I recover first.

"Dude! Not cool!"

I can see the fear seize him. He's older than I thought he was at first, and his face is rough and lined. Thick salt-and-pepper stubble covers his chin, and when his lips pull back in fear I can see crooked, rotting teeth. He's holding one of his hands tight to his stomach, and three of his fingers are badly broken. For a moment I feel pity for him. Nobody ends up looking like this if they have an easy life.

But then I remember he just shot me about thirty times in the chest and face. That clerk he was holding at gunpoint doesn't have bulletproof skin like I do. What would this guy have done if he thought the cash wasn't coming fast enough?

The robber gets to his feet and starts running the other way. Calamity steps into the alley from her end and casually shoots him twice in the chest. I can hear the breath explode from him, and he crumples up, falls to his knees. He raises his gun again, and she shoots him in his good hand as she strolls towards him. His gun goes skittering into the shadows.

"You good, hun?" she calls to me. Her gaze is locked on the thief, her aim steady, straight at his head.

"I'm fine. Turns out I really am bulletproof."

Calamity nods. "Good to hear. Let's get this feller trussed up."

Halfway through having his wrists zip-tied together, our thief starts blubbering. It's weirdly uncomfortable to hear. Even though he was a terrifying threat to an innocent clerk, we outclass him so much it's kind of pathetic. As we frog-march him half a block back to the liquor store, it's hard not to feel a little bit like we're bullying him. He sobs and sags, and we're carrying him as much as he's walking.

Calamity must see that on my face, because she says to me quietly, "I know it's weird at first. Remember, this guy is a violent felon. You don't gotta feel bad about playing dirty with his kind." She gives him a shake. "Ain't that right, Sweet Pea?"

The liquor store clerk's eyes get wide as dinner plates when we knock on the glass door and wave at him. He almost drops the phone he's speaking into. I hold up the bag of money, and he says something quick into the phone before putting it down and vaulting over the counter. He unlocks the door, and up close I can see his eyes are red and puffy. "You got him?" he shouts excitedly. "Oh, man, thank you!"

"Not a problem, partner," says Calamity. I hand over the bag of money, and the clerk clutches it like a lost child.

"I thought I was going to lose my job!" he says. "Thank you. Thank you so much."

"Glad to help," I say.

"Is this him?" the clerk says, catching sight of the thief where we've left him propped against a car. The clerk stalks towards him. "Not so tough now, are you, ya piece of—"

I catch him by the shoulder just as he's winding up to kick the robber square in the stomach. "No."

"Wh—what? He just robbed me!"

"I don't care. I'm not going to let you beat up a defenseless man right in front of me." I squeeze his bicep just enough to let him know how strong I am.

Calamity puts a finger to her earbud. "Cavalry's coming," she says.

"Good." I turn to the clerk. "We're going to be watching until the police show up. Tell them what happened so they can put him in jail. If you hit him before they arrive, I'll come over and report you for assault. Understand?" I let go of his shoulder.

He steps away from me quickly. His cheeks are turning pink. "Yeah, fine. Whatever."

I stay and watch him until he picks the phone back up and starts talking into it again. Calamity and I vanish back into the shadows. When we're back up on the roof overlooking the liquor store, we sit back and wait for the cops to show.

"You did good, partner," she says.

"Thanks."

"I ain't sure I'd be so eager to protect someone who shot me like that."

The bottom falls out of my stomach. Of course I'd screw it up at the end. Of course. It would have been better to follow Calamity's lead, but it's too late now, so I shrug and say, "Well, I... maybe if I thought about it..." and then sort of trail off. Like he said: I don't even have the sense God gave a tapeworm.

Her bandanna makes her expression hard to read sometimes, but there's a thoughtful look in her eyes. "You're the real deal, aren't you?"

"Um?" There's this weird little flare of hope in my stomach. Maybe I did the right thing after all.

Calamity nods. "You're gonna be a great Dreadnought someday."

"Oh. No, I don't think so." I curl my knees up in front of me.

"Why not?"

I think back to that meeting at Legion Tower, and how Carapace was so set against me taking Dreadnought's name. I could fight for it, make it a fait accompli, I know I could. But the mere thought of doing that fills me with shame. Dreadnought was a fearless champion. I'm a wimp, and an idiot. If I wasn't, wouldn't I be able to stand up for myself? If I deserved the name, I wouldn't keep letting Mom bribe me into helping her pretend everything is fine at home. I would have said something. I don't deserve to be Dreadnought. Hell, I don't deserve any of this. I may be a horrible person, but I'm not going to slander the dead by pretending to be something I'm not. "Dreadnought meant so much to so many people. Also, you know, I'm pretty stupid sometimes, and I'm always finding ways to screw up. If people found what a loser I really am…It just seems like I should have a different name. *If* I even keep doing this."

Calamity is quiet for a moment. She sucks in a breath as if she's about to speak, and then hesitates. The rain starts to patter down on us, and she pulls her jacket closed tighter. Something I've said seems to have unsettled or confused her. "For what it's worth," she says finally, "I think you deserve to call yourself whatever you want."

"Thanks."

The cops arrive in a swirl of flashing lights. They get out of their cars and rush around, securing the scene. Calamity and I melt back into the shadows on the rooftop and start moving out of the area.

"We should get home and get some shuteye. Tomorrow, we're going to take the training wheels off," says Calamity. Her eyes are alight with excitement. "Might be you'll feel a lot better about calling yourself Dreadnought after you help me take down Utopia."

# CHAPTER EIGHTEEN

Another note calling me to the office shows up when I'm in class. I walk through the empty halls of school with a cold runnel of dread pouring down my spine. Maybe Dad changed his mind. But stalling won't make it better, so I walk onward. When I get to the office, my parents aren't there. A slender man in a nice suit is standing in front of the receptionist's desk. He turns to see me, and I get a strange sensation of déjà vu, like I've met him before.

"Hello, Danny," he says. It's Chlorophyll, but he's not green. Or, no, he…what?

"Uh, hi."

"Come with me," he says. When he moves, it's like the pigment on his skin is a half second behind. As we leave the office, I notice no one else in the room was doing anything. They were only standing or sitting, staring at nothing.

"Are they going to be okay?" I ask as we walk down the hall.

"Of course," he says with a smile. "Although they might start sneezing a lot later today."

"So what are you here for?"

"Let's talk in my car. It's more private."

We walk quickly out of the school and into the parking lot. My head is swiveling to make sure nobody sees us, but Chlorophyll moves with supreme confidence. We get to his car, a nice blue sedan with tinted windows. He *bee-beep*s the locks open and we settle into the front seats. This car reeks of money. Soft dark leather, real hardwood trim, everything. Being on an established superteam is a lucrative gig.

"So what's this about?" I ask, voice flat.

Chlorophyll looks embarrassed for a moment, and then says, "First, I wanted to apologize."

Which instantly puts me on guard. In my experience, apologies are weapons. "I'm listening."

"When I said it didn't matter if you were Dreadnought or not, so long as we had your powers, that was out of line. The mantle comes with the title, and you deserved more respect than that. I'm sorry."

"Um. Thanks."

Chlorophyll nods, but stays silent.

"So, uh…is that it? I've got to get back to class."

"No. I also came to ask you to reconsider joining the Legion. We really could use someone like you."

I look away from him. Being pressured is always uncomfortable for me. It means I have to stand up for myself or let myself get pushed into something, and both of those options feel horrible. It's always a no-win scenario. "I'm not sure I really want to."

"Danny, this is a huge opportunity for you. You'd be coming in at the top of your field. You want to talk funding? We have expense accounts bigger than most people's yearly pay, and that's on top of our stipends. And it's good work, too. Important work. We save lives. You could be doing something great, be someone that nobody else could hope to be. It's an amazing life, and I think you'd be good at it."

"And what if I want to be an accountant?"

Chlorophyll laughs, and I stare at him until he stops. "You're serious."

"Not really, but still. What if I don't want to be a superhero? I finally have a body I can stand living in. Maybe I just want to spend some time catching up on what I've missed."

"Ah," he says delicately. "Well, there have certainly been plenty of women who have become capes. I don't see how being one precludes the other."

"Well, maybe, but, anyway, I'm too young."

He shrugs. "You won't be forever. You're what, fifteen? Eighteen will come up faster than you think."

"So? I still can't join right now."

"That doesn't mean you can't make any choices," Chlorophyll says. He reaches into his jacket, pulls out an envelope, and holds it out to me. "This is a statement of intent. If you sign this, when you come of age you'll automatically be inducted into the Legion."

"I'm not ready to make up my mind."

He holds it out for me. "You can still change it later, but this sets you up for not having any hassles down the road no matter what you choose."

This doesn't feel right. There's got to be a hook in there somewhere. "What about Graywytch?"

Chlorophyll smiles a funny kind of smile, as if suddenly uncomfortable. "What about her?"

After taking a deep breath, I manage to say it straight out: "If you want me, then you need to kick her off the team."

"I...that's not really how things work."

"Okay," I say, not taking the envelope. "Then I guess I'm not joining."

Chlorophyll presses his lips together for a long moment. "Danny, we need Dreadnought. The *world* needs Dreadnought. If someone like Mistress Malice ever shows up again, we're the ones who have to deal with it. If people were dying, could you really just step away from that?"

"No! I wouldn't just—I'd want to help." Wouldn't I? Or maybe I'd just be too scared.

"Well, this"—he smacks the envelope on the gear dashboard—"is how you can help. Every day we get out of bed knowing that someone like her could turn up. We need you suited up and getting experience as fast as we can. Because when the next big one shows up, we're not going to be ready." As Chlorophyll speaks, his skin and hair start to fade back to green. Whatever he's doing to make himself look normal is beginning to slip. "We're *never* ready for someone like that; that's why they're so dangerous. And every day you spend with a cape on your shoulders is one more day of preparation we have against the next time something like that happens."

And, you know, it's not like he's talking nonsense. Nobody has quite gotten up to the level that she did, but there have been some really close calls in the last half century. It will happen again. Sooner or later, someone will take another stab at conquering the world. That's why all the big cities still have public bomb shelters now, and why superteams with government contracts are so heavily funded.

"I know Graywytch is being difficult," he says quietly. "I don't agree with what she thinks, but sometimes we've got to put aside our personal issues. Lives are at stake here, Danny. I know you want to do the right thing."

I sink deeper into the leather seat. Maybe I'm being really selfish. But when I reach for the envelope I remember the shame that dogs me whenever I think about how I can't stand up to Dad. I pull my hand back.

"What if I'm not good enough to be a cape?" I ask quietly. "What if I'm a coward?"

He swallows, won't meet my eyes. "Then, maybe you should… we need *someone* to be Dreadnought, so—"

"No!" I shout, suddenly livid. "I'm not giving up the mantle! I'm not going to die for you just because you asked nicely!"

"Danny, wait!" he says, but I'm already out the door. I slam it behind me, and it pops back open, latches blown to hell, hinges bent out of true. Screw him. Screw the Legion. I owe Dreadnought, but his friends? His friends are assholes.

• • •

Calamity and I both get swamped with homework, so our campaign to find and capture Utopia has to be put on hold until the weekend. Reading about Andrew Jackson's kitchen cabinet is an intensely surreal kind of frustration when you know you should be tracking down a supervillain instead. It gives me more time to practice with my powers, at least. I buy a little bouncy ball out of a vending machine at the drugstore next to school and spend about an hour each night bouncing it around my room and watching the patterns of its momentum and impacts in the lattice. A few times I try to grab the strings of their momentum, the way I did with the airliner, but I can't quite get it to work. Maybe they're too small, or moving too fast, or maybe it was just a fluke and I won't be able to do it again.

Finally, we both get ahead enough in our work that we're able to spend a few hours caping. Calamity taps on my window at the agreed hour, and I'm already wearing the suit. She beckons me to follow her. After days of rain, the weather is clear tonight, leaving the sky black and the ground dark. We slip a ways down the alley and find a dumpster to hide behind before we talk.

"I've been doing some bookwork." Calamity clicks on a small flashlight with a red filter and holds out a sheaf of papers. "This here is all that's publicly known about Utopia."

It's a detailed dossier on Utopia. Every known sighting, every known associate, even a section on estimated capabilities and rumors. It's not a long article. "Where did you get this?"

"There's a wiki for everything if you know the right passwords. Anyhow, the main thing to know is that as far as anyone can tell she's only been active since 2011, and for most of that time, she mainly provided hypertech support to larger jobs organized by more established villains. That's the rumor, anyway. She's all but anonymous most of the time." As Calamity narrates, I skim through the important parts of the printout. There's a photo of her, in surprisingly high resolution. Utopia is not a tall woman, maybe five and a half feet if she stands up real straight. Her body is made of plastic and steel. Her torso is wrapped in a faceted corset that rises to meet two thick slabs of flat armor over her chest. Her legs aren't quite human—not like they've got a second joint or anything, but their proportions are all wrong, longer than they should be and bulging around the calves. Her fiber-optic hair is short and dark in a pageboy cut, and arms that are obviously robotic but designed to look mostly human.

Her list of known crimes is relatively short and sweet. She seems picky about what kind of work she takes. "What about this job last year?"

"The NASA lab raid?" Calamity steps close beside me to see where I'm pointing.

"Yeah."

"That's the only time she's known to have worked solo until she rode into New Port and shot Dreadnought."

"What was the lab researching?"

"They were mighty curious about some chunks of that asteroid Northern Union stopped last year." Northern Union is the international team that covers North America, and the Legion Pacifica provided a lot of the NU's muscle before Dreadnought died. For all intents and purposes, sometimes the Legion *was* Northern Union. "She made off with all the samples, but nobody really understands why she'd want 'em."

"Do you know what she was doing on the day she killed Dreadnought?" I ask. The memories come back sharp and hard. The guilt follows.

"I am not possessed of any firm notions, no," says Calamity. "The news says the place she hit was a software development shop. Their website says they do medical-grade software, but nobody answered the phone when I called. Probably still closed for repairs."

"If Utopia does hypertech, why is she bothering with a baseline shop?"

"That had struck me as eccentric as well."

But wait. Doctor Impossible and Carapace use baseline tech in their project. Doc said they were trying to make the technology generalizable. "Maybe she's trying to look for a way to bridge the gap between her hypertech and baseline tech, for some reason," I say.

"Possible. Difficult, though."

"Let's go check it out."

"Can't. I tried," says Calamity. "They had an entire floor, and the elevator to that part of the building is locked off."

"I wasn't thinking of using the elevator."

• • •

The shattered windows are gaping holes in the building's side. The shredded ribbons of the blinds wave gently in the night breeze. Calamity is rigid under my hands. I'm carrying her by her armpits, and since we left the ground she hasn't stopped praying under her breath. We glide into the building and I gently set her down before touching down next to her.

"There," I say. "That wasn't so bad, was it?"

"Maybe we can find another way down." Sarah is not doing the old-timey voice right now.

Shattered glass cracks under our feet. Calamity clicks her flashlight on again and plays the red beam across the room. There's burnt-out office furniture and smashed computers everywhere. Everything within six feet of the windows is still damp from the rain.

"What are we looking for?" I ask.

"This was your brilliant notion," says Calamity. "You tell me."

"Um. Well, let's see what she was doing up here."

Deeper into the building, past shattered cubicles and blasted walls, we start seeing evidence of workshops and laboratories. The rubble is inches thick on the ground, but in the few clear spots we can see sooty linoleum on the floor. The twisted mass of something that might have once been an MRI machine lies broken on the ground.

My heart sinks. I don't know what I expected. Maybe a big flashing sign saying THIS WAY TO THE CLUES. But I owe Dreadnought so much. Even if I'm not good enough to make good on the debt, I've got to try.

"Look here," says Calamity, as she pulls something from the

rubble. It's a complicated tangle of wires that are studded throughout a piece of cloth.

"What is it?"

"I don't know, but there's about ten of them here in this little chasm." The way two broken walls lean against each other has created a sort of cave from which Calamity pulled the...thingy thing. She unfolds the cloth entirely, and it appears to be a skullcap of some kind. "Was that an MRI machine in that last room?"

"Yeah, I think so."

"Then between this and that I think we can make a leap and say these fellas were interested in brains."

The facts loom over me, incomprehensible and yet somehow urgent. It feels like getting hit with a final exam I haven't studied for. "So first she knocks over a lab studying bits of an asteroid, and then she hits a place doing neurology research. How does that make sense?"

Calamity shrugs. "Maybe she's got attention deficit disorder?"

On a hunch I take a look at the lattice around here, and the bottom falls out of my stomach. "Calamity, something's wrong here."

A revolver is in her hand almost before I'm finished speaking. "What is it?"

"The lattice...it's been *torn*."

"What in hell is that supposed to mean?" asks Calamity, tension unwinding from her shoulders.

"I mean...I can sort of see the back side of reality, like it's a net of light, and everything is just a tangle in the lattice. It's where I get my powers. I've never seen the end of a thread before but now..." But now there's a big tear, right across the floor. The ends seem frayed, and they leak sparks of heat and potential. They wiggle and squirm. Nausea begins to swell in my stomach, horror like cold grease settling in every tissue of my body. If I step a few feet to the side, I can get a different angle on it, and I see that it's a laser-straight line starting near the middle of the building and shooting out the window, where it eventually fades away in the distance. Another rent in the lattice sweeps across the room, chest high, a broad slash in the fabric of the world. "Before he died, Dreadnought said Utopia had some kind of new weapon. I think...I think it's a gun that unmakes reality."

"Oh. Well. That's new."

• • •

It takes me a few minutes to settle myself enough to fly us back down to Calamity's bike. I can't get the image of those shredded reality strings out of my head. It's wrong for something like that to be possible. It's wrong in a way I can't describe to someone who hasn't worn the mantle. Everyone is better off not knowing. I wish I didn't have to know.

"We need to tell the Legion about this."

"Screw the Legion." Calamity takes off her hat and stows it in an aerodynamic storage container bolted to the back of her bike. "Utopia is *ours*."

"Calamity, this is serious." I need to make her understand. This is way bigger than we thought it would be. "That gun of hers is a crime against *reality*. They're looking for her too, and if they find her they need to know what they're going up against."

"I thought they didn't want you to be caping in throwaway colors," she says.

"Yeah, well. Crap." I hadn't thought of that. Maybe I should tell them anyway, and—no. No, that's a bad idea. Saving the jetliner is one thing, but Magma specifically told me not to do any kind of investigation. If they knew I was caping behind their backs, they wouldn't trust me anymore. They'd know that I'm not good enough for my powers. That I don't deserve them. Graywytch would turn them all against me.

"They know to be careful. She killed Dreadnought, so they won't take any chances." She puts her helmet on and straddles her bike. "We'll run it from our end, and they'll take it from theirs."

She's right, of course. I can't tell the Legion what we found.

Valkyrja might think I'm ready, but that doesn't change the fact that they were pretty firm about me not doing any investigations in throwaway colors. In my head, I can see it clearly: Doc Impossible and Valkyrja and Magma looking down at me, disappointed, but nodding as if it finally makes sense. As if they've realized what kind of a person I really am. I won't tell them. I *can't*.

But the horror of what I've seen won't leave me. I hug myself tight around the middle and look back up at the burnt-out floor of the skyscraper, some blocks distant from us now. Utopia needs to be stopped, if only so she'll never fire that gun again.

Calamity reaches over and touches my shoulder lightly. "Come on, we still have a couple hours before we need to call it a night."

"Where are we going?"

"There's a bar I know."

# CHAPTER NINETEEN

The bar is called the Flying Dutchman, and it has no sign. It's called the Dutchman because for a long time it moved from place to place, and the only way to find it was to know someone who knew where it'd be. Calamity explains that since then, they've worked something out with someone, so now it doesn't have to move every night. The details of the arrangement are something she says we're not supposed to be curious about. To get there, you've got to go to this anonymous stairwell down into the pavement along the back side of a building in the meatpacking district. Behind the door is a long hall that kinks and twists until eventually you're at another door, one that looks like it was built to withstand a military assault. Calamity stops me before we go inside.

"You said your suit could change colors, right?"

"Yeah."

"Then change them to something that's not an obvious Legion hand-me-down." Calamity gestures up and down at my suit. "You go in there looking the way you do right now, and laughter is about the best thing you can hope for." The Flying Dutchman, Calamity has explained, is a bar for graycapes, nonpartisans, and associated hangers-on. Occasionally, the lighter shades of black-capes show up, and plenty of baseline muscle looking to get hired on for "odd jobs" hang around the place, too. Whitecapes aren't exactly unwelcome, except they're totally unwelcome.

"Uh, I don't know if this is a good idea."

Calamity steps up close to me. "Do you want to catch Utopia or not?"

"Yes."

"Then pick some goddamn colors."

"Hold on," I say as I fumble my cell phone out of the little pouch on my belt line. A few moments later I've got it plugged into my suit and I'm booting up the color-changing app. To make it easy, I just select the whole garment and stab at one of the preselected colors, a dark green. A new blister pops up on my wrist, and I push it down. The gray camouflage melts and swirls and becomes a solid emerald across my entire body.

"Good enough," says Calamity. "Come on."

We approach the door. There's a security camera behind a thick shield of bulletproof glass that watches us as we approach. Calamity knocks at the door, and the camera turns to center on us. After a long moment in which I start to hope they won't let us in, thick magnetic bolts thud open and the door swings outward. We step through and find ourselves on a small landing above a short flight of stairs down into the rest of the bar. Glossy old wood is everywhere, and the light is a bit dim. An old jukebox plays music about a decade out of date. The place is not quite packed, but it's still the largest gathering of metahumans I've ever seen.

A bouncer approaches us. He's a lot smaller than you'd think a bouncer should be. His skin moves strangely, like it's locked in place except for short, rapid shifts, as if he's a bad example of stop-motion animation. I get the feeling that if I punched him as hard as I could, he *might* feel it. Or maybe that's just the way he carries himself. Calamity draws her pistols and hands them to him without being asked. He nods, places them in a cubby, and hands her a chit with a number on it.

"Come on, let's get a table," says Calamity. I follow her down into the bar and weave between occupied tables. A lot of the people here look baseline, but a few have things like reptile eyes or glowing hair. Maybe a quarter of them are dressed in colorful outfits like Calamity or myself. We find a small table far from the bar. It's not against a wall, but at least we'll have a good view of both doors. I only know this because Calamity gently prompts me to sit across from her in such a way that my field of view covers all her blind spots, and hers covers mine.

A waitress floats over to us, toes pointed toward the ground some six inches beneath her. "You ain't been around, Calamity," she says as she pulls out an order pad.

"Been lookin' into things."

"What kind of things?"

"I'm looking for Utopia."

The waitress blinks. "Oh. Who's your friend?"

"A new girl. I'm showing her around."

"I'm D—" Calamity kicks me in the shin. "Emerald."

"Pleased to meet you, D-uh-Emerald," says the waitress. "That's a nice suit you've got there."

"Thanks. I'm, uh, really into cosplay."

"Sure thing, kiddo." She turns back to Calamity. "Anyhow, the usual?"

"Yeah, and for her, too."

The usual turns out to be a pair of Diet Cokes with straws. We sit and sip our drinks. "What are we doing here?" I ask. Calamity has obviously had practice slipping a straw under her bandanna without looking like a dork. "Putting our ear to the ground," she says.

"Oh."

It turns out putting one's ear to the ground means sitting around doing not much, but trying to pay attention to everything. The murmur-burble of two dozen conversations at once, with music on top of that, basically makes eavesdropping impossible. A few people come by to chat briefly with Calamity, but nobody has anything important to say. It is supremely boring, and after a half hour of it, I start to get antsy.

"How often do you do this?"

"Eh, once a week or so." She shrugs. "Been busy lately."

"Is there something we're looking for?"

"We'll know when we see it."

The main door to the bar is over Calamity's shoulder. It opens, and a familiar figure shuffles through. "Crap."

"Hey, caping ain't all roof running and firefights, you know."

"No, I mean I see what we're looking for." I lean closer to her, drop my voice, and point. "That guy who just walked through the door is my dad."

"Sit back, don't point," she says calmly. Calamity moves her glass across the table and examines it intensely. After a moment I realize she's looking at the reflection of the bar behind her. "Does he know?"

"About my powers? No."

"Fine. Don't look at him, and don't draw attention." Her voice is level and smooth, but it's got the same kind of solid control you imagine a surgeon might use during a tricky operation. "He doesn't happen to have superpowers of his own, does he?"

For a wild moment, the world seems to shift under me as a whole new realm of horrifying possibilities plays out in my mind, but no. No, Dad is not the kind of guy who would keep his powers quiet. Especially not these past few years, since he lost his good job and has gotten so much louder about being "strong" and how important it is for "a man to provide for his family." (And here, my train of thought briefly segues into a bitter accounting of all the things he has provided for me. Shame. Fear. Hearing loss.) Doc Impossible said most people with superpowers—ahem, that is, "special abilities"—use them to make a lot of money. There's no way Dad would still be slaving away in a crummy little retail tax preparation job if he could do that.

"No, he's baseline."

"Do you have any notion why he would be here, then?"

Not at first, but just a moment of thinking about it suggests a really awful possibility. "Oh. Oh no."

"Care to share?"

"He's looking for a cure," I say. Calamity raises her eyebrows, inviting me to explain more. "For me being trans, I mean."

"He may be a long time searching." She slips the straw back under her bandanna and takes a sip.

"My luck isn't that good. What if he finds a shapeshifter who can shift *other* people's shapes?"

"My, that *is* a nasty little mind you have," Calamity says approvingly.

The first whispers of panic are beginning to float around in the back of my head. "What am I going to do?"

"First, calm yourself." She puts her hand on my wrist. "I've not heard of anyone who can do that, and I doubt anyone else has, either. Even if they do exist, *he* ain't gonna find them on his first night slumming. Second, they'd have to have tumbleweeds rolling between their ears to do something that would piss you off that much. Really, hun, you ain't got much to worry about on this score right now."

With an almost physical effort of will, I cram the panic back down. Calamity is right. He can't take this from me. I disappointed myself when I thought I could stand up to him, but I'm still determined not to give up the mantle. I will stay a girl until the day I die, and there is nothing he can do about it. Holding onto that thought tight, as tight as I can, helps. A little. Seeing Dad here is unpleasant in ways I wasn't prepared for. Running around in a costume with Calamity has been an escape. Since I went back to school, I can barely show my face at home. Every night is spent quietly poking around the internet or doing homework for fear of waking the mountain again. Climbing out the window into a world where I get to be someone else, someone who isn't scared all the time, even if that someone doesn't have a name, has been magical. But now he's invaded that, too. It leaves me feeling cold, and a little queasy, but I can manage. Dad hasn't noticed us, although he's constantly scanning the room. It's okay. It will be okay.

"How in the hell would he even find this place?" wonders Calamity.

"He's pretty smart. And, I guess, determined."

Dad sits at the bar, and keeps looking around and adjusting

his seat. The bartender brings him a large glass of some kind of hard liquor, and Dad knocks it back like apple juice. A few minutes later, he gets up and starts trying to strike up conversations, most petering out quickly, causing him to move on to another.

"Uh-oh," says Calamity.

"What?"

"He's barking up a mighty bad tree." She nods at my father, who is talking to a man with biceps like my thighs and no neck whatsoever. "That's Bosco. He's nonpartisan, but he's also a separatist."

"There are metahuman separatists?"

"*All* minorities have separatists, and he's a real nasty one. Your father doesn't want to be talkin' to his sort." Calamity puts her hand on my arm again when I'm halfway out of my chair. "Easy. Might be Bosco just tells him to—aw, hell."

Dad is looking really happy, relieved even, and he and Bosco are getting to their feet. There are two doors in the Flying Dutchman, and they head toward the one in the rear. Calamity clamps down on my wrist to keep me from following.

"Is he going to hurt my dad?"

"Not immediately. We should give them a few moments to clear the door. No sense advertising that we're following them."

An achingly slow thirty seconds passes, and then we stand and follow Bosco and Dad out the back exit. More than a few patrons spare us a glance as we go by, but I am so far beyond caring I can't see it anymore. The air outside is wet and cold. The door closes behind us with a solid *thuh-thump* of magnetic bolts, and there is no handle on this side. We're in an open storm drainage channel, set a little ways above the main spillway on a raised platform that's part of a series of catwalks. Across the channel, just twenty or thirty feet distant, I see Dad following Bosco up some stairs to street level. In the sudden quiet of the outdoors I can hear him talking, excited, almost babbling, about how he is so glad he could find someone to help his son. For a brief moment I almost want to let him take his chances with Bosco.

Calamity begins walking down the side of the canal to get to the catwalk bridge. Her gait is so fluid that even with her boots on she doesn't clang against the metal. That's not a trick I can duplicate, so I tap her on the shoulder and point up. She nods, and I lift into the air and put a good thirty feet between me and street level.

With my suit turned to green, I'm more visible than I like. I press the second blister on the inside of my wrist, and my gray camouflage pattern comes back. In this darkness, that kind of stealth might be useful. In the light of the full moon, I can see everything clearly. Bosco can too, so every edge counts. As I tail them, I realize I forgot to ask Calamity what kinds of things Bosco can do. I look around for her, but she's vanished into some deep shadow.

Bosco is leading Dad into a vacant lot behind two low brick buildings. The fence facing one road is made of panels and beams, and Bosco holds a loose board open for Dad. Only when my father is halfway across the lot and sees the chain-link fence on the other side does he realize he's trapped. He turns around, a kind of confused smile on his face.

"It's blocked," he says.

"I know," says Bosco, stepping closer.

Dad takes a half step back. "So, you can do it from here?"

"It don't matter," says Bosco. "I could kill you anywhere."

# CHAPTER TWENTY

*Yes.*

Bosco says to my father, "I could kill you anywhere," and the first thing that pops into my head is: *Yes.*

*Kill him. Please.*

I'm a horrible person.

*But so is he!*

But he's my father, I can't let him die.

*But he deserves it!*

I'm a horrible person, and it's the guilt that drives me onward.

Bosco starts laughing, and I start diving for speed. I jerk myself to a stop ten feet above them. They don't see me, but I realize that once I'm down there, it's almost certain Dad will recognize me. Even in the dark. Even with my cowl on. Even though he never liked to look at me once I became a girl. At that range he'll know who I am. Crap. I can't let him die, but I can't let him see me. As I'm frozen with indecision, Bosco seems to grow a few inches and stalks towards Dad. The moonlight now glints off his skin like it's polished steel and his footsteps sound heavier, sharper.

Calamity saves the day.

Something clatters on the ground between them, and a trilling instinct warns me to screw my eyes shut. An instant later, a bang like the end of the world washes over all three of us. I open my eyes to see Bosco and Dad both wobbling on their feet, stunned and frozen. I drop down, seize Bosco under the armpits, and pop back into the air. He's much heavier than I expected. A few seconds later, and a few hundred feet up, he comes to his senses.

About a half second after that, I've dropped him and I find myself spinning wildly on three axes, with my neck sore and the left side of my face stinging. He has somehow managed to hit me in the face hard enough that I feel it way more than I did when I got shot. I get control of myself about twenty feet before I hit the ground, and a moment later I hear the sound of something heavy hitting the ground after falling from a great height. The world still seems to spin, and I'm disoriented, which is going to be my excuse for why I just hang there in the air while he does a sprinting leap and slams into me like a truck. We land in the middle of a street and I take the worst of it, crushed between the ground and what appears to be a Bosco made of living steel.

He finds his feet, grabs me by the front of my suit, and throws me straight through a parked van. The van detonates shattered glass in every direction and I end up crumpled against a brick wall on the other side of it. When I push myself to my feet, he's right there to put his fist through my skull and I just manage to jerk out of the way. He goes wrist-deep into the wall.

So, uh, maybe I ought to hit this guy—

His elbow takes me in the nose and I go skidding down the sidewalk, crack over a fire hydrant. Yellow pops of pain are dancing up my back. This is really not my night.

He's up in the air again, coming down with both fists. I scramble sideways, pull into a roll, and he lands where I was with a night-shaking clang. Even as I get to my feet, throwing a half-hearted jab at his jaw, he's moving into me, knocking me down.

His punches are like enormous, cracking strikes of lightning. He's digging a new pothole with the back of my skull. But when I get a hand between my face and his fist, I'm able to stop him cold. His knuckles clap against my palm with a sound like a gunshot, but my arm doesn't budge more than a centimeter or so. For a moment we're both too surprised to continue.

"Stop hitting me," I tell him. With a convulsive ripple of my stomach muscles, I get my knees between him and me, and he backs way the heck off before I can launch him into orbit. Okay, maybe not literally. But almost.

"You'd attack one of your own?" Bosco says. His voice is wary, but sullen. Is this what a bully sounds like when he's scared? He backs off, a good ten yards or so, arms loose and ready. "For a *flat*? What the hell is wrong you?"

"What the hell is a flat?" Being able to fly gives you all sorts of nifty choices for getting up off the ground so it's not super obvious you're worried about being unsteady, and I take advantage of that, pivoting up from my heels to rest gently on my feet.

"You must be new. Flats are *them*. The baseline."

"That is the most boring slur I have ever heard."

Bosco doesn't seem to expect me to be as fast as I am, because his arms are barely starting to come up when I slam my fist into his nose with the power of a locomotive. He goes backward end over end and I stay with him and wind up for a kick. My toe catches him in the gut and he goes *up*.

Once he's up there, he's stuck in a nice, predictable arc. Not that I planned it this way; kicking him high in the air just seemed like a good idea. To be honest, I don't really know what I'm doing. I haven't been in a fight since the fifth grade. It's, uh…it's different than I remember.

Bosco begins his downward trajectory, and with a jolt of fear I realize there's a not unrealistic chance he could land on someone. It takes every bit of acceleration I have, but I manage to get to him before he hits the ground. What I was planning on doing when I got there, I haven't the foggiest. The impact is enormous, an almost cataclysmic smashing of bodies that jolts me all the way through. My collarbone complains sharply, and my rib injury from the jetliner rescue starts to act up again. But somehow I manage to get my arms around his waist and keep them there, so we're gaining altitude fast.

Mechanical punches begin to fall on my head, neck, and shoulders. These are blows that could shatter concrete and bend steel. Yeah, they hurt, but none of them are doing any real damage.

My skin holds, and my bones don't shatter. With my shoulders drawn in tight and my head ducked low, he can't get the angle he needs to make me regret it.

"Hey, lemme go!" Bosco shouts over the wind. "You ain't supposed to be fighting in throwaways!"

"You're not supposed to be setting up to murder people. Let's go squeal on each other to the Legion and see whose ass they kick!"

Bosco's answer is a double-fisted hammer blow, right to the back of my head. It jolts me around a little, but I maintain my grip. "Hey, hey, this ain't funny!" he shouts. "I was just gonna rough him up, I swear!"

"Aw, come on, hit me like you mean it, you weenie," I shout. Something wild has come to life inside my chest. Pure, savage joy pours through every part of me.

Standing up for myself has never been something I've been any good at. There was a time in middle school when I knew the names and habits of my bullies better than my teachers. No matter how much I wanted it, I just couldn't get them to treat me with respect or even just leave me alone. Maybe it was the way I liked to carry my books—that hadn't been beaten out of me yet—or the way I liked to cross my legs. Maybe it was just that I was a quiet, shy kid who thought all the boisterous exuberance of early testosterone exposure was somehow distasteful and uncomfortable. So I got bullied a lot. When I told my parents, Dad said I needed to handle it myself, that it was an important step in becoming a man. I didn't have the courage to tell him I wanted nothing of the sort, and so for years I endured torment at school in silence, because I knew if I said anything about it at home again, I'd be blamed for it. There was nothing I could do, so I endured and learned which parts of school were safe to hang out in. The anger was there, but I packed it up and stored it away, deep inside me where it piled up into great heaping mountains that I pretended I didn't have.

But that feeling of helplessness is falling behind me as fast as the city lights. Bosco's blows get weaker but faster as his panic begins to take hold. His terror makes me feel amazing. I begin to laugh. Every stupid half-formed fantasy of standing up to the bullies and beating them into a hospital bed comes back to me at once. Years of bottled rage are uncorked. Someone has to pay for what was done to me. Now, I'm strong enough to *make* him pay. For a heady moment I consider trying to get Bosco up into orbit for real.

But then he starts weeping, the bastard. His weeping ruins it, and probably saves me from doing something I'd regret for the rest of my life.

My ascent slows, and he's not hitting me anymore, just bawling. He's trying to say something through the tears—and I'm sure there are tears, I can hear them, although I can't get a good look at him in the dark and have no idea what a metal man's tears would look like—but I can't make it out.

"*Shut up!*" I shout at him, and by some miracle he pulls it back to a wet sniffling. "You're a bully and a coward. If I hear about you threatening baselines again, I will drop you off in Antarctica and let you walk home. Do you understand?"

"Yeah, yeah, please. Just lemme go."

We're over the water now, and I can't resist. He makes a big splash.

• • •

Our fight carried us about a mile from the Flying Dutchman's rear exit, and it takes me a few minutes to find my way back. Calamity waves me down with a glowstick from a rooftop.

"You okay?" she asks as I touch down. "That was some racket."

"Yeah, fine. I dropped Bosco into the Sound. What happened with, uh, you know?"

"He got the hell out of dodge." Calamity tips her head back to gesture over her shoulder. "I followed him to make sure he got to his car all right."

A little pang of regret shoots through me. We might have

arranged to arrive too late. I might have been free of him. But now I've got to go back home and face him again. Damnit.

"Thanks," I say, suddenly exhausted. "We should probably head home."

"Sure, but come with me back to the Dutchman. I need to pick up my guns."

We make our way through the empty streets, sliding around the pools of yellow streetlight and flitting from shadow to shadow. When we're back inside the long hallway, Calamity speaks again. "That was amazing, you know that, right?"

I shrug. "I guess. Is he really nonpartisan? If he's going around trying to kill baselines, that seems pretty blackcapey to me."

"He's a thug, for sure, but he's too stupid and lazy to be a blackcape. He works in construction, I hear, and hauls things around." She pauses for a moment. "Come to think of it, I don't think he's actually killed anyone. He just likes to make them scared when he beats them up."

"And what, people just put up with someone like that?" I ask.

"What, exactly, do you expect anyone to do about him? As long as he restrains himself from making corpses, the cops ain't interested in a tussle, and the Legion is far too high and mighty to worry about every rat in the gutter. You're about the first person in this town who is *able* to fight him that has bothered to."

A little nugget of outrage starts to burn in my gut. "It's not like he waited to see if I could take it before he hit me at full strength. If I were anyone else, he'd have killed me."

"Yes. And that's why I'm glad you stopped him," says Calamity. "Danny, I know I was pretty harsh on the Legion, but I see this kind of crap every other week. They don't bother with small stuff like Bosco beating up a baseline every now and then."

"They wouldn't—I mean—they've got to have their reasons, don't they? Maybe it'd cause too much chaos or something. They need to keep the peace, right?" Even to myself, that sounds lame.

"Ain't no peace without justice, hun," says Calamity. "I don't care why they sit up there in their little tower and let bullies like Bosco run around free. I just care that they do."

"I'll ask them," I say. "Maybe I can change their mind."

She nods, and we keep walking. A moment later she says, "Danny, promise me, if you ever do join up with them, like, full-time, that you won't forget tonight. You won't forget us small fry."

"It'd be pretty hard to forget you, Calamity."

For a moment I'm scared I've offended her. She straightens up, looks at me funny. Finally, just as I'm about to apologize, Sarah says, "Thanks."

# CHAPTER TWENTY-ONE

So we don't find Utopia that weekend. Or the next night, or the next. Then we get walloped with homework, and we have to take the rest of the week off to catch up. Sarah says once she turns sixteen she's going to test out and get her GED so she can start caping full time. She never says so out loud, but I get the feeling her parents know what she's doing. Testing out won't be an option for me. I'm stuck here until I can turn eighteen and become a legal adult. There's no way my parents would let me leave school.

Speaking of, here comes Dad. He lumbers into our kitchen, stepping over the broad, curling crack in the linoleum we've trimmed down but don't have the money to fix. The house is starting to fall apart in a dozen tiny ways. Someday, we are assured, there will be a summer of do-it-yourself projects to mend the place up. Mom and I aren't holding our breath, though.

My gaze drops to my cereal, and I try to eat quickly without being obvious about it. Watching Dad closely is a habit that's so natural I don't even notice I'm doing it half the time. I don't think he's been sleeping well. His eyes have bags under them, and when the weekends come he doesn't bother to shave. He'll pad around the house for hours, sometimes all day, in nothing but his boxers, undershirt, and bathrobe. He never says anything about what happened with Bosco. As far as he wants to pretend, nothing happened. That's fine; I don't like thinking about it either. That whole episode is soaked in regret and guilt for me. Contempt, too. He talks a big game about being a strong man, and then he needed to get bailed out by a little girl. Calamity had a quiet word with the bouncer at the Flying Dutchman, and Dad won't be allowed in again, so at least I won't need to tail him to keep him from going back.

It really worries me that Dad is out searching for metahumans to "fix" me. Not that I'm scared he'll find a fix. Calamity is right: once I explain I have the mantle, nobody would be stupid enough to try shapeshifting me against my will. My concern is that Dad's already found one metahuman who was willing to smash his bones for fun, so who's to say what else he'll find as he staggers through the underworld, shrieking for help?

"What's this I hear about you quitting the football team?" he asks as he fills the coffeepot with water. His voice is mild, but I know not to let that fool me.

Swallowing my food is a good excuse for taking a moment to think of my reply. "I didn't quit. Coach and I agreed that since I'm not a boy anymore—"

"Danny, you *are* a boy," snaps Dad. "You were born a boy, and I raised you as one."

There's like ten million things wrong with that sentence, but all I can think of to mutter by way of reply is, "Yeah. Well. Things change."

He puts the pot down. "Son, I know it's scary right now—"

"I'm fine." He didn't call me "son" very often before my change, but now he can't get enough of it, like if he denies I'm a girl enough, he can make it untrue.

Dad sighs, and pulls out a chair. He sits down next to me and puts his hand on my shoulder. "Son, you don't know what you're saying." Ugh. The Concerned Father. I hate it when he does this. He's not any less likely to erupt when he does this, but it gets under my skin so much that I'm more likely to say something that will set him off. "This is stress that nobody could be ready for, and you're doing the best you can. I'm proud of you for holding up so well. But pretending like it's fine, and like you could be happy this way—that's not going to make it better. You've got to face your problems, not deny them."

With every word, the resentment builds in me until I can barely keep my face clean of it. In a voice so steady it surprises me, I say something really stupid.

"Dad, I'm transgender. I like being this way. I'm not going back, and you can't make me."

He gets this confused look on his face, with an undercurrent of something that scares me, so I push on quickly to get it all out while I've still got my nerve.

"I've known I wanted to be a girl for years. This change is the best thing to ever happen to me. I won't go back."

He sits back in his chair, and looks at me like he's never seen me before. The deep flush starts low on his neck and moves upward. His eyes go hard, and I brace up for another Vesuvian detonation of Mount Screamer.

His words are lost in the sheer noise of it. He gets up and paces around as he bellows, as if his rage is too wild for him to be still. When he blew up after I went back to school I thought we'd touched bottom, but I was wrong. He's letting loose with everything now.

*Freak. Tranny. Faggot.*

He goes down the list.

*Worthless. Disgusting. Failure.*

There's no end to it.

*Abomination. Sinful. Unnatural.*

I'm fighting to become safely dead inside.

*Queer. Homo. Shemale.*

But he knows how to dig in under my guard.

This is my fault. I am so stupid. Why am I always so stupid? What is wrong with me? I should have kept my mouth shut. I should have let him believe the lie. Pathetic. I'm pathetic and stupid.

He runs out of steam, the way he sometimes does, but his rage is still there, so he makes me an accomplice. "Well?" he demands. "What do you have to say for yourself?"

"I'm sorry," I mutter.

"Speak up when you're talking to me!" he snaps.

"I'm sorry!" I say. This is the only safe thing *to* say when he's like this.

"Get out," he snarls. "Get out, you disgusting little freak."

Every ounce of my self-control is needed not to use my powers to bolt up into the stratosphere. With my eyes on the floor and my heart slamming in my chest, I leave my bowl where it is and walk-run out of the room and up the stairs. My hands shake as I throw some textbooks and paper in my backpack, and I seriously consider leaving through the window. But no, if he doesn't hear me come down and leave through the front door he might come up to investigate. So I leave through the front door, as swiftly and silently as I can. It's not safe to come back here for a few hours at least.

I should have let him die.

I'm so stupid.

• • •

By the time I get to the library the shaking and the fear has dribbled away. Now I'm feeling angry and mean. On the train, a man old enough to be my father—and right then, even that was enough to hate someone—leaned forward and said, "Smile dear, it can't be that bad."

For a moment I was stunned. A boiling fury consumed me. Here I was, glowering in peace, and this…this insufferable jackass decided to insert himself into my life and pass judgment on all its events and my feelings. For a few seconds there, I seriously considered the merits of kicking him through the side of the train and down onto the streets below. But I didn't, which I'm sure I'll be glad of later. Right now, though, I just want to find someone and make them pay. For something. For anything.

I texted Sarah on the ride over, and she meets me at the broad granite steps leading up to the library. The library is a palatial building, and even though it's only three floors high it seems to tower over us with its soaring columns and mournful gargoyles.

She skips and runs down the stairs toward me, a huge smile on her face that melts away when she sees the look on mine. "Are you okay?"

"I'm fine," I snap as I pound up the steps. She blanches, and I pause at the doors. "I'm sorry. I had a bad morning."

"What happened? I thought you were grounded."

"Doesn't matter."

I keep marching and stiff-arm one of the front doors. Sarah falls in behind me, and we pass through the foyer. We find an open table in a reading room to sit down at. The reading room is a kind of Gothic chamber, with vaulted ceilings and richly carved old wooden trim you don't see in modern buildings. The floor is polished marble with strips of red carpet running down the main walkways. Tall, many-paned windows let the soft gray light of late morning in, and I don't care about any of it. This is one of my favorite places in the city, but the dull ache of anger is blotting everything else out.

I'm supposed to be catching up on history. The third time in a row I get to the end of a page before realizing I haven't remembered a word I read, I close my book. "Screw homework, let's go find a mugger to beat up."

Sarah looks up, lips pressed tight. "No. We're not going caping while you're angry."

"Why the hell not?" I snap.

"Because when you go into it angry you make mistakes. And the kinds of mistakes *you* can make would be real bad."

"I can control myself."

"I don't think that you can," says Sarah evenly. "And in any case, I'm not going anywhere with you while you're being like this."

"Being like *what*?"

"A bitch," says Sarah. "Danny, what is up with you?"

I almost cuss her out, pack up my laptop, and leave. Almost. But when I realize what I'm about to do, the anger rushes out of me, and all that's left is the pain. She can see the change come over me, and her expression softens.

"I came out of the closet to Dad," I say quietly. "About how I'm transgender, and I don't want to go back to being a boy."

"Oh," Sarah says.

"And he called me—" My throat clenches up, and I wait for it to pass. "Why can't he just be happy for me?"

Sarah opens and closes her mouth several times, and then finally says, "That sucks. I'm sorry you have to put up with that."

"Not your fault."

"I know. Still. Do you want to talk about it?"

I sigh. "Not really. I'm sorry. I was an ass."

"Plenty of bridges in this town, I'm sure we can let some water pass under one of them," says Sarah, with hints of Calamity.

I open my textbook back up and try to pick up where I left off. What Doc Impossible said comes back to me. I've got to get better at dealing with my anger. I wish I could just flip a switch and make it go away. At least I have a friend like Sarah to set me straight. That's nice, really. David was never one to talk about feelings. Said it was too girly.

Girly suits me fine.

# CHAPTER TWENTY-TWO

By the time I finish the final draft of an essay about Mistress Malice's campaign for world domination (short version: with over a quarter million confirmed dead including 39 heroes and 182 fighter pilots, Mistress Malice remains the undisputed heavyweight champion of supervillains, even almost 60 years after her death), Sarah has become Calamity in everything but costume.

She's scribbling in a notebook, pausing to think, scratching things out, scribbling again.

"You got a plan?" Without really talking about it, we seem to have come to the agreement that Calamity is in charge, which is fine with me, since I don't really know what I'm doing.

"I'm starting to. Utopia hit that medical lab downtown, right?"

"So?"

"So she doesn't have everything she needs. I'm betting she's hitting other places, too."

"Have you checked the police blotters?" I ask as I slip my books and laptop back into my bag.

Calamity raises her eyebrows at me. "Danny, you ever even seen a police blotter?"

"No."

"They have basically zero information. *A burglary was reported at 123 Hypothetical Street* is about all you'll get. We head down that road and we'll be sifting through every reported crime in the New Port metro area for the past six months with no way of telling which ones even looked like something our girl was involved in. We don't have that kind of time. We need something else."

"Okay. So what do we do?"

"I've got a couple of contacts I can put the word out to, but mainly I want to go back to the Dutchman."

Ugh, I really do not want to waste another night sitting on my ass in the Dutchman, trying to look hard. Sarah doesn't seem to notice that they think we're the bar mascots, but I do and it's not something I'm super thrilled about. "Yes, because that's worked so well thus far."

"Don't you sass me, sidekick," she mutters around the edge of her chewing pendant.

"*Sidekick?*"

"That's a funny-sounding echo," says Calamity as she closes her notebook and locks it. It looks like one of those locking diaries, except the lock has a thumbprint reader on it. "Now, as I was saying: the Dutchman is one of the main networking points for the metahuman underground in New Port. If Utopia is pulling off other robberies, she'll need lackeys. Supervillains ain't known for doing their own menials. Someone's got to drive the getaway van. If she was looking for muscle that wouldn't lose their heads when things got weird, the Dutchman would be a good place for her to shop. Last time we were there, I didn't exactly make it a secret we wanted to find her. We show our face again, shake the tree a bit more, and I'm betting something interesting will fall out."

"Okay, when do you want to do it?"

Sarah considers for a moment. "You feeling better?"

"Yeah." In fact, I'm kind of embarrassed by how angry I was.

"Then let's do it right now. Daylight's burning, partner."

• • •

Finding a safe place to change into our capes and stow our stuff in the middle of downtown during the day is a larger challenge than I'd have expected, but soon enough we're riding on the roof of a blue line train out to the meatpacking district. Calamity sits cross-legged with one hand holding down her hat, the other clenched on some pipes running across the carriage's roof. We have to sit close to each other to be able to speak when the train is moving at speed. Calamity keeps flicking her eyes away, probably to make sure nobody is watching us and calling the cops.

The Flying Dutchman seems to be a twenty-four-hour kind of place, and the door opens right up when we pound on it. Calamity hands over her guns to the bouncer, who smiles at me, but doesn't card either one of us. Do metahuman bars just not bother with liquor licenses or something? Anyway, we've barely sat down when somebody bolts up from his seat and takes off for the back door. He's got short brown hair and isn't very tall. It's not too crowded today. He might as well have walked up and introduced himself: *Hi, I'm the lead you've been looking for.*

Well, he might have introduced himself to Calamity that way. This is all still new to me, and I don't understand the significance of it until she's tapping me on the hand and gesturing with a tilt of her head. I make to get out of my seat and she clamps her hand down on my wrist. "Hold it, partner. Don't want it being too obvious we're taking an interest in him. We'll give him time to get home."

"You know where he lives?"

"Not as of yet, but I'm possessed of a notion as to how we're going to find out." As the rear door snaps shut, Calamity gets out of her chair and crosses to the table the man left behind. There's a crumpled napkin and a half-finished pint of beer. She pulls some tweezers and a plastic baggie out of her jacket, picks the napkin up with the tweezers and runs it around the glass's rim before folding it into the baggie and sealing it.

"Um, ew."

"Caping ain't always glamorous, hun."

"What are we going to do with that?"

"Us? Nothing. But my ex might be able to do a thing or two about this."

"How?"

She shrugs. "He's a wizard. He's going to do wizardy things."

• • •

The wizard likes to hang out in a musty used bookstore out at the edge of town, on the second floor in a corner near the back. It's dim here, and the fluorescents flicker. The books are all leather with fading gilt letters. He's a black kid, skinny and crouched behind a stack of fat books—ratty, leather, with dimly gilded pages.

"Hey Charlie, we got a job for you," says Sarah. We can't exactly walk right in the way we were dressed at the Dutchman, so we're going as Sarah and Danny. There's an almost sacrilegious feeling in the air. We're doing cape work in street clothes. It's just *wrong*. Caping is supposed to be the thing we do when I want to stop being in the real world for a while.

"Who's this?" says Charlie. He pushes his glasses farther up his nose.

"This is Danny," says Sarah. "She's cool."

"Yeah? How cool?"

"She's a cape."

Charlie brightens. "All right, just needed to be sure we could talk. Have a seat."

"Ain't no call for that," says Sarah in the Calamity voice. "Wouldn't be bringing her around here if there was."

"I'm just being careful, Sarah."

"Sure." Sarah pulls out a chair and sits down. "Careful. That's you all over."

I sit too. "So, uh, Sarah says you're a wizard. Like figuratively? Or…?"

"What, you don't believe in magic?"

Flashes of Graywytch flick through my mind. Surely they wouldn't keep someone like that around if she couldn't deliver the goods. And Valkyrja is a straight-up mythological being. So, yes, I do. But it's one of those things that doesn't sit easily. Technology can be explained. Even hypertech sort of makes sense most of the time. Magic is something else, though. Magic is things like witches spinning thread out of moonlight, and using that to weave a cord for binding lies. It's dangerous and unpredictable and not easy to replicate. Supposedly it's more common in parts of Europe and a lot of India, but even there it's a relic of the past.

"No, I believe in magic." I'm not sure I believe someone at our school can work any magic, though.

Charlie must have heard some of that subtext in my voice. He smiles like he knows something I don't. "So what can you do?"

"Um, here." I pull a marble out of my pocket. Nervous butterflies tickle my stomach. This is something I haven't shown anyone before, and even with all the extra practice I've put in, I'm suddenly afraid of screwing it up and looking stupid. When I close my eyes to get a good look at the lattice, I'm taken aback by what I see. Things seem somehow more distinct in this corner of the shop, distinct and yet looser. I open my eyes in surprise. Charlie's got a look on his face like I've suddenly caught his interest.

"Go on," he says.

"Am I missing something?" asks Sarah.

"Yes." He waves at her to pipe down. "Go on, Danny."

*You practiced this*, I remind myself. The lattice is searingly bright in the darkness. The marble rolls out of my hand, and as it rolls I see the first trails of its momentum. Quickly I seize them, twine them about my mind, and…pulling? Pull? Push? Pull them through my own pattern in the lattice. A strange sensation, like thread running through the flesh of my fingers, mirrored somewhere deep in my chest, a strange rustling, almost cold and buzzing. The marble stops falling, then goes up. Its momentum expended, it pauses at the top of its "fall" and then gravity reasserts itself. It begins to fall again, and again I use the energy of its fall to send it upwards. The marble is now moving smoothly, up and down, up and down, never falling and yet always falling.

I open my eyes, and am almost surprised to see the marble bouncing in the air. It's difficult to focus my gaze while I'm concentrating on the lattice, and the world keeps splitting in two. Prickles of sweat break out on my forehead. "See?" I say, and that's enough to push me over the edge. The threads slip through my mind and the marble plummets to the floor.

"That's uh, hm. That's…really neat," says Charlie.

"I can also bench press a school bus," I mutter, cheeks hot.

"She saved that airliner last week," says Sarah. I shoot her a grateful smile. Sarah's own smile is a little awkward.

Great. She thinks I'm an idiot.

"Oh!" says Charlie. "That was you? Nice!"

"Thanks."

"So what's this job you've got?" he says to Sarah.

Sarah pulls the plastic baggie with the paper napkin in it out of her backpack. "This was being used by a fellow we're interested in following. I wiped it all over his beer glass, too."

"You didn't touch it, did you?"

"No," says Sarah, as if he's asked a stupid question. "It's pristine. Can you work with this?"

"It'll take a few minutes to get ready, if you don't mind sticking around?"

"We don't have any place to be," I say.

Charlie carefully sets his books on a chair next to him and clears the space on the table he's claimed as his own. He pulls a small silver bowl from his backpack, about six inches across, so shallow it's almost a dish, and engraved with intricate etchings of strange symbols across its entire surface. After snapping on some gloves like the ones doctors wear, he pulls the napkin out of the baggie and sets it in the bowl. For a few moments it looks like he's lost something as he pats his pockets and sweater, but then with a look of triumph he produces a cigarette lighter.

"Uh…are you going to…?"

"The smoke detector in this part of the building is always on the fritz," he says absently.

"Funny how that works out," says Sarah.

"Shh!" says Charlie. He lights the napkin, and as it burns he sprinkles a pinch of granular powder into the flames from a small pouch on a string around his neck that he pulls from under his

T-shirt. The flames flare, bright and aquamarine blue. When they die, the ashes sit limp and black in the center of the dish. Charlie sifts through them with his finger and finds something: a small, clear bead.

"Either of you two bring a map?"

"Um, we could try to find one around—" I begin.

"Will a computer do?" asks Sarah as she opens her backpack.

"It's worth a shot," says Charlie. Reaching into his pocket, he pulls out a thin leather cord and loops it through the bead, tying it off with a knot.

Sarah pulls a tablet out of her bag and brings a map of New Port up on the screen. Charlie holds the bead over the map, and lets it hang from the cord like a pendulum. Slowly, the cord begins to drift toward the south half of the map, and then stops, hanging at an angle in midair. Hairs stand up all the way down my back, tight and chilly. Yeah, yeah, I can fly and shit, but...well, magic is *spooky*. I don't know how to explain it. It just is.

"Wow," I whisper.

"You like it?" Charlie smiles hugely. "I wasn't sure it'd work with a computer. This implies a lot of things for my next project."

"Looks like it's pointing to somewhere in Lacey," says Sarah. Lacey is a suburban neighborhood in southwest New Port. "Can I zoom in?"

"Go for it," says Charlie.

Sarah puts two fingers on the map and slides them outward. Our view zooms in closer and the pendulum takes a sharp swing to the west, ending up hanging at an angle greater than forty-five degrees and pointing off the map.

"Okay, pan over."

Sarah flicks the map to the west, and the pendulum begins to move again. Through trial and error, we find the place. An apartment block in Lacey. When we move the map around, the bead stays locked on it, moving perfectly in sync. When Charlie moves his hand the bead stays locked in position, no matter where he pulls the cord.

"That's your spot," says Charlie.

"That's where he is right now?" asks Sarah.

"No, that's where he spends most of his time. You might not see him right away, but he'll be back sooner or later."

"This is so cool," I say. Charlie smiles. Sarah scribbles down the address on a scrap of paper. "Yeah, he's a dork, but he's useful."

"Shove it, Sarah," he says amiably.

"Can you find the apartment number?"

Charlie shakes his head. "The map doesn't zoom in that close."

"If we took you there, could you find it?" says Sarah.

"Uh, look, I'm not really into caping anymore. I'd rather focus on my projects."

Sarah sets her pencil down. "It's just for one day…"

Charlie takes his glasses off and inspects them for dirt and smudges. "Sarah, we have been over this—"

"This is important!"

"It's *always* important. But you can handle it without me."

"Oh, come on!"

"No, it's fine." I lay a hand on her arm. "We can figure out which one is his on our own."

Sarah looks like she wants to argue more, but nods. "Fine. Thank you. We really appreciate the help you've given us."

"No problem." He slips his glasses back on and smiles. "If you wanna swing by again, feel free."

"We might do that. See you around." I snag Sarah's sleeve and pull her with me before she can say something else. We're almost out of the store before I think to let her go. I was sort of expecting her to shrug me off.

Sarah is blushing and won't meet my eyes. "I'm sorry. I didn't—sorry."

"Don't worry about it. You know, I think I've seen him before. How many of us at school are…you know?"

She looks relieved to have a question to answer. "Well, technically Charlie *is* baseline, but he has an esoteric skill. The vocabulary isn't too precise. To answer your question, uh, there's maybe ten I know of. That's probably not everybody."

"Have you gone caping with all of them?"

Sarah shakes her head. "No. Just the ones that—" She seems to think better of saying something. "Well, that seem like they'd be good at it."

We get back to her bike. Sarah slips her helmet over her head, cranks the engine on, and begins backing her bike out of the spot she parked in. "Let's go pay our buddy a visit."

Something tickles the back of my mind. "Wait, what time is it?"

"About four, why?"

"Shit. I can't. I have to get home." Yeah, Dad chased me out of the house, but I know from experience that a little thing like getting shouted out of the building doesn't mean I'm not grounded anymore. The longer I'm away, the worse it might be. Or maybe it won't be an issue at all. It's unpredictable, and that always makes me reluctant to go back home when things are like this. But I have to go. I've spent too long out already. I try to keep the worry off my face.

"Oh," says Sarah, disappointed. "What do you have for seventh period on Monday?"

"Study hall."

"Wanna cut?"

"Sure. I want to get this Utopia thing wrapped up."

Sarah smiles behind her helmet and slams the visor down. She peels out from parking lot with a sky-shaking roar and is gone.

Well. Now I go home and see if I'm lucky today.

• • •

Monday comes, and it's harder than ever to care about class when I know that once school is over I get to go caping again. Finally, the bell rings and study hall begins. I'm getting pretty good at cutting study hall. Someday that's going to catch up with me, but not today. Calamity meets me at the agreed spot, an out-of-the-way nook in a parking garage downtown. Top level, below a shopping complex, and behind an elevator shaft. The place is littered with cigarette butts and stamped-flat plastic cups. A cold, wet breeze brushes in through the open gap above the waist-high cement walls. Calamity noses her bike around the corner, and coasts to a purring stop next to me. She rests her boots on the ground and sits up in the saddle. She flicks the visor up and squints at me.

"Hun, it's still daylight out," she says.

"So?" I step away from the wall I've been leaning on.

"So I've been thinking: if you're gonna be caping in sight of the sun, you really oughta pick some real colors."

"Ah. Uh, hold on." I press the third blister on my wrist, and my suit shifts back to green. "Better?"

"I'd prefer something in blue and white, but that'll have to do."

"Yeah, well…" I reach for my pockets but this suit doesn't have any. It makes feeling awkward so much worse.

"Honestly, hun." Calamity puts her hand on my shoulder. "You deserve to call yourself Dreadnought as much as anybody."

"Well, I dunno. Let's just find this guy, okay?"

She snorts. "Got the GPS all set. Stick close; ain't gonna wait on a stray."

Calamity slams her visor down and cranks her throttle. The bike traces a screeching half circle of smoking rubber across the ground and then bolts down the ramp and out of the garage.

I step over to the garage's wall, swing my legs over it, and let myself fall for a few moments before I catch myself in the lattice. Calamity has pulled back to street-legal driving, so I have plenty of time to fume as we make our tortuously slow way through the city. Why is she hassling me to be Dreadnought? There are times when there's nothing I want more in the world. But I'm also ashamed to even think about it. Dreadnought knew no fear, and I'm a coward. When I first got my powers I thought courage would come with them, but I can't even stand up to Dad. How the hell am I supposed to save the world, too? It would be easier for both of us if she'd stop poking at it, if she'd realize I'm pathetic and weak, and let me do this my own way. We're gonna find Utopia and snitch her out to the Legion. I owe Dreadnought that much. And then I'll go be a girl in private, and stop teasing myself with these day-dreams about being someone important.

I stay tight with her, only fifty feet up and thirty back, all the way down to Lacey. She pulls off the freeway, and drives through the surface streets until we're at the apartment block Charlie found with his spell. It's a long, low two-story building in the shape of a squared-off crescent. Along the inside of the C is a walkway with occasional staircases. Everyone's front door faces into the central courtyard area, which could really use some grass but is covered in concrete. Cheaper, maybe. Calamity pulls in to the parking lot off to one side of the complex and wedges her bike into an open space between the last parking spot and some shrubs. I tap down lightly next to her.

"You possessed of any ideas for which one of these is his?" she asks me.

"I was thinking we'd just look in their windows."

"Shoot. Better than nothing. Come on. I'll take the ground floor, you do the second."

This is not as easy as we'd hoped it would be. More than half of the windows have their blinds closed, and in one tense moment, Calamity almost gets caught in the open by an inattentive res-ident who's wandered outside to get better cell reception while she's trying to squint through his window. For what feels like ten minutes but is probably more like thirty seconds she gets close and stays in his blind spot as he meanders around the yard, until I can get a clear path to drop down and hoist her into the air. We make three passes of the entire building, checking off which apartments we've confirmed our guy doesn't live in, and focusing on the others.

It's getting late. We skipped study hall, but we've almost burned through the time that bought us. In a whispered conversa-tion we agree to one last round, and then we'll have to pack it in and try again later.

We slip over a fence into one of the tiny back yards, and come face to face with the guy we're looking for. He's standing in sweats and flip-flops, with a cigarette half raised to his lips.

We all stand there blinking in surprise for a moment.

Then it's running, shouting, fighting, tackling, and we've got his face pressed into the carpet in his living room. He sucks in a breath to scream. I clap my hand over his mouth, and he tries to bite me. It's kind of adorable, actually. He squirms and struggles but with my legs clamping his arms to his sides he might as well be trussed up with steel cable for all the good it's doing him. Calamity pats him down and pulls his phone from his pocket.

"I'm bulletproof and I can juggle dumpsters," I say quietly. "Give it up. We just want to talk. If I take my hand off your mouth, are you going to be quiet?"

He nods. The moment my hand clears his lips he begins to shout. I muzzle him again. "If you keep doing that, I'm going to take you ten thousand feet straight up and let you scream to your heart's content, okay?" He goes still. "Can we just talk, please? I need you to tell me all about Utopia."

When he nods again, I take my hand off his mouth, and this time he doesn't scream. His voice is a shaking whisper. "Please, just leave me alone! I don't know who you're talking about!"

Calamity holds up his cell phone. "Is that why you know Utopia is a person and not a place, and also have her listed in your contacts?"

He starts to open his mouth, and then seems to think better of it.

"Start talking."

# CHAPTER TWENTY-THREE

His name is Gerald and he just wanted to be special. Huddled on the couch across from me, clutching the mug of water Calamity brought him, he doesn't seem like the type to go in for being a supervillain's henchman. He's got a round face and a scrawny neck. His hair is short and bristly, and his fingertips are ragged where he's chewed the nails too close. Regret is stamped all over his face, and if he didn't have what we needed I'd be out the door right now because I hate doing this to him. There's something about him that's tugging at me. Something familiar.

"I don't know how she found me," Gerald says. "One day I came home, and here she was. She kinda waved her hand and I couldn't move or say anything. She said she knew what I wanted, and she could give it to me. I just had to help her out with a few things."

I'm sitting across from him on a cheap folding chair. The furniture around here isn't exactly high-end. "What is it you wanted?"

Gerald looks down at his hands for a moment. When he speaks, his voice is so soft I barely hear him. "She said she could give me superpowers."

Calamity is leaning against the arm of the couch farthest from him, ankle over ankle, hand clasped on her wrist. She rolls her eyes. "Groupie."

Gerald scowls. "I know I'm not the brightest stick in the pile—" Calamity snorts. "Crap. Sharpest stick, brightest bulb. The point is, I know I'm not that smart, and my health has never been very good. I didn't graduate college but I've got so much student debt I can't go back to school. That's how it goes for people like me, okay?" He crosses his arms over his stomach and seems to sink in on himself. Gerald seems to be in his thirties, and he's getting interrogated by girls half his age, either one of whom could take him apart without much effort. That must sting. "My whole life I've been middle of the pack or falling behind. Utopia said she could change that. If I had powers, I could get a good job, or sponsorship from a cape team somewhere. I could be somebody. You don't know what it's like living the way I do, how nobody sees you and nobody cares."

Something clicks, and I realize what it is about Gerald that seems so familiar. He's the man I was scared I would grow into. "Yes, I do," I say.

"No, you don't!" he spits. "Look at you. You're stronger than you have any *right* to be, and you say you can fly? You don't know anything about me." His shoulders slump. "The world has been *handed* to you, and I'm stuck in the gutter."

"Returning to the subject at hand," says Calamity with a significant glance at me. "What is it Utopia had you doing?"

"I can't say."

"Now *that* is a point worth contesting," says Calamity. She uncrosses her legs and brushes her jacket back. Grenades, knives, and an enormous black revolver leer out at him.

Gerald goes pale—well, paler—but he clenches his fists on his knees and holds firm. "You can't possibly understand how important this is. I'm not going to let you bully me."

"Oh sure, because *you're* the victim here." Calamity leans over and smacks him upside the head, hard.

"Hey, easy," I say, raising my hand to stop her.

"Oh, fer Christ's sake, you're not buying this sob story, are you?"

"I think he's telling the truth," I say, and Gerald unclenches for a moment until I continue, "but that doesn't mean we're leaving without what we came for. You need to tell us what she had you doing."

"No," says Gerald. "I don't care what you do to me, I'm not screwing this up." The way he's standing up to us is kind of impressive, in its own way.

"You can talk to me, or we can go to the Legion Pacifica." This is mostly a bluff. There's no way I'm going to tell them I've been caping unless I absolutely have to. It's not worth the risk.

"Chlorophyll's got pollens and flowers that can make you talk," says Calamity. He does? That's news to me. I just thought the Legion would, I dunno, be better at this than we are. "So you can spill now and keep your little scraps of dignity, or you can tell him every secret you've ever had. And THEN they'll hand you over to the cops."

A plaintive whining noise starts to leak out of Gerald, and he begins to rock back and forth on the couch. Welp. There goes my sympathy, torn away like a fart in a hurricane.

Calamity pulls some handcuffs out of an inner pocket. "He ain't talking. Let's take him to Chlorophyll."

"Look, I don't know anything!" Gerald scooches away from her. "She just had me drive the truck."

"What truck?" I ask.

"She had…pickups to make." He takes a breath. The weight of his confession seems to settle down on him, and almost push him deeper into the couch. "I would stay with the truck and make sure nobody was around."

Calamity and I trade a glance.

"Can you tell us more about them?" It's an open-ended question on purpose. Back when we had cable, I saw this show about interrogation tactics, and right now I am furiously trying to remember more details, but the one thing I know for sure is you're supposed to ask open-ended questions.

"Sometimes she would have me move boxes, real heavy boxes, from one place in the city to another. But she must have more than one driver, because sometimes the boxes weren't where I left them and I'd have to go pick them up somewhere else."

"Mm-hmm. And these heavy boxes, did she seem to already own them?"

"Well…maybe not exactly *own* them," mutters Gerald.

Calamity pulls out a notebook. "Dates and addresses. Start talking."

"I don't remember."

Calamity closes her notebook, stands up, and stomps hard on his shoe. Gerald yelps and grabs his foot. "Did that help? I can do it again," she says.

"Take it easy," I say.

"This chickenshit is just gonna whine and pout until we go away unless he knows we're for real," snaps Calamity. She rounds back on Gerald. "Talk. *Now!*"

"I really don't know! Uh, two nights ago, out in South Hill!"

"And?"

"Monday! We did something last Monday. In Puyallup."

"I'm going to need you to be specific."

"I don't know, I swear!"

"Was your phone with you?" asks Calamity, snatching it up off the coffee table.

"Yes, yes it was. Why?"

"Do you keep your GPS turned on?" she asks, but isn't really listening for an answer. A few seconds later, she nods sharply. "Hold on." Calamity reaches into one of the little pockets on her tactical vest and pulls out a small slab of plastic, sort of like a USB flash drive. She plugs it into the phone and a green light winks on and starts blinking. When it's solid she pulls the drive and tosses the phone back to Gerald.

"This should be enough to tell us where and when the burglaries were," she says to me.

"Excellent. Did she say when she's going to pull off whatever she's planning?" I ask Gerald.

He's been cringing on the couch, quiet, like he was hoping we'd forget about him in the whole thirty seconds it took to download his phone's data. "No, I didn't ask! I didn't want to upset her."

"It's a wonder to me you haven't gotten further in life with that kind of courage and curiosity at your command," says Calamity.

"Go to hell," Gerald mutters.

"We need more than that, Gerald," I say. "We need to know what she's planning and when it's going to happen."

"No! If you stop her, she won't be able to hold up her end of the deal!"

Calamity sighs. "You *are* aware she's a murderer, right?"

"I'm…I'm sure she—"

"'Has her reasons,' yeah, sure." Calamity leans in close. "What makes you think she wasn't planning to kill *you*?"

His eyes open up round. "Oh."

"Yeah."

"She said she could get me my powers at the end of next week. That's all I know, honest."

• • •

"Are you going to be able to do anything with that data?" I say as we get back to the bike.

"Oh yeah," says Calamity. "From the list of places they robbed, we'll start putting together an inventory of whatever it is they stole. And even better, we've got a time frame now."

"So? We still don't know what she's planning."

"Not yet, no, but the timing on these things can be mighty important." Calamity shrugs. "Might be there's new reactor coming online somewhere, or a new satellite getting put in orbit, or an important vote in the EU. If we compare what she's stolen to what's happening in the next week, we might have some idea what she's trying. I happen to know a man who is right perfect for this kind of puzzle. Once we've got enough to take to him, we'll pose him a tricky question and see what his answer is. After that, it's only a matter of finding the best monkey wrench to throw into this particular set of gears."

"Excellent." Shit, we're really doing this, aren't we? It feels like I'm someone else. Someone competent.

"I'm gonna go home and crunch the numbers. It's going to take some time, and I've still got a lot of homework I need to do. We'll link up tomorrow and start running down leads, okay?"

One of the residents does a double take as she walks past us with a full garbage bag in each hand. I wave at her and smile. She smiles back uncertainly and keeps walking. "Sounds good. Meet me at my place at ten?"

"Sure." Calamity takes off her hat and pops open the storage blister on the back of her bike.

"That was nice good cop, bad cop we did back there."

Calamity freezes with her helmet halfway to her head. She looks blank and confused. "We were doing what now?"

· · ·

We spent too long with Gerald. I end up tickling the sound barrier to get back home before my curfew kicks in. I'm still in my super-suit, so I go straight for the rear of the house and slide my window open. Taking my suit off is easier than a snug, full-body garment has any right to be, but I still make enough noise as I step out of it for my mom to hear me. Should have done it in midair.

"Danny?" She taps lightly on the door. "Are you in there?"

"Uh, don't come in, I'm changing."

"I didn't hear you come in."

"Yeah, I got in a few minutes ago."

"That's strange." She wanders off, muttering about losing track of things. A few minutes later I wander downstairs. Mom is in the dining room, papers from her latest freelance gig spread out in front of her. A mug of tea steams by her elbow, and when she looks up it takes her a moment to come back from far away. "I don't remember getting you that shirt," she says. I'm wearing one of the outfits Doc Impossible made for me.

"A friend gave it to me."

Mom looks surprised. "Oh, who? David?"

"Uh, no. We don't really talk since, well, he doesn't like that I'm transgender."

"Oh." Her face clouds. "I'm…I'm sorry to hear that."

"Thanks. Did Dad go into the office or something?"

"I think so," says Mom. "Tax day is only a month away now."

That's a relief, at least. If I play my cards right I might not have to see him today at all. "I'm gonna grab a snack; do you want anything?"

"No, I'm still in the middle of this." She's already sunk back into her paperwork.

In the kitchen I slice up some cheese and put some crackers on a plate. Mom clears some space for me at the table and I set it all down with a glass of water on the side. When Dad's not home I like to do homework in the dining room, so I go get my books and notepaper. It's hard to focus. My mind keeps flitting back to what Calamity and I are going to do tonight, but I've got a test tomorrow so I need to get this knocked out before I go caping again. I open my math book and gird myself to do battle with binomial equations.

Halfway through the crackers and not nearly far enough along through my homework, Mom speaks, her voice quiet, almost musing. "I used to wonder what you'd be like if you were a girl."

I look up. "Really?"

"Yes." She seems surprised to hear herself talking about it. "When you were little, you once asked me if you could be a princess."

"I don't remember that." Except now I'm starting to think I do.

"You did. You never went through a cooties phase, either. You got along so nicely with girls from your class."

That, I do remember. I also remember how I slowly began to drift away from them. Or did they push me out? It's not clear. There are so many things that happened in middle school that I can't remember anymore. I've buried them so deep, I don't think I'll ever find them again. Not that I really want to, of course.

"Why didn't you tell me?" My voice sounds like it's coming from far away.

"Because," says Mom. "Because you seemed like a happy little boy. It never crossed my mind that you could be anything else."

"I was too scared to say anything." My pencil feels clumsy in my hand. My throat is tight. So much time lost, so much of my childhood gone, because nobody ever asked the right questions.

Mom nods like it makes sense, like any of this makes sense, and dives back into her reading. Or, no. Tries to. A few minutes later she looks up. "Danny, are you really happy like this?"

The answer comes immediately. "Yes."

"You're not going to consent to hormone shots." It's not a question.

"No." We both know that's the end of the line. I'm fifteen, which is old enough to put up a fight. My situation is too strange, too exotic, for the doctors to have any firm ethical guidelines. I doubt any of them would risk doing something that could get them sued once I turn eighteen.

And that's *before* we get to the part where I'm an invincible superhuman.

She stares into her mug of tea. "I feel like I've lost my son."

"Mom, you never had a son."

Mom seems to crumple. "We tried so hard, Danny. Is it something I did wrong?"

"Jesus, no! Mom, it's nobody's *fault*. It's not a bad thing."

"Are you sure? I just…it's going to be so hard for you. I think of what…trans?…transgendered people go through, and I don't want that for you. I'm scared of what will happen to you, Danny."

"Mom, that stuff doesn't matter," I say. She doesn't look like she believes me. I need a way to make her understand. "If it happens or not, whatever it is I'll live with it. What about the stuff that was happening to me when I was trying to be a boy?"

Mom leans back in her chair. "It wasn't so bad, was it? You were growing up so well."

"It was torture! You know what I was doing when Dreadnought—when that supervillain attacked me?" I don't believe it. It's like she's willfully misunderstanding it. They never take my word for it; *why can't they take my word for it?* "I was painting my toenails behind the mall because that's the only way I could keep sane. Does that seem normal to you, Mom? Does that seem healthy?"

"I just…I don't see you as a girl," she says. "Even now, even looking like that. You were going to be such a fine young—"

"I was going to *die.*" The pencil snaps between my fingers, one end cartwheeling off across the table and onto the floor. "And I *am* a girl. Even if you don't see it."

The chair scrapes the floor as I stand up. My homework crinkles as I slam my books closed, scoop them up in my arms, and head up to my room.

Do I want her to call out after me? I don't know.

She doesn't.

# CHAPTER TWENTY-FOUR

Sarah calls in sick on Tuesday and doesn't show up to school. Over the next few hours, several industrial sites in the Pacific Northwest get phone calls from a "reporter" asking about what they lost during their recent burglaries. She dragoons me into the effort as well, sending me a list of phone numbers to call over lunch. I don't get much to eat, but I send what I find back to her. I get a text message around dinnertime: *I've got the list. We need to double-check some things, but we're close. Be ready by ten.*

As the day dims toward night, our inventory of stolen goods begins to firm up. Exotic coolants and ceramic heat sinks. Optically flat mirrors and several very expensive motion picture camera lenses. A thousand gallons of low-viscosity hydraulic fluid. Somehow Sarah tracks down news about some bulk industrial good shipments that got hijacked, and so we add eight tons of a nickel-chromium steel alloy and five tons of assorted industrial ceramic tiles to the tally. The list goes on and on. Utopia is gathering a grab bag of high-end industrial and commercial electronics goods, with no obvious unifying theme.

Calamity throws pebbles at my window to tell me it's time. We slip over the back fence into the alley and make our way to where her bike is parked in a pool of shadows. The night is crisp and clear, and the dim stars are pinpricks in the sky. We're headed to the most recent place Utopia hit, hoping to find some clues about what was boosted.

The capacitor manufacturing plant is part of a light industrial park that's surrounded by a twelve-foot chain-link fence with coils of razor wire over the top. The fence isn't the kind that can even slow us down, and we can see the place where it didn't slow the thieves down, either. The wire in the fence is covered in black rubber everywhere except for part of a perfect circle that intersects the ground and leaves a man-sized hole. Here, the fence has been roughly patched over by a square of naked wire mesh fastened to the two posts on either side.

Calamity bends over to examine the place where the fence was cut. "Look at the wires here."

They look like they've been perfectly sheared. No tool marks, no tear or stretch in the rubber. The wire simply comes to a stop, smooth, naked, and gleaming. It's like that all around the circle.

"Ain't no regular clippers did this."

"So we're on the right track. Let's take a look inside."

Calamity steps up to me. "Hoist me over."

I lace my fingers together like a stirrup and she sets her boot in my hands. It's a little tricky figuring out how much muscle to put into the lift, and she ends up going twenty feet high to clear a twelve-foot fence. This gives her enough altitude to perform half an acrobatics routine on the way down, though, so it works out okay. Thankfully, the place seems to be deserted on the weekends. We slip across the empty parking lot and press ourselves up against the long, low building of the main manufacturing floor. Sliding along the nondescript brown wall, we come to a side entrance still blocked with police tape. Calamity takes off her hat, gets down on her belly, and shimmies along the wall so she can look in the glass door with her head against the ground.

"It's clear," she says after a long moment.

Back on her feet, she pulls something out of her jacket that looks like a tiny toy gun with a pair of thick wires poking out the front. She jams them into the lock, squeezes the trigger a few times, and we're in.

"Lockpicking with actual lockpicks is for eccentrics, hobbyists, and morons," she says.

"You're not an eccentric?"

"Hush."

Inside the building, we find a front office, the assembly floor, and a storeroom for completed capacitors. The lights are off and it's a little dim. The floor is carpeted in that thin, hard stuff that doesn't cost too much and is easy to clean. The door to the storeroom has had its lock cut out. Again, a perfect circle with smooth edges. Without the lock, the heavy security door swings freely. "I'm going to have a looksee in here," says Calamity. "You see about any missing files in the office."

In the office, there are several rows of filing cabinets. The key is in the top drawer of one of the desks. I start flipping through the files, trying to find anything obviously empty or missing. There's a file here that catches my eye: a shipping manifest for some Cerita power couplings, with a handwritten note in red ink reminding someone to include them among the losses from the recent theft. Something about that trips my memory, but I can't remember where I've come across that name before. I take the file and make a photocopy of it for Calamity.

"Wackachicka wackachicka wackachicka wackachicka…"

Calamity pops her head out of the storage room. "What in the hell are you doin'?"

I pause like a deer in headlights between a *wacka* and a *chicka*. "A cheesy '70s investigation montage?"

"Damn it, D—girl!" She stalks down the short hallway and slips into the office. "Caping is a mite bit more serious than that."

"Oh come on, you talk all old-timey and you call yourself *Calamity.*"

"That is a *persona!*" says Sarah. She snatches her hat off and throws it to the floor. "It is a vital element of the form, one that you have ignored for too long. I don't even know what to *call* you when we're out like this!"

I shrug as I take the copy out of the machine and fold it up. "'Hey you' is working fine so far."

Sarah throws up her hands. "Do you even want to be a cape?"

That's a very good question. At first, I sort of assumed I would be. But then. Well. But *then*. But then my parents found out I was a girl. But then I met the Legion. But then David torched our friendship. Running around hunting Utopia is fun and all, and yeah, I promised I'd find a way to honor Dreadnought, and taking down the supervillain that killed him is a good way to do that, but Calamity has a point. I've been able to choose permanent colors—not even Dreadnought's colors, just *anything*—for more than a week now. And I haven't. And maybe I never will. So I don't say anything because I don't have any answers, and after a moment it gets weird.

"Hey, look, I didn't mean anything by that," says Sarah. It's a little weird talking to Sarah when she's got the Calamity outfit on but she's not doing the voice.

"It's okay." Like a bubble rising from the depths, the question forms and is out of my lips before I really think about it. "Is it selfish that I kinda just want to be Danielle right now?"

"No. I don't think so." Sarah bends down, picks her hat up, and fiddles with the brim. "I think we've already gotten everything we're going to get from here. In fact, I was just being thorough. We probably have enough for my contact to go on already. Do you, um…do you wanna go buy makeup?"

"I don't have any money."

With that bandanna over the lower part of her face, Sarah's eyebrows become much more expressive. "My bike cost seventy thousand dollars, and my guns are eleven hundred each. You think I can't afford a tube of lipstick?"

"Where the *hell* do you get that kind of money?"

Sarah shrugs. "I rob drug dealers."

"Oh."

• • •

About an hour later we're back in our street clothes and facing down the makeup aisle in a twenty-four-hour drug store. Racks of foundation and concealer stretch from the floor to the ceiling.

Row upon row of mascara, lipstick, nail polish, and eye shadow are arranged in neat ranks. It's a little overwhelming, and even though I'm not scared, exactly, to be seen in a makeup aisle like I used to be, it's still a bit strange to be standing here, openly shopping.

"What kind of makeup do you like?" asks Sarah.

"I have no idea. I used to just grab the first nail polish that looked pretty and get out."

"Okay, so let's get you some foundation and mascara to start. Maybe some lip gloss, too."

"Not lipstick?"

Sarah shakes her head. "Maybe. Lipstick is a little heavy. Unless you're going to a formal event, or there's a particular look you're going for, it will seem out of place." About this time, I realize I've never seen Sarah actually wear makeup, and yet she speaks as an authority on the subject. When I say as much, she shrugs. "I am the only daughter in a family of boys, and if you think my mother didn't force me to learn about this stuff, then you are out of your goddamn mind."

A little stab of envy goes through me. That one day shopping with Mom seems cheap and flimsy in comparison.

Picking the correct foundation turns out to be a lot more involved than I thought it would be. There's a special lamp that's supposed to give the right kind of light for color matching, and I've got to hold different shades up against the inside of my arm to see which ones match my skin tone the best. Of course, before I can do that I've got to decide between liquid and powder foundation, and really, I have no idea which is better. When I reach for a tube of black mascara, Sarah shakes her head, and points me toward some dark brown instead. Because I'm blonde, I'm told, black mascara would stand out strongly against my coloration, which is useful for achieving certain looks but not something I want to tie myself to, at least not until I know what I'm doing.

It's like this all the way down to the smallest detail. There's nothing simple about makeup, and she assures me that I'll want to practice putting it on a few times in private before I leave the house with any of it on, because apparently it takes considerable skill to put the stuff on and make it look nice. Then she says I might not even need it, and I nod and say its one of my superpowers to be impossibly beautiful, but it still looks like fun to get made up. Sarah sputters for a little while.

Eventually we get a basic makeup set selected, with enough everyday colors and enough experimental stuff to keep me busy for weeks or months. A bottle of liquid foundation, two mascaras, two tinted lip balms, some eyeliner and multipack of eye shadow comes out to about forty dollars, which seems terrifyingly high until Calamity says she's glad we got the stuff while it was on sale. She swipes her debit card like it's no big deal to drop that much money on a lark, and then all that stuff goes in a bag, which she hands to me. My throat is a little tight, and when I hug her there's an instant of tension in her shoulders before she relaxes and hugs me back.

"Thank you, Sarah."

"You're welcome, Danny."

We step apart and her cheeks are a little pink. "Crap, was that—I mean, well, girls seem to hug so much…" My tongue is tripping all over itself.

Her cheeks graduate to a full-on blush and she laughs. "It's fine, Danny. Let's get out of here."

We get some food at a diner, and this is something I can afford so I insist that she lets me treat her. She spends the meal smiling deeply, staring out the window and flicking occasional glances my way. It's nice having a friend.

# CHAPTER TWENTY-FIVE

Calamity taps on my window almost exactly at 10 p.m. on Wednesday. My nerves are so strung tight waiting for this final, enormous phase of our investigation that I actually jump up from my chair and stay hanging in midair for a moment. When I slide the window open, her eyes sparkle above her scarlet bandanna.

"Nervous?"

"Yeah. Hold on, let me get changed." I seize the bottom of my sweatshirt and pull it up over my head. Underneath, I've got my suit on already, but Calamity's eyes are very wide. "Warn a gal before you do that."

We're good at leaving my back yard without any noise now, and we wait until we're most of the way down the alley before we say anything else. I notice for the first time that somehow all the streetlamps in this alley are out. When I examine them in the lattice, I see they have been shattered. Almost as if someone with a silenced pistol came through here and shot them all.

"So tonight's the night?"

"Tonight is *a* night. Gonna come calling on a business partner of mine, fella going by the name of the Artificer. He's a grayish sort of hypertech merchant. We tell him what we know about the robberies and the time frame, then maybe he can tell us what she's planning. Probably won't be too exciting. I was thinking we'd do a little patrolling after we talk to him."

"All right. Cool. Lead on."

Calamity drops the helmet over her head and cranks her bike to life. A few minutes later I'm following her down the highway, headed east. We pass out of New Port and through a few suburbs until finally we get to an industrial park.

It's a dozen or more square miles of gravel with corrugated metal hulks sleeping between pools of sodium-orange light. We go around two and a half sides of a trapezoid and down a long, rutted, weed-grown gravel road before we find our entrance. Calamity pauses to open an unlocked and unguarded gate, then shuts it behind her. Without anyone around to see, I drop down to fly next to her as we head deeper into the gravel field, passing between two shuttered factories and under pipes that link them. In the distance, a few of these old buildings still blurt gouts of steam into the air as trucks back up to their loading docks, but that's literally miles away, behind hills of gravel and forests of holding tanks.

Calamity kills the engine and pulls her helmet off. Her motor-cycle ticks and clicks in the cold night air. "This is it. I called ahead, so we shouldn't get shot at, but just in case we are, try not to get hit. He's got things that could even put a dent in *you*."

It takes a moment for my mouth to catch up with my brain. "Jesus Christ, what the hell are we walking into?"

Calamity draws a pistol and begins swapping out jelly rounds for hollowpoints. "He's a mite bit eccentric, but he only tried to kill me the one time. We're square. Square-ish. It'll be fine."

"That's why you're loading lethal rounds, because this is fine?"

"Only in one gun. Nice to have options." She snaps the cylinder closed. "Let's go."

We walk toward the shuttered factory. There are no lights on in this area, no sodium orange to keep the night away, and so the Artificer's factory seems like a hulking black void in the silver moonlight. When we're within thirty yards, I start to hear a low buzzing noise. My hair begins to prickle and float. A white spotlight clacks on and pins us to the ground.

"That's far enough, children," says a voice. It's coming through a speaker somewhere, loud and humming with static. "Identify yourselves."

"Oh, you know who it is, Art," says Calamity. "Quit fooling and let us in."

"I know who *you* are, Calamity. I've not seen your friend in the throwaways. What's your name, girl?"

Crap. "Um, I've been going with Emerald."

"I don't get it."

"Uh, hold on." I push one of the blisters on my suit down, and it shifts to the green I've been using.

The voice is silent for a long moment. "Adorable." He means it as an insult.

"Told you ya needed to own your colors," Calamity mutters under her breath.

"You may enter." The spotlight clacks off and leaves us in absolute darkness, our night vision erased. A white rectangle of light appears as a door opens inward, and we step forward. Inside, the building is almost completely black except for a line of soft white track lights, tracing a path to an elevator across the empty space to another door. As we cross the factory, our footsteps echo back at us. The second door opens, and we step into an elevator. I suppose I was expecting it to travel halfway to the Earth's core or something, but it only goes down what feels like one level or so before the door opens again. We enter another huge space, but this one is well lit.

Holo-projectors and flat screens throw pale glows on the cement floors, and bright white banks of LEDs hug the ceiling. Huge dynamos and racks upon racks of computer servers dominate the walls to either side. Deeper into the Artificer's lair—and this place is *so* obviously meant to be thought of as a lair—I can see individual experiments in progress. A half-refurbished matter fabber sits in a corner, its guts splayed out on the ground. Its functioning sister is humming quietly, steam leaking from its sealed production cubby.

The Artificer is standing at the foot of a small set of stairs leading down from the elevator into the main part of the room. "Calamity, you had better be prepared to pay your bill," he says as we come down the steps. "I refuse to be strung along any further, young lady. No more ammunition until you settle your debts."

"Don't let your horses lead you, Art. Here's your money." She reaches into her jacket and pulls out a fat brick of twenty-dollar bills. She holds it up and he snaps it out of her hand, rubs his thumb down the edge to make sure they're all the same denomination.

"I'll count this later," he says.

"Your trusting nature in these cynical times is a balm to my wounded soul."

The Artificer is obviously American, but he affects a slight accent. Maybe he thinks it makes him sound sophisticated. He's got eyes set deep in the hollows of his skull, and thick black hair pulled back high from a severe widow's peak. He's wearing—and I swear to God that this is true and I'm not making it up—he's wearing a double-breasted white lab coat and thick purple gloves.

No, really.

That's what he's wearing.

He notices me staring. "What's the Legion's pet doing in my humble shop, hm?"

"Uh…" Now how the *hell* did he know I'm with the Legion? I look at Calamity. She shrugs.

"Please, don't delude yourself," he says. "Only the Legion's kiddie club wears throwaways."

"Oh." I'm starting to get the feeling that the Legion are the only people in town who don't realize that. "We're, uh, we're looking for Utopia."

"Dear God, why?" asks the Artificer, aghast.

"It's, uh, complicated," I say.

"Child, she killed *Dreadnought*. Why on Earth would you want to find someone who could do *that*?"

"Well…because she killed Dreadnought."

Calamity nods. "Someone's got to stop her."

Something changes in the Artificer. He seems older for a moment, opens his mouth like he's going to say something.

"You are *not* about to tell us that kids got no place in this," says Calamity.

The Artificer presses his lips together. "Fine. On your heads be it. How am I relevant to your errand of madness?"

"She's been stealing equipment all over Washington and Oregon for the past few months," I say. "It looks like she's gearing up for something big. We were hoping you could figure out what it is."

"We brought a list of the gear she rustled," says Calamity, holding out a twice-folded square of paper. "Our sources say it's going off in the next week or so. Think you can figure it out before she blows?"

"That's a difficult, dangerous, *expensive* question to ponder. I will require significant recompense for my efforts," says the Artificer. Calamity sighs and reaches into her jacket again. Christ on a cracker, how rich *is* she? "No, money is not sufficient. I'll need something else."

"Name it," says Calamity in a guarded tone.

"I'm almost out of $N^2$ fluid. Obtain more for me, and I'll see what I can do about solving your puzzle for you. Two canisters should be sufficient."

"Done."

The Artificer takes the paper from Calamity and unfolds it, then stares at it for a few moments. "This may take some time. Get my $N^2$ fluid. I'll call you when I've got something."

"Remember, we only have a week."

"Yes, yes." He waves his hand dismissively and turns to head back into the chaos of his workshop. I'm sorry, I mean, his *lair*.

Calamity and I take the elevator back up to the surface level. The factory's side door shuts behind us with thudding magnetic bolts.

"What's $N^2$ fluid, and where do we get it?" I ask as we scrunch across the gravel.

"Non-Newtonian fluid," says Calamity. "It's a staple of a lot of hypertech. He uses it in my bullets, in fact. We're gonna pick some up at the university."

"How much does it cost?"

"Nothing," says Calamity as she stows her hat in the cargo pod on her bike. "It ain't for sale."

"So then how—wait, we're not going to *steal* this, are we?"

She looks at me like I've said something strange. "Of course. What do you think being a graycape means? We ain't gonna let the law stand in the way of doing what's right."

"Stealing isn't right!"

"If we were talking about stealing from people who can't afford it, I'd agree. But we're not. We're talking about an ivory tower situated in the middle of a river of cash."

"Look, if this stuff is that common to hypertech, I'm sure I can get some from Doc Impossible. Just hang on for—"

"NO!" Calamity's shout echoes against the factory wall. "We are *not* going to the Legion for help!"

She's so forceful I take a half step back and pause to collect my wits. When I find them, a slow burn of anger comes with them. "Why the hell not? I've been letting you call the shots so far, but this is stupid!"

Calamity swings her leg over the saddle of her bike. "The Legion's not just gonna hand the stuff over."

"How do we know? We haven't even asked them!"

"They ain't trustworthy! It don't matter what they do and don't give us, there'll be some hook behind the bait and we'll end up frying!" She slams the helmet down on her head. "We're doing it my way."

I walk over and grab the center of her handlebars. "No. We're not. Why do you hate them so much?"

She looks at me, tries to stare me down. It's hard to tell in the moonlight but I think her eyes are wet. There's something else there, something harder and deeper than I can relate to. I look away first.

But I keep my hand clamped on her handlebars.

"They arrested my dad." Sarah's voice is thick and choked. "The government framed him for murder, and the Legion just went along with it. He's doing twenty to life in a federal pen."

"That doesn't make sense." It feels like I understand all the words she's using, just not the order in which she said them. Maybe I misheard her. "Why would the government want to frame him?"

"My dad was a cape, called Ricochet. He worked just above street level," says Sarah. "He found proof the CIA was smuggling drugs for the Colombian cartels and pocketing the cash to fund their black operations. He tried to go to Congress about it. The Legion arrested him a week later."

"No, that…they must have been tricked."

"They invited him to their tower and then ambushed him in an elevator."

"They wouldn't do that—"

"*They did!*" she shouts. "I only see my dad from the other side of a glass wall now! He missed my brother's *funeral*, Danny!"

"Then they were tricked!"

"Or they didn't bother to check out the evidence," says Sarah, seething with contempt. "Or they were *in on it*. They can't be trusted. We have to do this on our own, because there is nobody else. I'd love to be able to play by the rules, but the people who make the rules are crooked, so that's not a choice we get to make right now. So are you with me, or am I riding alone now?"

"This is…I don't know, Sarah this is *not* what I thought we were doing—"

"Then let go of my bike and get out of the way," she growls.

I open my mouth to say—to say what? I don't know. Something. Something I hope will make this okay again, and put us back where we used to be. Where it feels like we're supposed to be.

A flash, blue on white, and sharp black shadows racing to the horizon.

The pressure wave rips us from our feet and slams us across the gravel. I go end over end in a shower of rocks. Calamity's bike spins and crunches into the ground inches from her skull. I reach out for her, find her hand in the dark. She squeezes back.

The night is broken by a pyre rising from the shattered factory. The mushroom blooms red and black over dancing flames.

A second flash. A piercing cobalt beam lances down from the sky and into the flames. New explosions blossom and thunder.

The wind shifts and the smoke clears for a moment. A small figure floats down from the sky, wreathed in blue and silver.

Utopia.

# CHAPTER TWENTY-SIX

"Calamity?" I whisper. "Calamity, get up. Utopia is here; we have to leave." She moans, gets one arm under herself, and begins to shove herself to her feet. "Are you okay?"

"My bike…" she says.

"We can fly, just hold on."

Calamity gets to her knees and pulls her helmet off. It's carpeted with gouges. The eye shield was up, so she's got some cuts over her eyes and across the bridge of her nose. Calamity gingerly touches her face, blinks. "We ain't running," she says. Her voice is hard and steady.

"Are you insane?" I hiss. Glancing over, I can't see Utopia anymore. She's dropped down into the fire, probably to finish off the Artificer. "We've got to get out of here!"

Calamity is already on her feet, seeing what she can salvage from the twisted ruin of her motorcycle. "Why? Utopia didn't show up here by accident; Gerald must have warned her we paid him a visit, then she got the same notion we did. Since she's gone to all the trouble of keeping us from needing to track her down, it seems a mite bit inconsiderate to let that pass without so much as a how-do-ya-do."

I throw my hand out at the inferno. "She just blew up an entire factory!"

Calamity snaps her hat by its brim to shake the dust off and sets it on her head. "I did notice that just now."

"We are not ready for this kind of fight." I step over to grab her, and in a single fluid move she has somehow locked my wrist against my elbow and thrown me clear over her shoulder. I land and slide for a yard or two.

"You get along home if you want to, but that woman just killed our last lead." Calamity begins unloading her pistols and stowing the ammo in her pockets. "Without the Artificer we've got no prayer of heading off what she's got planned. So if you want to avenge the guy who gave you that mantle, now is your one and only chance. But if you wanna quit the moment it gets hard, then I'll not cry to see the back of you."

I get to my feet. "We don't even know if we can hurt her!"

She holds up a bullet with a very pointy tip. "Tungsten penetrators. These will kill anything."

A huge gout of sparks and embers leaps into the sky as something inside the fire collapses. Somewhere in there, Utopia is erasing her trail, or maybe stealing what she can use. This is an amazingly bad idea.

"We should call for backup," I say, but I know there's no point. By the time they get here she'll be long gone.

"Ain't no cavalry coming." Calamity finishes loading her weapons and snaps the cylinders shut. "We do this now, or we don't do it."

With a revolver in each hand, Calamity marches toward the flames.

● ● ●

Calamity's plan is simple: split up but stay close enough to support each other. Whoever finds Utopia first starts fighting as hard as she can, and then the other comes and attacks from Utopia's blind spot. In the close quarters down there, it seems unlikely she'll use her anti-reality beam against us.

Inside, the factory is a howling hell. Hot winds tear at us as we make our way through the flames to the elevator. The doors are jammed, so I pull them open with a scream of twisting steel. Calamity holsters her pistols, hops into the shaft, and slides down the elevator cables like a fire pole. I follow a moment later, letting myself fall before catching myself in the air a little ways above her. It's a little cooler down here, but not quiet. She pries the emergency hatch off the elevator roof and swings down into it.

"We gotta do this quick," she says. "The oxygen down here won't last long with that inferno upstairs." She gestures with a gun. "Get the door."

I wrench the elevator doors open, and we stumble into a scene from a nightmare. The equipment is all slagged and burning. Rubble and wreckage clutters the ground. The roof has caved in at two places, and beneath those spots pools of liquid rock are beginning to cool. Calamity motions me to go right and she pulls left. When I close my eyes to look at the lattice, I find it's easier to navigate. I can see the threads and tangles of the smoke and the flames, and the rubble, but those don't actually block my sense of our surroundings. It's not like seeing, exactly. It's more like knowing, like walking through my bedroom at night and remembering where everything is in the dark. Those two rents in the fabric of reality where she fired her weapon leap out at me, almost vulgar and difficult to look at.

There is a limit to how far and how much I can "see" this way. I was hoping I'd notice Utopia immediately and attack her before Calamity had a chance to draw her fire, but it's not working out that way. I'll have to search her out and hope I can get the drop on her before she brings that hideous weapon around to blast me. I fly deeper into the ruined laboratory, searching half by sight and half by the lattice. Maybe we're too late. Maybe she's been here and gone—

Sharp, popping gunshots to my left.

I snap my head over and put all my effort into peering through the chaos of the lattice, past the broken concrete hanging down from twisted rebar, past the flames, the smoke, the ruined equipment. I can see two figures dancing around the rubble. One is human. The other...the other is *not*.

My cape is suddenly heavier, pulling at my shoulders as I

accelerate at eight Gs. The concrete, the row upon row of computer racks, the dense machinery of the Artificer's manufacturing equipment, they all slow me down. A little.

Calamity is in close, blasting away at point-blank range. Utopia is dodging back, taking a round in her shoulder instead of her throat. Her left arm folds open into a submachine gun and burps fire at where Calamity was just standing. Calamity has rolled behind her, jams the muzzle of her gun into Utopia's back and fires. Utopia jerks with the impact, swivels 180 degrees at the waist to face her—

That's about the time I body-check her at 350 miles an hour. Utopia goes flying. I reach out for the lattice and stop myself cold. "You good?"

Calamity's eyes are wide, but she nods. "Get her!"

Utopia is clambering out of a pile of destroyed machine tools when I hit her again, a pile driver of a blow that punches her down into the cement. Her chest is crumpled metal, her shoulder socket bent out of true, and her arm is hanging by thick black cables. Utopia's good hand rotates open and she points a bulging glass lens at me. As it is beginning to glow I stomp on her hand and smash it flat.

"Wait!" she says. My fist jerks to a stop inches from her face. Her voice is trilling, musical, shaped by electronic undertones. Up close I can see that her hair is synthetic fiber, her face silicone pseudoflesh, pale and sparkling. "You must understand what is at stake."

"You murdered Dreadnought."

"I kill only when compelled to. He would not see reason."

"What reason justifies murder?" I shout.

"The Nemesis is coming, and sooner than we think."

"Who is the Nemesis?"

"Not who, what." Utopia blinks, a strangely unsettling action. Her eyes have no whites, only a pair of glowing blue irises. "You wouldn't believe me if I told you—"

"Do you have *any* idea what kind of month I've had?"

Utopia smiles. "I take your point. The Nemesis is the name I have given to a mass of exotic matter that is currently traversing the solar system. Should it arrive before I am ready, the consequences will be severe. For everyone." She sounds honest and calm.

"What does this have to do with killing Dreadnought?"

"Very little, but he forced the matter. Let me be on my way." Utopia tries to push herself up on her broken arms. "I haven't harmed anyone but those who stand between me and what must be done to protect us all."

"No." This is nonsense. I'm actually letting the supervillain talk me down from beating her. I shake it off. I reach down and grab a firm hold of her good shoulder. "You're going to prison."

"You don't understand what is at stake, Danny."

"*What?*" It's hot in here and growing hotter, but I am suddenly cold.

"I saw you hiding down there with Dreadnought," she says quietly, barely louder than the snapping flames. "After killing two of your predecessors, I knew the mantle would pass on. It always does. I chose to let you have it, and to let you live. You were no threat to me, so there was no need to kill you. Since then, I have been following your development with some interest."

A cold, draining horror sucks at me. A supervillain knows who I am. Knows, probably, where I live. Could kill my family whenever she wants. This whole time, she's been watching me. Even if I win, I'll never be able to stop looking over my shoulder. I step away from her, almost dizzy with panic.

"For what it's worth," says Utopia, "I applaud your discretion in refraining from announcing yourself as the Dreadnought. It demonstrates forethought and clarity of mind."

"You gonna let her jabber on forever," says Calamity with a cough. She steps around a fallen metal beam. "Or are we going to finish this?"

"She knows," I say.

"What?"

"She knows who I am!" I'm pacing, hugging myself, holding back from the edge of terror.

Calamity's answer is immediate: "Let's kill her."

"No! We're not killing anybody!"

"We can hardly let her go or drop her off with the cops if she knows your name. Ain't got no real good options here, do we?"

"I—I don't know."

"There's another factor to consider," says Utopia as she reaches a sitting position. I stop pacing. "It takes some time to recharge my inversion beam, but it does recharge."

Her chest cavity pops open, and the searing cobalt beam leaps out at me.

I jump clear in time.

Calamity doesn't.

# CHAPTER TWENTY-SEVEN

The blast flings me into some fallen machinery. The beam's fuzzy green afterimage swims in my eyes and blots out the world. I shut them and try to see through the lattice instead. Utopia's weapon—the inversion beam, she called it—has shredded reality in here. Torn, dangling ends of the lattice seem to writhe in pain. Nausea bubbles in my stomach. With a conviction I can't account for, I know that nothing will ever really work quite right in this place again. Machinery will fail, animals will cower, and people will feel unaccountably disturbed. Even though I'm still half blind, I open my eyes and focus on the visible world again. Anything is better than being confronted with the damage she's done to the foundations of reality.

Utopia has found her feet, her nimbus of blue and silver beginning to flicker back to life. She turns toward me. There is an infinitely small and infinitely bright point of light hanging inside the open cavity of her chest, like a fleck of a blue star ripped from the cosmos and hung between her ribs. She still has some of her organs in there, run through with plastic tubing and synthetic replacements for her lost biology.

"The key component of this weapon is material that was salvaged from the asteroid the Legion Pacifica stopped last year," she says. "That asteroid was part of the Nemesis once, flung ahead of its master by the tides of gravity. This is what a single kilogram of that thing can do to the world, Danielle. Imagine what thirty million tons of it could unleash if it even passed by our moon."

I push a fallen industrial lathe off of me and clamber to my feet. "Then come with me and tell the world what you know so we can defend ourselves."

"My long experience with the governments of humanity has left me with no confidence in them. I dislike killing children, Danielle." Utopia points to something behind me. "Attend to your friend, or she will die."

"What?" The fear in my chest explodes into ice. I look around frantically. Calamity lies on her back, her hat knocked away. Her breath is coming in short, hard gasps. The left side of her body is a ruin. Her charred skin weeps at the cracks. Her arm...oh God... her arm. It's nothing but ash and gore, more bone than flesh. The melted remains of her pistol have fused with what was her hand.

A stupid, feeble protest bursts from my lips. "No!"

It's not fair. That's what gets to me. It's *not fair*. This isn't right. *She* was the one who knew what she was doing. *She* was the one who had training and experience. *She* was the one who was really a hero, who didn't flinch at going into danger. This doesn't make sense. It's not supposed to go this way. Calamity is too smart to lose, too brave to die. I am a child. In one hideous epiphany I realize that, powers or not, I'm just an idiot little girl who is in way over her head.

Utopia is rising on pulses of blue light that flash from the small of her back. "It would be prudent to kill you now, but I am serious when I say I have renounced unnecessary violence. Do not come for me again; I will not extend my leniency twice."

She powers away on jets of blue fire, up through the holes in the ceiling and out into the night. I could follow her. Utopia fired twice, and then needed to reload before she fired once more. I'm thinking that means she's got, at most, one shot left in that inversion beam. I could dodge it and then she'd be helpless for long enough to comprehensively destroy her.

And then Calamity would be dead.

It's not a hard choice. It's barely a choice at all. I rush over to Calamity and scoop her up in my arms. Her gun is fused to the ground, and her hand with it. She comes with me. The hand stays behind. We fly out through the roof. Once we're clear of the fire, the air is shockingly cold and clean.

Sarah sucks in a breath, and then begins to cough convulsively. She vomits against my chest, and her breathing slows. I turn toward downtown, ready to push for all the speed I have, but pull back when I realize Sarah probably wouldn't survive being exposed to the winds at my full speed even if she were in the peak of health. Mach 3 winds would rip the skin from her body.

"Take me home," she mumbles against my chest.

"I'm taking you to a hospital."

"No hospital. I'd get…" She has to swallow. It's costing her a visible effort to speak. "I'd get put into the foster system. Never see them again. Take me home. I want my family."

"You're going to die!"

"Danny." Even saying this much seems to exhaust her. "I've been ready to die since I was four years old. Take me home."

We hang in midair while I try to think. It feels like my gears are locked, like I can't put two ideas together. The words come to me before I really know what they mean. "I can take you to someone who will help. Not a hospital, but a doctor." It occurs to me, finally, that I'm talking about Doctor Impossible. She'll help. She'll have to.

"No hospital…" says Sarah, and then she passes out.

I fly her as fast as I dare, barely more than eighty miles an hour, straight toward downtown. It is more frustrating than anything I have ever done. I can feel her growing weaker in my arms, literally feel her breathing get shallower and her muscles go slack. Her life is slipping away by seconds, and there's nothing I can do about it. The mantle makes me stronger, faster, and tougher than almost anyone else in the world and none of it matters.

Legion Tower is at the north end of the main skyline, which runs north to south along the southeastern edge of Puget Sound. Flying in a straight line from the industrial park, it still takes more time than I would have believed to get to Legion Tower. Minutes tick by. Sarah passes in and out of consciousness. She shivers in the icy wind. Her moans are getting weaker. I bump the speed up a little. Her bandanna gets ripped away. I press my cheek to her forehead—it's the only exposed skin I have—and she's ice cold.

"Calamity! Wake up!"

Nothing.

"Sarah! Sarah, can you hear me?"

Her eyes flutter, and then nothing. She's stopped shivering.

We come to Legion Tower at speed and I don't slow down before the long skid across the landing pad that barely brings me down to a running pace before I hit the glass doors. One of them shatters under my boot, and I punch the elevator call button. "Come on." The elevator is taking forever. "COME ON!"

An intercom clicks on. It's Graywytch. "What are you doing?"

"It's my friend! She's really hurt!"

"I'm sending an elevator and waking Doctor Impossible," says Graywytch.

I'd be surprised but the relief so strong it blots out all my other feelings. The elevator doors open, and I step inside. Why are these elevators so goddamn slow? Who decided to make them this way? Finally they open again. Doc Impossible is waiting, her face tight with concern. The airlock is already open, and she beckons me inside.

"What happened?"

"We were looking for Utopia—"

"*What?*" Doc Impossible is staring at me in open-mouthed shock.

"We found her. She shot Calamity with the beam she used to kill Dreadnought."

I can't meet her eyes. She doesn't say anything while we wait for the decontamination beams to clear us.

Two of her robots are waiting on the other side of the door with a gurney at the ready. I lay Calamity down as gently as I can. Her skin is pale and waxy. If not for the slight wheezing of her breath, I would think she was dead. She is much smaller than I remember her being. Just a kid, really. We were so stupid.

"I'm going to have to take her into surgery," says Doc Impossible. She is clipped and distant. "Wait upstairs in the lounge." She strides off deeper into her lab. The robots follow with Calamity.

The airlock closes behind me with a *thuh-thunk* of magnetic bolts, and it's hard to shake the feeling that I'm never going to see her again.

# CHAPTER TWENTY-EIGHT

With hot water and several wads of paper towels, I wash Calamity's blood and vomit from my chest. There's some dark stuff caught in the seams, which, after a moment, I realize is her ash, and I almost barf with disgust. I peel my mask and cowl back, and find myself sitting in the lounge, dazed and staring out at the fallen-star canyon of the city at night.

The lights here are kept dim enough that there are no reflections in the glass, but a man the size of Magma is not the kind of person who can sneak up on you. I sense his bulk before he sits down on the couch next to me and holds out a steaming mug. I take the hot cocoa but don't drink.

"What happened?" he asks softly.

"We found Utopia."

"I see." There's no judgment in his voice, and for that I am more thankful than I can express. He doesn't push. He waits for me to keep going.

"I'm not…I'm not sure I'm cut out to be Dreadnought. I wanted…" God. What had I wanted? Why had this seemed like a good idea? It's so hard to remember now. "When he gave me the mantle, and my body changed, I was so grateful to him. It was every dream come true. The flying and the strength, that's cool and all, but being able to look the way I'm supposed to, that's the important part. That's the best thing anyone has ever done for me. I promised myself I would repay him, ya know?"

Magma makes a noise of understanding and nods, but no more.

"So Calamity shows up at my bedroom one night and says we're going to go find Utopia—" Wait. No. I'm sick of lying. "That's not true. She came to me, but she just wanted to go caping. So we ran up to McNeil Island and looked around until we found a liquor store robbery to stop. And it was fun, and I liked it, but I knew you guys wouldn't want me to be doing that, so—"

"This isn't about what you did wrong, Danny. Just tell me what happened."

"I told Calamity I wasn't sure I was good enough be Dreadnought."

"That's why you're wearing green?"

Crap. Yeah, I still am. "Yes. Nobody would talk to me in throwaways and it seemed wrong to wear his colors." I tell him about the research we've done into Utopia's robberies, about staking out the Flying Dutchman, about how we tracked down Gerald and got him to give us some idea of when it was all going down. I tell him how we went to the Artificer, and about our argument over how to get the $N^2$ canisters. I tell him she said they'd arrested her dad, and Magma only says, "It was more complicated than that, but go on." I describe how Utopia showed up, and how we went in to fight her, and about the things she said to me down in that small pit of hell. When I tell Magma she knows my real name, he shows emotion for the first time. Grief, but not surprise.

Magma is silent for a long moment. Finally, he speaks. "Danny—"

"I know, I screwed up. I should have come to you the moment we were done with Gerald."

"Yes, you should have, but I was going to say you did the best you could under difficult circumstances, and I think we owe you an apology for not being a more hospitable source of guidance for you."

I look up at him, not quite sure if I should believe what he says. "Really?"

"Yes. Absolutely. And if I'd known Calamity was Ricochet's daughter I would have contacted her as well. This isn't high school.

We don't give detention for sticking your nose in where it doesn't belong. If I'd known you were this close to being ready, I'd have found something for you to do. Sidelining someone as strong as you, with as little experience as you have, was a damned dangerous mistake. Power is difficult to live with sometimes, especially when you're young. You shouldn't have been left on your own to learn things the hard way. There are excuses I could make, but they don't matter. We failed you, and she paid the price. But you? You did the best you could."

Goddammit, I'm crying again. Magma plucks the mug from my hands as they go slack, and I lean into him and sob. They are convulsive, twisting sobs that come hard and seem to rip at my throat. I feel stupid at first, but he rests his hand on my shoulder and the weight of my tears flushes all self-consciousness downstream.

I come back to myself in bits and pieces, and realize I'm still leaning into him. I sit up straight and pull myself inward, suddenly embarrassed. "Thanks," I whisper.

He pats me on the shoulder. "You're a good kid, Danielle." His smile disappears. "Are you going to be okay?"

"Yeah, I think so."

"Good. I have to make some calls. I'll be back in a bit."

"Okay."

Magma gets up, and the whole couch seems to leap with relief. "Is…is Valkyrja around?" I ask as he leaves. I hate how plaintive I sound.

"I'm afraid not," he says. "She and Carapace are out of town. I'm going to see if I can get them back. We need to see if this information helps us understand what Utopia is planning."

"Okay."

"I'll have the doctor check in on you when she's out of surgery."

"Thanks."

Magma leaves me alone with a mind blissfully free of thoughts. I feel empty, which is a relief. The cocoa is sweet, but it's gone tepid. Nuking it in the microwave helps, and I curl back up on the couch, sipping hot chocolate and feeling nothing at all. Somehow

I find myself dozing, and I wake with a start when Doc Impossible sits down next to me. Her braid is loose and her face is drawn. An unlit cigarette dangles limply from her lip.

"Hey, kid."

"Hi, Doc. Is she okay?"

"*No*, Danny! She's not okay. I had to cut her goddamn arm off." Doc Impossible presses her eyes closed with her fingertips. "Shit, I'm sorry. It's...I just hate treating kids. I never had the stomach for it. She'll live. She's stable for now, but her body needs rest. She and I have some decisions to make in the morning."

"Okay."

"Did you get hit in the fight?"

"No."

"Good." She pulls the cigarette from her lip and takes a long sip from her own mug. Her hand is shaking.

"Can I see her?"

Doc Impossible shakes her head sharply. "She's asleep. She needs rest."

I bolt upright with a sudden realization. "Somebody's got to tell her family."

"Unless you know who that is, it will have to wait until she's awake."

"Her dad was Ricochet."

"Really? Shit." Doc Impossible sets her mug down and starts fishing around in her pocket for a lighter.

"What happened with him?"

She flicks open a flame, and sucks it into the cigarette until the end glows. "It's a long story."

"We've got time."

Doc Impossible tilts her head back and shoots a pillar of smoke into the air. "He was an associate member. Part-time, only pulled in for the big stuff. We were fine to let him do his own thing, but he started going after the government."

"She said he had proof the CIA was smuggling for the cartels."

"He was probably right," says Doc Impossible. She shrugs.

"That guy he killed worked for them. We sent a delegation to his funeral to mend some fences."

"Why?" I feel like I've been kicked in the gut.

"Look, we know the government is dirty. Parts of it, at least." Doc Impossible's shoulders sag a little, and disgust is written all over her face. "That doesn't change the fact that he crossed a lot of lines we can't let one of our own cross. You think tonight was bad? Things that are ten thousand times worse happen when capes try to police the government. It would turn us into a police state overnight, and if we were *really lucky* that's all it would do to us. It's happened elsewhere, and it almost happened here once. Ricochet shouldn't have killed that man, no matter how crooked he was. Too many things rely on us and the government staying out of each other's way. Even when it sucks. Or, especially then. Government corruption is out of our jurisdiction, and he knew it."

"Maybe you were wrong," I say. "Maybe he was framed."

"He wasn't." She shakes her head. "The video that convicted him wasn't faked; I know, I examined it myself. Ricochet hand-cuffed a CIA officer, and then shot him in the back of the head. It doesn't get more premeditated than that, and we do *not* let our people sink down to that level." She takes a long drag, taps her cigarette in an ashtray. "But no, that doesn't make it any better for his kids."

Does it make me a horrible person that I feel nothing but relief from hearing her say this? Calamity has done so much for me, believed in me more than I ever did myself. I should be loyal to her and her family. But I don't want Doc Impossible to be one of the bad guys. I don't want Magma or Valkyrja to be people I can't trust. I don't think I could stand that. Not right now, and probably not ever. Tomorrow it might get complicated again. Tonight, I just want it to be simple. They're the good guys. They're helping Sarah. That's the important part.

"Danny, why do you want to be a superhero?" Doc Impossible looks at me. She seems so incredibly tired.

"I don't." The answer comes before I think about it, and I feel vaguely guilty about it.

"You wouldn't have been out there tonight if this wasn't what you wanted," she says. "You just haven't given yourself permission to admit it."

I think of Charlie, and how reluctant he was to come with us, and I realize she's right. There's too much self-loathing bottled up inside me. It gets in the way, keeps me from seeing myself, and what I really want.

So finally, finally, I tell her the truth and hope it doesn't sound vain. "I want to help people."

"And that is *beautiful,* and you're amazing." She takes my hand and squeezes it. "But there are a million things you could do to help people that don't involve pissing off superpowered psychopaths. You could be the best firefighter in the history of fire. You could be a one-woman space program and explore Mars for us. Every single person who has put on the mantle and used it to fight has been killed in action. Every one of them. It is a job with a one hundred percent mortality rate. You could be anyone you want to be, do anything you want to do. Why do you want to get murdered?"

"I don't! I just...I got pushed around a lot when I was little. Even after it eased up when I hit my growth spurt, I still don't feel safe at school unless I'm hiding in a corner where nobody goes. But now, I've got these powers so nobody"—my father looms in my mind's eye—"can push me around anymore. And I don't want to let them hurt anyone else, either."

"Damn," says Doc Impossible quietly.

"What?"

"That's one of the classics, all right. You might be in the right place after all." She smiles. "God help you, kid."

The way she says it makes something click. For a moment I stare into my cocoa and try to figure out how I want to phrase this. "Doc, can I ask you kind of a personal question?"

"Go ahead."

"How long have you known you've made the wrong choice?"

Doctor Impossible grunts. "Ouch. Ya got me." Her cigarette flares orange in the dim light. "It's been five years."

"Have you ever tried to get out? Go back to being nonpartisan, I mean?"

She shakes her head. "Can't. I made an enemy who will follow me no matter where I go or what I do. It's not real safe for me to leave the Tower, so I do my work from here. Sometimes we make choices, and we don't realize they're permanent until it's too late."

"I'm sorry." For what it's worth, I really am. I'm beginning to understand why someone wouldn't want to do this forever. I'm also beginning to understand that not once this whole time have I ever thought about tonight as *the horrible thing I'll never let happen in my life again*. No, I've been thinking about it as *the first time things got bad*.

The *first* time.

"C'est la vie," she says. "I'm fine. I've made peace with it. I just want you to know what your choices mean before you make them."

"Um, thanks, but I don't think I have a choice anymore," I say. Doc Impossible looks at me, confused. "Utopia knows my real name."

Her face twists. "Oh, *shit*. I'm sorry, hun. That's terrible."

"Yeah," I say. "Is there something we can do to keep her quiet once we beat her? Maybe offer her a nicer prison cell?"

"Unfortunately, yes, that's about the best…we can…huh." Doc's face goes blank. I can see the wheels turning in her head. A half second later, she bolts up off the couch, staring off into nowhere. Her hands come up to her mouth in horror. Her voice is quiet and shaking. "*Oh*. I can—I can fix this."

"You can? How?" If there's some way to keep her from attacking me at school or something, I'm all for it.

Doc Impossible looks at me, confused for a moment before she seems to remember where she is. "I mean…well, she hasn't come at you at home yet, so she probably won't unless you push her. We can make her silence part of a plea deal or…I don't know…we'll fix this. Okay? We'll fix it. There's some guest condos on the fifteenth floor, you can sleep here tonight."

"Oh, damn!" I say, getting up off the couch. "What time is it?"

"It's about three in the morning," says Doc Impossible absently. She seems to be making a checklist in her head, counting tasks on her fingers.

"I need to be getting home." I slip my mask and cowl back over my face. "My parents will freak if they wake up and I'm not there."

Doc Impossible seems more put together and confident again by the moment. "Are you sure?"

"Yeah, thanks for everything. I'm probably going to cut school tomorrow to come see Calamity, is that okay?"

"Yes. Danny, be careful. Utopia is dangerous."

"I know."

Oh God. Do I ever know.

# CHAPTER TWENTY-NINE

The wind snaps at my cape as I power across town. The lights of the sleeping city slip past and by now I don't have trouble finding my street from one hundred feet up in the dark. From above, my neighborhood is row after row of small cottages and bungalows, their windows dark and blinds pulled.

Except the lights in my house are on.

A thousand horrible possibilities jump to mind. They could have found I was gone. Or Utopia could be holding them hostage, and waiting for me to come back. Or she might have—no, she said she didn't like to kill, and she could have ended me. My heart rate slows as I tell myself this. I have to believe they're not dead.

The urge to burst through the door at the speed of sound is almost overwhelming, but new instincts for caution are taking root in me. I circle the house twice from as low as thirty feet and try to see if anything is amiss. The blinds are drawn, but yellow light spills out from the windows anyway. When I check the lattice, I don't think I see anything inside that looks unusual, but looking on the other side of solid matter can be difficult.

My bedroom light is on. They definitely know I'm gone. Crap. Crap, crap, crap.

I hang in the air in front of my house and three stories up. Utopia was pretty banged up when she left. She'd be a fool to face me again with two broken arms, even with her inversion beam. But I have no idea how fast she can repair herself. Not *this* fast, right?

Then there's the other possibility, that Mom and Dad figured out I was gone all on their own. That's almost worse. I can't go in the front door dressed like this, but if I go into my room through the window, then they'll want to know how I got in the house once I got home. There doesn't seem to be any easy way out of this.

The front door opens. A figure steps out, dark and wearing some strange draping garment. It turns to say something to my father as it leaves. The light doesn't seem to catch the person as clearly as it should, but when it turns in profile I see a raven perched on its shoulder. Graywytch.

She's fifty yards down the street from my house, almost to the corner of the intersection, when I slam down from the sky. My feet crack the pavement as I land, and I've got murder on my face. "What the hell are you doing?"

"Putting an end to this tragic farce, young man." If Graywytch is nervous about making me angry, she doesn't show it. "You nearly got that girl killed tonight. This needs to end. There's still time for you to do the right thing."

"You *told* them?" The sheer gall of it rips my breath away. All this talk about how the Legion protects secret identities, and then *poof*, she takes mine away from me.

"Talk to your parents, Daniel." The moonlight and the light from the streetlamps don't hit her the way they hit everything around us but through some kind of magic leaves her all in blackness except for her eyes. They are gray and very tired. "They want to help you. Goddess only knows why, but they seem to think there's still hope you'll step back from your perversion. Talk to them, and when you're ready, come to me and we can discuss how to remove your powers and return you to your proper self."

I find my voice again. I find it to be much louder than I intended. "You had no right—!"

She cuts across me. "Don't you dare speak to me of rights. You are the purest distillation of an evil that has haunted half the human race since the priests killed the Goddess."

"What did I ever do to you?" I shout.

"It's not about what you've done. It's about what you'll do. Dreadnought cannot be a transwoman, I won't allow it. The damage you could do to women once the media gets wind of you would be incalculable. Already you've nearly killed one of us. How many more must suffer to satisfy your sickness?"

"Snitching goes both ways. When the Legion hears about—" And then my voice disappears. I don't mean I stop talking—I can feel the vibrations in my throat and mouth. But my voice is gone. Once upon a time, Graywytch casting a spell on me would have been terrifying. Then I fought Utopia and learned what real fear is like. This is petty.

"Hears about what?" asks Graywytch with a smirk. "Do you think I would let you tell them? Do you think I would let them believe you even if you did? This is between you and me now. There will be no more muddying the waters. No more playing on unearned sympathy. You will never be one of us. Real women—"

As if moving off the topic of the Legion has freed my voice, I find that I can shout at her, "It's not my fault I'm trans! You think I wanted to be born this way?"

"Not really," says Graywytch. "I don't blame you any more than I would blame an ebola victim. Society has fed your generation so many toxic ideas about gender, it's only natural some of you would crack. But that doesn't mean you aren't dangerous. It doesn't mean you shouldn't be expunged. You reify the holocaust of gender, you invade my sex, and you poison my sisters by your simple presence. You cannot possibly understand what it means to be a woman, and you rape us all when you try. If you will not surrender the mantle, I will be forced to destroy you."

"You wanna try?" I stalk forward. "Any time, bitch!"

"The instant resort to violence." Graywytch seems to collapse in on herself, and the night's shadows become somehow more solid, even alive. They rush to embrace her, and she's gone. Her voice comes to me as if from a great distance. "How essentially male."

"Coward! We'll beat you!"

For a moment, I think she's gone. When her voice comes again, it is tight with fury. "Magic leaves no fingerprints, Daniel. You *will* surrender your powers, or by the end of the month you will die in agony and damn the mantle if it is lost. Nobody will believe you. Nobody will help you. Nobody can. Not your parents. Not the Legion. Not your fists. Your only hope is surrender. I will leave you to think on that."

A sudden gust of wind whips up and pulls at my cape. Dust and dead leaves swirl, and then settle. I turn to take off, intending to fly straight back to Legion Tower to settle accounts. I will *break* her.

"Danny?" calls Dad. "Danny, is that you?"

He's standing under a streetlight in front of our house in boxers and a tank top, staring at me, squinting like he's not quite sure he sees through the darkness correctly. He sounds shaken, and scared. Screw him. My feet leave the ground, but Mom's voice halts me.

"Danny, please. Come home."

Dammit.

My feet touch the sidewalk again. It's a long, slow walk to my house. When I pass into the light from the streetlamp nearest our house, and they see me clearly, they draw back a little.

I pull back my mask and cowl. "Hi."

"Get inside before somebody sees you," snaps Dad. Good old Pop, always reliable.

We file into the house, and he bolts the door. There's something in the air, some crackle of tension. Dad turns and looks at me, lips tight. Mom is trying to fold up into nowhere in a corner. She's got a clear line to the kitchen door from here; I imagine she'll duck out quickly once this gets going.

"Have a seat," commands Dad, pointing at the couch. That's a thing he does when he wants to show how big and tough he is.

I look at the couch. Look at him. Sigh. "Earlier tonight I saw my best friend get her arm burned off with a laser cannon, so if it's all the same to you, can this wait until tomorrow?"

"You won't speak to me like that, son," says Dad.

"I'm your daughter." I'm just as surprised as he is that I've found a spine at last.

Dad puts his hands on his hips, takes a deep breath, and blows it out through his nose. It doesn't scare me the way it used to. It feels weird. "So, you stole Dreadnought's powers when he died."

"He *gave* them to me. He was dying, and he gave them to me so they wouldn't be lost. That's what changed my body. Not any supervillain."

"Why didn't you tell us?" asks Mom. It takes me by surprise. She doesn't normally talk during times like this.

"Because…" I trail off. It's a harder question than I expected. I never really considered telling them, and I never stopped to ask myself why. After a few moments, I find an answer. It doesn't feel like the whole answer, but it's part of it, at least. "Because I was scared you'd try to take them away from me." Like everything else I ever wanted to be.

"You don't need superpowers to impress me, son," says Dad. There's a look on his face that's hard to process. Something like sympathy and concern, but that can't be right. "You don't need them to impress anybody. You're just fine without them. It didn't make sense, before. All those things you were saying, all that nonsense about being a girl—it was crazy. But now I get it. Daniel, pretending to be something you're not just so you can hold on to some power that doesn't even belong to you, that's not healthy. It's not healthy for your soul."

"I'm not *pretending*, and it is my power. He gave it to me."

"Graywytch said that without the powers, you'd go back to being the way you were," Mom says.

Of course she did. "Nobody knows if that's true or not," I say.

"Have you tried?" asks Dad.

"Why would I want to risk it? I'm happy this way. I told you, I'm transgender, and this is the best transition I could ever hope for."

"No, Danny. No, that's not true," says Dad, shaking his head. "We raised you better than that. We kept you away from all that queer stuff, we made sure you weren't neglected. You're not trans-swhatever. No more lies, son. I know you're scared, and you feel like you're backed into a corner. It's okay. Just tell us the truth. We're your parents. We love you no matter what. You don't need powers to feel special. You'll always be special to us."

My eyes start to prickle. I clench my jaw. That bitch. That horrible bitch. I've been waiting years for him to say something like this. Seems like my whole life, all I ever wanted was for him to tell me it was okay to be who I am.

Now he is.

And it hurts like nothing I've ever felt before.

My vision is blurry. My throat is tight. Dad steps forward, arms wide for one of those stupid manly hugs he's obsessed with. "DON'T FUCKING TOUCH ME!"

Dad jerks to a halt, eyes wide. We're all surprised. His face darkens and Mount Screamer gets ready to blow again. But now that I've started, I can't stop. "I am *not* your son!" I shout. "I have never been your son! I am your daughter! And you have never once told me that you loved *me*!"

"Now wait just a goddamn minute!" he shouts. "We're trying to help you, you ungrateful little faggot! We want you to be who you really are and not some—"

"Don't talk to me like you give a shit about who I am! I *told* you who I am, and you called me a liar!" I am shaking with rage, and my feet do not touch the ground anymore. "And you knew! You knew I didn't want to be a man, that's why you forced all that shit on me! Well, I'm never going back! I'm a girl, and they're *my* superpowers, and I'm not changing back, and there isn't a god-damn thing you can do about it!"

"Don't you think you're being a little selfish?" asks Mom.

The world lurches out from underneath me. "What?"

"You've said what you want," she says. Her arms are crossed, her shoulders pulled up, but she's looking me dead in the eye. "We want our son."

"Mom, no." My feet touch ground again, but it doesn't feel solid. Everything is sliding away, spiraling down into chaos.

"Yes, Danny. I thought we just had to make the best of it. But you've been lying to us this whole time, making this huge decision that affects all of us all on your own, and not even telling us what options we had. It's got to stop."

"It's *my* decision!" This is insane. The world has gone mad. How can this be anything *but* my decision?

"You're only fifteen," she says. "You're too young to make this kind of choice. You need to give Dreadnought's mantle back to the Legion, and when you're eighteen, if this is what you really want, we can talk about it."

"There's nothing to talk about." It's a struggle to keep my voice down. "I'm a girl, and I always have been. The difference is now you can see it."

"You don't make the rules, young man!" barks Dad. "Your mother is right, you are being very selfish right now! As long as you're going to act this way, you are not welcome in this house."

Someone has sucked the air right out of me. I gawp at him for a moment. "You can't do that! Mom, tell him! He can't do that!"

Mom looks at Dad, and then back at me. She closes her eyes, and forces the words out. "I'm sorry, Danny, I really am."

"So what's it going to be, huh, tough guy?" asks Dad. "You gonna keep throwing this fit?"

I clench my fists, painful tight. "I am *never* going back."

"Fine then." Dad walks over to the front door and rips it open. "Leave."

From way at the back of my skull, I watch my body turn and leave the house I grew up in. The door slams behind me.

# CHAPTER THIRTY

My eyes snap open. Daylight filters through the trees.

The nightmares came thick and deep last night. In them, I'm a monster, but I don't know what I look like because I can't see myself in the mirror. Everywhere around me, people are getting hurt and killed, and it's all my fault. No one will tell me why.

The dream's details burn off like morning fog, leaving me with a disquieted feeling. The forest on the flanks of Mount Rainier smells of pine and mud. Birds chirp and sing. A bug I don't recognize is exploring the surface of my kneecap. Everything that happened last night comes back to me in a rush, and I consider rolling over and trying to go back to sleep. The pile of pine needles I've assembled isn't all that comfortable, but there doesn't seem to be any point in going anywhere. My stomach gurgles, giving me a good reason to get up.

Check inventory. I have one cell phone, one hypertech supersuit, and…uh, that's it. No money. No ID. No schoolbooks. No computer. No place to stay. No food to eat. My parents really kicked me out of the house with nothing but the clothes on my back. Even sitting here, living it, it still doesn't feel quite real.

I should have let him die. I regret that he's still alive, and I'm ashamed that I regret that, but I'm also frustrated that I'm ashamed because it's not like I don't have reasons. This sucks.

Sleeping in pine needles has left me covered in patches of sap, which have helpfully picked up all the dirt they touched. A ways off, I can hear the rushing of a stream. I push myself to my feet and get some altitude, skimming treetops until I reach the water.

Up close it turns out to be less a stream and more a small river. After rubbing the patches of sap off with handfuls of dirt, I take my phone out and set it on a rock. The water is grippingly cold, but it doesn't bother me. Extremes of temperature are more interesting than uncomfortable to me now. I'm spin drying above the river, whirling so fast the world smears into green and brown blurs, when it occurs to me I should be more upset. Like, I'm out here in the woods because I'm *homeless*, right?

And yeah, I am *bothered*. I'm more than bothered. I'm pissed and scared and I feel lost. But I'm not shattered. Last night, I expected to wake up broken, nothing more than a torn-up, chewed-out, smaller half of what used to be a person. But I feel whole. Really, completely whole. Strip away everything: my house, my stuff, my family. Strip away the Legion, and Calamity, and my secret identity. Everything. What's left? What's left are the things I can count on. I have my body, my powers, and my freedom. Maybe that will be enough. It will have to be.

For the first time in my life, I am completely in charge of myself.

With that realization comes a misty relief that settles in the bottom of my chest. It's over. All that shit with Mom and Dad—it's done. My whole life has been leading up to this moment, and now there's nothing else they can do to me. No more lies, no more pretending, no more shouting. No more pain. I'm free. Whatever else will suck about this week, I'm free.

My phone is complaining of a low battery when I check to see if I can get a signal up here. Damn. I shut it down. Should have turned it off last night. Oh well. Take it as a lesson.

I press the blister for the throwaway camo, and the emerald of my suit shifts and flows into the fuzzy grays and blacks. It's best at night, but I'm going back into the city and every bit helps. If you asked me what I'm preparing for, why I'm concerned about being spotted, I wouldn't be able to give you an answer. It just feels like the right thing to do. The smart thing. I've got to be smart now, and cautious, all the time. There's nothing to fall back on anymore.

I need a plan. First, food. My body is astounding and super-human in all sorts of ways, but I still need to eat as much as anyone else. Once I've had a meal, I can see about getting my phone charged. There are some calls I need to make once I'm back in range of a cell tower. I think I can trust Valkyrja to help me, but I don't want to go back to Legion Tower. Graywytch is there, and I'm not ready to face her again yet.

There's no rush to get back in town, and I've got plenty of thinking to do, so I get up to about five hundred feet and tool along at a leisurely hundred miles an hour. Rural Washington slips past beneath me, green and sleepy. Fields and forests are shot through with asphalt ribbons and tiny model houses. People think the world looks small when you get up high, but that's not true. It looks huge. The horizon leaps away from you, further and further the higher you go. The world is gigantic from up here.

About thirty miles out of town I start overflying the first sub-urbs of New Port. Our city is enormous, but dense, and even this close there are long stretches of forest dropped right in between, for example, a high school and a strip mall. A diner seems to call my name, but I have no idea how I'm going to pay for food. I'm not too proud to panhandle, but dressed the way I am, I don't think I'd have any luck. The diner passes beneath me and away and I fly on, trying to come up with something. Three or four miles later, it hits me that I've got this backward. I shouldn't be trying to get food and then call Valkyrja. I should call Valkyrja and she can bring me food. I feel like an idiot for taking this long to figure that out, but at least I got there before I did something stupid.

This far into suburbia, I'm bound to be near a cell tower. I turn my phone back on, hoping I can get one quick call out before it dies. Immediately, I get text message notifications. I come to a stop in midair and scroll through them. One from Doctor Impossible and one from Valkyrja.

Doc Impossible: danny, please come to tower. calamity is awake but wont talk to us. shes asking for you

Valkyrja: How do you fare, young champion? I have returned

from my journey, and would welcome a visit from you, should you care to give me the pleasure of your company.

"We have gone backwards," I mutter to myself as I pull up Valkyrja's number for a voice call. I don't have the charge needed to keep my phone on while I wait for a text message reply, but her phone rings once, and then I get the most ornate and formal voicemail greeting I have ever heard. Frowning, I try Doc Impossible's number, and get a (much less flowery) voicemail message as well. Since they're not answering their phones, the best I can do is shoot them a message and then power my phone up for a few moments every half hour or so until I get a response. I tap out quick texts to both of them saying my parents kicked me out, that I have no food or money, and I'll be waiting for them on the roof of the main library downtown. When I try to mention that Graywytch is a doxxing asshole, the keyboard on my phone stops recognizing my inputs. With a sigh, I send the message. Maybe I can pantomime it or something.

Maybe I'll need to grow up and go to Legion Tower in person, but I'm hoping that won't be necessary. I'm not sure what I'll do if I see Graywytch again, but I think there's a real possibility I might try to pulverize her on sight. There's something else, too. The Tower is *their* ground, and now that I'm on my own, I feel reluctant to go anywhere that's not neutral territory.

I slip the phone back into the little pocket on my belt, snap the flap shut, and boost for speed toward downtown New Port. The city's outer districts snap by beneath me, and I peel into a circling dive around an office tower to come at the library. The looming neo-Gothic building seems somehow even more imposing and fortresslike from the air when you can see how both of its wings spread and then double back on themselves.

The roof is surprisingly steep and made of slate, with blisters of windows and stonework erupting like barnacles. At the center of the building, the roof levels off and there's a shallow depression with access hatches and air conditioners tucked away from the sight of the street. I find a heating duct that's reasonably clean of pigeon crap and get comfortable.

This may take a while. My stomach growls. The minutes begin to slide by, and I try not to think too hard about the pizza Doc Impossible still owes me. But that leads me to think about how I'm not thinking about the pizza, which inevitably returns to the pizza itself, and so I start trying to figure out how I'm going to get my school supplies from the house so I can go back to school tomorrow. I've still got another year before I can test out, and until that happens I'd like to avoid tanking my GPA.

At first I don't recognize the sound over the noise of the city. Engines running, tires hissing, and the faint suggestion of human voices wafting up from the ground level. But then it comes again. Deeper. Louder. I stand up and cock my head, trying to figure out which direction it's coming from. Again the noise floats over the city, and I think I hear the sound of human voices hitch for a moment as people start to notice.

Explosions.

Big ones.

# CHAPTER THIRTY-ONE

Gnarled fingers of black smoke curl like some enormous claw rising from the train yards. In the eastern part of New Port, a few miles from the shore of Puget Sound, sits Grand Union Station, where row after row of train platforms wait for passengers to board. But a mile south of that there is an industrial rail junction that makes Grand Union Station look like a model train set. Cargo trains load there, on braided lines of rails that split and split again until dozens of miles of track lie next to each other in the space of a single stadium-sized loading port. An entire freeway off-ramp is dedicated to the cargo truck traffic that comes to load and unload the thousands of boxcars that roll and click through the junction every day. It's here the fires are burning.

Hundreds of boxcars crowd the lines, and a double handful of engines sit puttering diesel fumes into the air. And there, in the center of the crowded rail yard, a twisted battlefield. Trains have been derailed. An engine is set up on its nose, leaning against the crumpled side of a boxcar next to it. A liquid storage tank on one of the cars has burst open. Everything within thirty yards is coated in some kind of sticky, burning substance that gives off coal-black smoke. Other cars add more smoke to the air, with their cargoes burning crimson, howling for more oxygen. Flat cars, stock cars, boxcars, and more are all scattered and twisted and stamped flat in places. A path of destruction fifty feet wide meanders westward from the disaster's epicenter toward the edge of the yard. People are dodging among the broken trains and twisted track, running and screaming and shouting into radios.

From fifty feet up, the smoke stings my eyes and nose. I'm trying to get a sense of where the greatest need is, but it's so hard to see what's going on. Everything is chaos. There—a clump of rail workers huddling against an overturned boxcar. A pool of flaming liquid is seeping across the ground toward them, and they're penned against the wreckage. I drop from the sky and they look at me like I'm an angel.

"Get clear of the car!" I shout as I slip my fingers into a gap between the crumpled side of the train car and the ground. It's heavy, damn heavy. My fingers strain and my legs shake, but I get it up to waist height. With one convulsive heave, I hoist it up past my belt line and reset my hands to get it over my head. Metal screams and bends, and the car starts to slip out of my grasp, sliding away from me and back down to the ground. I take a desperate step forward to get under it, and then another, my hands walking inches-deep divots in the side of the car until I've got it mostly balanced over my head on shaking arms.

"Go! Get out of here!" I shout. I count heads as the rail workers slip past me, making sure all five are clear before I let it come smashing down.

"You guys okay?"

"Yeah, but I heard gunfire over there," says one of them, pointing deep into the heart of the destruction.

Gunfire? The hell? I get up in the air fast, looking around for where the destruction began. A man is at the epicenter; he looks like he's in his forties. He wears a blue jumpsuit with a black bulletproof vest over it. In big yellow letters the word TREASURY is stamped across his back. His rifle is lying on the ground next to him, and he's down in the gravel and the mud, trying to shift a twisted lump of steel off the leg of one of his coworkers, another man, somewhat younger, also dressed in overalls and armor.

I land next to them and grunt out a greeting as I slip my fingers under the black and twisted steel. It's pretty light, only a thousand pounds or so. The treasury guard looks at me in surprise for a half second, and then quickly pulls his partner free.

"What's going on?" I ask him, as he bends over his friend's leg to inspect the damage. The guy who was trapped is clenched tight with pain. His leg isn't ever going to be the same again. "People say there was gunfire."

"They robbed the cash train," says the older one absently. "Dammit. Bill, this break is pretty bad; we gotta get you out of here."

"What's a cash train?"

"Look, kid, if you want to help, check on the other side of this wreckage," he says, looking up. "I think some of my guys went down over there."

"Tell me what happened," I say, getting a little frustrated. If I don't know what is going on, there's not much I can do to help. That's obvious, right?

He looks at me with his lips pressed tight for a moment. I don't budge, so he finally says, "It was five guys in big suits, hyper-tech stuff." He says this and my blood freezes in place. Utopia has started whatever she's planning. We were supposed to have another week. "They knew we were running a few carloads of old bills out to the treasury incinerator to get taken out of circulation. That's supposed to be secret, but they were waiting inside some boxcars for us. We stopped to refuel and that's when they hit us, made off with about a half billion dollars. Now, if we're done with show and tell, could you maybe go see if my people are dead or not?"

"Right." My voice doesn't shake with the terror that's coursing through me, which is a small blessing. "Back soon."

I don't find anybody else. Either they're smashed flat under hundreds of tons of steel, or they're making a trip the long way around to regroup with their boss. I make a low, slow pass by him to shout the info down, and then I light out for the edge of the rail yard. This can't be all that Utopia was planning. This is bigger than a robbery. It has to be. Dreadnought dead and Calamity maimed, just for some money? I won't believe that's true. I've got to warn people.

Fire trucks and police cars are starting to nose onto the train tracks, and at the loading dock I find a harried police lieutenant in the middle of a throng of officers, who are using the hood of a police car as a table for a map. I'm a little ways out from them, and a few feet in the air, so they haven't noticed me yet. I need to warn them, but something holds me back. The treasury guard's reaction has me shaken. What am I even doing here? What if I'm just in the way?

Another explosion ripples out in the distance. The cops go silent for a moment, and then the fear sets in. I can sense the moment when they realize the devastation hasn't ended. It's just getting started. Over their radios I hear the panic building. The entire police radio net is a snarl of conflicting reports and pinched voices. It sounds like there's a whole army out there, but nobody can agree on what it looks like. Again and again and again the only thing that is consistent in the reports is that the police desperately need Legion backup.

And they're not getting any.

The cops need help. They need something that will put them in control again, give them a way to see how they're going to do their jobs. They don't need some kid nobody's heard of or has any reason to trust. Right now I'm just some loser in throwaway colors. I look at the inside of my left wrist, where the color blisters stand out. With a trembling hand, I put my thumb on the one that sets the suit to Dreadnought's colors, and I push it in until it clicks. The camo pattern swirls and fades away to solid dark blue and clean, glittering white.

My feet tap down on the cement, and as I approach the knot of police, some start to take notice. One by one they stop speaking and step aside until the lieutenant looks up, confused. They're all staring at me, and I start to think maybe this was a big mistake.

"Are you having trouble getting through to the Legion, too?" My voice sounds like it's coming from someone else.

"They're not answering our calls," he says. That's unheard of. The Legion is always ready to defend New Port; everybody knows that.

"Mine, too. There are some guards from the treasury department back there in the rail yard," I say, sounding much more confident than I feel. "They need an ambulance, and they also said that five guys with hypertech made off with a half billion dollars. Your men shouldn't approach them."

"This is our town, kid. We don't let people bust it up." The gathered cops give a murmur of agreement. Brave, but, wow. Just…just amazingly stupid. Have they not seen what those guys did to the rail yard that's, like, *right over there?*

"They'll be in my way," I say evenly.

Staring down a cop turns out to be a lot harder than I thought it would, but after a long moment the lieutenant nods and gives a few terse orders into his radio. Nothing ironclad, no call to retreat or anything, but he tells them they should give the capes room to work. I notice he doesn't use the word that's hanging in the air.

"Get everyone to the shelters, and keep trying to get through to the Legion." I turn and step away to get space to take off. "Tell them Dreadnought wants backup downtown."

# CHAPTER THIRTY-TWO

Air raid sirens rise in wailing crescendos over the city. Like all big cities since Mistress Malice's war for world conquest, New Port has bomb shelters everywhere for people to hide in if a supervillain attacks. But not everybody can always get to a shelter, and it's been over ten years since anyone had to use them in this town. A lot of people might have forgotten what they're supposed to do when the sirens go off.

From five hundred feet it's easy to trace the path the thieves are taking. I just have to follow the wreckage and the burning cars. They must be hauling ass to have covered so much ground so fast. They're headed straight for downtown.

As the trail of devastation reaches the city core, it begins to meander through the canyons of stone and steel and glass. The damage is the worst at intersections. Burned-out cars and flipped trucks litter the road. There are shot-out windows and burning buildings. I see the first bodies there, lying sprawled out in puddles of blood, shockingly red in some places, so dark they're almost black in others. A few cars are trying to turn around and escape the city, but it's gridlock. Most people have abandoned their vehicles and fled on foot. A lot of them are still out on the street, running in confusion or walking around dazed. Some are trying to help the injured, and at some of the buildings marked with the discreet symbol of a bomb shelter, a few are holding the doors open and shouting for everyone to come inside.

The news choppers are all orbiting the downtown core, each jockeying to get the best angle on whatever is happening. I can tell the exact moment one of them spots me, because the nose-mounted camera turret on one of them snaps over to track me, and a few moments later three other choppers are banking hard to get pictures of me. Uh, great. No, really. Whose dumb idea was it to wear Dreadnought's colors, anyhow?

The sounds of violence are more distinct now. The burping roar of machine guns echoes around corners. Explosions, and the flat hissing sizzles of rockets. I'm close now, but it's hard to tell where the noise is coming from. The sounds bounce off the buildings until it sounds like they're now to my left, then to my rear, now to my front. I round a corner, and I'm almost surprised to find the source of the noise. As I see them, my breath catches in my throat.

When the guard said they had hypertech suits, I thought he meant, like, armor and maybe fancy guns. These things are walking tanks. If I stood next to one, I might be chest-high to its knee-cap. The roughly humanoid machines are piled with thick slabs of armor, but they are not ponderous. They bound forward like grasshoppers on screaming jets of fire. They bristle with weapons. Cannons, machine guns, racks of missiles and rockets, and the short, stubby housings of high-powered lasers. None of them are alike, differing in shape, size, and armament. Each is a different color: green, blue, yellow, and red. Two of them have hands ending in stubby-fingered claws, and between them they carry an entire boxcar. It is dented and smudged with soot, but it's holding up well enough for them to leap forward fifty feet at a time on pillars of smoke and flame. The other two are out-riding, leaping ahead and behind, to the left and the right, switching up and keeping vigilant at all quarters. Some of Utopia's thefts suddenly make sense. She was stocking up to build herself an army.

Traffic here is a snarl as drivers panic, reverse into each other, and get up on the sidewalk in their desperation to escape. The mecha land in the center of an intersection, and as they're coming down they're already firing into traffic and the surrounding buildings. Cars are shredded in seconds; the entire front of a building melts away under the punishing fire. A laser licks out and sets a newsstand ablaze. Without breaking momentum they're up again, bounding toward the next intersection.

I'm in shock. They just murdered a dozen people at least, and they're moving on like it's nothing. A blank, empty moment gives way to a molten rage the likes of which I didn't even know was possible. It's all just to throw anyone following them off the trail. They're making as much chaos and carnage as they can to distract and delay anyone who comes after them.

These guys are about to have a *very* bad day.

I gather my power and explode into motion. Zero to three hundred in forty yards and then they're snapping past me to either side and I'm spinning around and sliding to a stop on the roof of a city bus that's slewed over to one side of the road and abandoned. I square my shoulders and try to look imposing with all five feet and six inches of me. The mecha see me, and come to a clanking, clattering halt.

"That is *ENOUGH!*" I shout. "You've got one chance to surrender! Come out of your mecha with your hands—"

The green one shoots me in the face with an autocannon.

# CHAPTER THIRTY-THREE

In the fight's first half second, explosions ripple up my chest, neck, and face. It is stunningly painful, and for a moment I lose hold of the lattice and get punted fifteen yards into the back of an abandoned delivery truck. The last time I was shot, it was by a submachine gun firing pistol ammo that's about the size of two knuckles of my pinky finger. *That* was uncomfortable. *This* is an autocannon, and it fires rounds that are longer than my hand. My face has gone hot scarlet with pain. I'm still staggering to my feet when the missiles arrive. They burst like tiny suns, and a driving rain of shrapnel tears into me. Then something hits the bus from behind and drives it forward into the truck, crushing me between them. A few seconds later, one of the mecha hops over and douses the whole area in napalm.

This is not going how I pictured it in my head.

My ears are ringing and my skull throbs. My body screams for release from the steel pressure that's pinching me between the truck and the bus. The flames haven't reached me, but drips of liquid fire are starting to pour in from all over. With a great rippling effort, I peel the bus and panel truck apart, and slip out the gap to the side. Almost immediately, I'm fired on with a minigun that sounds like chainsaws against sheet metal. An almost solid stream of bullets shatters against me, a stinging, vicious assault ripping across me in lines of pain.

With a burst of speed, I leave the street in a blur and smash through the window of a luxury clothing shop. Around me, thousands of dollars' worth of suits and ties are ripped to tattered threads. Deep in the store, I take a sharp turn behind a wall and skid to a stop. The place is empty, everyone gone to the shelters, and I let go of a sigh of relief. It was a gamble coming in here to get away. I can't afford to keep taking this kind of chance; sooner or later, I'll find a group of people who weren't able to make it to a shelter in time. Should have gone straight up. Stupid, Danny. Real stupid.

My face feels a little funny, and I wipe it on my forearm. In one horrifying moment I learn two things. First, I'm bleeding, which I'd kind of hoped wasn't ever going to happen again. But much, *much* worse, my mask and cowl have been shot away. All over my suit are little rips and burst seams, but starting around my collarbones, the suit's outer layers been stripped away, leaving the dark gray undersuit and hypertech circuitry exposed to the air. Where the suit should climb up my neck, it's simply fallen away in tatters. From the top of my neck up, my face is completely bare.

There's a sound like the breath of a hungry dragon, and then fire is pouring around the corners and splashing against the walls. This store takes up the entire ground floor of this building, so I fly for the other side, impeccably dressed mannequins pulled along in my wake. Just as I'm about to exit the other side of the building, I see something that makes me halt like I've hit a wall.

A news helicopter with more nerve than sense has flown into the downtown core, weaving among the buildings as it tries to get a clear shot. It's headed right down this street.

With an icy twist in my guts, I back up into the shadows. Over the crackling flames, I can hear the mecha bounding away on high-pitched jump jets. They've left me for dead, or have decided that whatever timetable they're on doesn't give them time to follow me and finish me off.

I could leave.

I *should* leave.

Let's be honest, these guys are kicking my ass. I'm not cut out for this. And if my face gets on the news, that's it; I'm never going to escape. There's a subway entrance right over there. I could put a shirt over my head, go down into the tunnels, fly until I'm out of the area, get back up into open sky, and not stop 'til I'm back on the mountain.

I can't go out there.

Another explosion shakes the windows.

No.

I can't *not* go out there.

I step out into the sunlight, and take to the air. It's hard to push the chopper out of my mind, but this is too dangerous to let myself be distracted. Half of a steep looping spiral brings me back onto the street where the four mecha are bounding forward with their stolen boxcar, maybe three hundred feet above them and a few dozen back.

I need a better plan of attack. I can't afford to get up close and slug it out with them when they're grouped up like that. They'll just mob me again, and those weapons hurt. Maybe none of them is carrying something that can take me out in one shot, but if I let them gang up on me they'll grind me to paste one way or the other.

Wait a minute.

Weren't there supposed to be *five* of these things?

The screaming of jet engines gives me a half-second warning before something big and purple and made of pain swats me out of the sky. I hit an office tower roof, bounce once in a spray of gravel, and slam most of the way through the building's air conditioner, a big box full of metal about the size of a minivan.

Ow.

As I'm peeling myself out of the metal that's bent itself around me, something heavy lands outside. It's the fifth mecha, royal purple and crackling with energy. Eight feet tall, it looks like a fighter jet crossed with a suit of medieval plate armor. A pair of hissing beam sabers, blue-white and painful to look at, burst from its wrists. Its jets scream up power again, and it launches itself across the roof at me.

I rip myself from the crumpled air conditioner's grasp and flip out of the way as the beam sabers cut a yellow molten *X* where I'd been trapped. Even as I'm pushing for distance, the mecha boosts at me and whips its sabers toward my chest. The blades crackle and hiss and the air smells burnt when I twist clear of another attack.

I'm half expecting to leave it behind any moment now, but it feints with its saber and then shoulder slams me like wrecking ball. This one doesn't jump; it flies. It flies fast. Crap, *very* fast!

But it flies only in one direction, which is not a problem I can relate to. I juke backwards and then fly *down*, feet first past and then up behind him. A pair of howling jet engines blasts my hair back, and they don't like it *at all* when I ram my fist up the afterburner. The right engine coughs and barfs a hardware store's worth of broken metal bits out the rear end. Sparks and black smoke begin to trail from the mecha and it begins a slow corkscrew to the ground. I stay with it, and rip the guts out of its second engine, too.

The mecha screams—like, literally a speaker crackles on and then some guy is screaming in rage at me. "This doesn't involve you; just leave us alone!" There's something about the voice that strikes me as familiar.

It fires its attitude jets and spins over on its back to slash at me with a hissing saber. I dodge, and it sprays me with a burst from its chest-mounted machine gun.

My fingers crunch through steel and ceramic, and I flip it back over by its legs. With a firm grip on its flaming engines, I start powering toward the ground. There's a nice open stretch of road I'm aiming for; I don't want this to fall on anyone. The pilot tries to wriggle out of my grip, but I stay tight against his back. Just a dozen feet up or so I let go and it plows into the ground in a shower of sparks and shattered asphalt, bounces, skids, and comes up to its feet in a fighting stance.

Which, you know, isn't even *close* to fair. It's all dented and banged up, but I think I should have gotten a little more out of pile driving it from fifty stories up.

"Why don't you give up?" I ask him, from what I hope is a safe distance in the air. "It took all four of your buddies just to slow me down—you don't think you're really going to win here, do you?"

"Get out of here! This has nothing to do with you!" the pilot shouts. I swear I know this voice from somewhere. "Just let me have this!"

"Wait, *Gerald?* Seriously?" Wow. Um. Okay. Sure. The mecha—or really, Gerald—flares his attitude jets and lunges at me. I bounce for altitude and he sails beneath me, sabers ripping at the air and not much else. On the way down he spins and fires off another burst of his machine gun. I loop under the tracers and shoot in to hit him in the waist. We hit the ground with a clang and I plow a deep furrow with the back of his mecha. His machine gun is in a little ball turret and it swivels down to shoot me. I grab the barrel and twist it with a whine of tortured metal. He fires again and something bad happens deep inside the gun.

Gerald slashes his beam sabers at me too fast to dodge. I get my arms up to block them, and molten pain sings out from my forearms. I bound into the air and frantically pull for distance.

The outer edges of my forearms each have a long, narrow burn crossing them. The suit has been almost entirely burnt away, the charcoal-gray undersuit visible along the length of each burn, and a few places where I can see red, angry burns on my skin. It feels like he hit me with some white-hot rebar. Already the blisters are starting to rise. I need something to counter those swords or I won't last long up close with him. A quick glance around, and I don't see any other mecha sneaking up on me. I need to finish with this one fast and get back to the others before they can hurt anyone else.

While he pulls himself from the trench we dug, I fly over to a nearby parking lot to get a weapon. Because I'm a fangirl and fangirls read too much, I know that you don't want to hit people with cars like they're baseball bats. A modern car is mostly made out of plastic crumple zones; it's not going to hit the kinds of things a superhero fights very hard. But if you rip out the engine block, which is a few hundred pounds of solid metal, then you have something to work with.

With a few sharp tugs I'm able to liberate an engine from the front of an SUV. I charge the purple mecha and use my big hunk of metal to smash its beam sabers aside, then slam it down on the mecha's shoulder. Once, twice, three times, and it gives way just about the same time as the engine disintegrates in my hands. He slashes at me with his good arm and starts screaming about how he's going to kill me for trying to mess up his "big chance." I get my arms around its good arm and set my feet against the shoulder socket. With a great twisting tug, I rip the arm off, hydraulics bursting in a spray of soupy blue fluid. Gerald screams again, and before he gets a chance to think of something clever I've anchored myself to the mecha's chest and I'm pounding at the release catches for the cockpit hatch. A few sharp blows and the hatch's locks are done; I rip it and reach out to grab him by the front—

Holy shit, what the *hell* is that?

Gerald is glaring up at me with all the hate he can muster, and I can't tell where he ends and the machine starts. Segmented metal tubes plug straight into his skin, all red and swollen where he is joined with the machine. His arms are gone, and in their place thick bundles of cables run into a pair of cavities that used to be his armpits. It's hard to see from this angle, but I'm pretty sure his legs are gone, too. He's nothing but a torso encased in a metal cradle that's been slotted into the center of this thing.

"Why can't you just leave me alone?" he mutters.

So I punch him, and man, it feels good. He cries out and snorts blood from a freshly broken nose.

"What's she planning?" I snap.

"Go to hell." I think it would be easier to accept if he were just angry and frustrated at being beaten. But his head is hanging, and his voice drips with self-pity. Because *he's* the victim here, don't you know?

There is a pair of yellow handles on the cradle, one near each of his shoulders. The more I look at it, the more I think what's left of his body is just plugged in there like a socket. With a sharp heave, I pull him straight up and out of the cockpit. The whole metal casing surrounding his body comes out cleanly, cables separating along magnetically sealed break links.

As it turns out, all of his nerve endings were still connected to the mecha. Whoops. He doesn't stop screaming until we're almost up on the roof of a thirty-story building. I toss him down on the gravel next to the building's air conditioner. He lands face-first and begins to sob.

For the briefest moment, I feel pity and remorse. Another explosion echoes in the distance, and I remember what Calamity said. *You don't gotta feel bad about playing dirty with his kind.* I'm not sure I agree with that, but I'm starting to understand why she would say it.

"I don't even want to think about how many people you've killed today, but whatever Utopia promised you *isn't* going to happen," I say. "You're going to tell me everything you know about her plan, or I'm going to leave you up here and forget about you."

"No!" he snarls, face down, glaring at me from the corner of his eye. "She said she was going to give me a real body, one like hers! You think I'm going to screw that up?"

"Dude, *look* at you! You can't even wipe your own ass anymore! You are already so fucked we don't even have words for how badly you're screwed. How often do you think the maintenance guys have a reason to come out here?" I ask him. "Once a day? Twice a week?"

He screws his eyes shut.

"I can't stay here long. I have to stop the others. I'm giving you until I reach the edge of the roof to start talking, and then I'm going to leave you here and see how long it takes for someone to find you."

I make it four slow paces before he cracks.

"This is all she told us about! I promise!"

"Not good enough," I say, and keep walking. Just a few steps more.

"Wait! Wait, there's a submarine! We were supposed to make our way to the waterfront, and she's got a sub waiting to meet us! That's our escape plan."

"Better." The gravel crunches under my feet. "But not enough."

"But that's all I know, I swear!" There's real panic in his voice now. "We grab the money, we fight through town, and we get in the sub and escape."

I pause at the edge. So maybe this is really just a big robbery? That seems so petty to go to all these lengths for. Why not just hijack the train when it got out of town? She clearly has the capabilities to pull something like that off. Gerald is pleading and sobbing now, and I'm pretty sure I won't get anything else out of him.

I turn back to him. "Thanks, Gerald. When this is done, I'll tell them to come find you." Shooting down between the skyscrapers, toward the sound of gunfire, I mutter to myself, "Eventually."

# CHAPTER THIRTY-FOUR

Four mecha, one of me, and last time I tried this they kicked me around like a soccer ball. I find them back in formation and bounding toward the waterfront. They land and spray another intersection down with fire. It seems like most people have cleared the area by now, but I still see a few stragglers trying to hide behind mailboxes or press themselves down under cars.

Anxiety clenches at me. I spent too long taking down Gerald. They keep blasting the city and I have no idea how I'm going to stop them. If I get close enough to hit them, they're going to mob me again. I'm not good enough for this. I'm not smart enough, not brave enough. These people are all going to die because of me. I can't think, I don't know what to do, everything is going wrong. I need Calamity. She'd know what to—

And then a plan just clicks into place.

These guys need to be as scared and confused as I am, and achieve to that, I need to hit them where it hurts. I need to split them up and hunt them down one at a time.

The wind tugs hard at me as I angle down and push for speed. The mecha notice me on the way in and fill the air with autocannon and laser fire. Ruby fingers of light lick out at me, and orange tracers crowd the air. I loop and roll under their fire. They score a few light hits but I crack the sound barrier and keep coming. Two hundred yards, one hundred, fifty—

Impact.

I hit the boxcar with an apocalyptic bang and punch through the other side in hurricane of cash. The boxcar rips in half like a burst piñata, spinning out of their claws and spraying millions of dollars out onto the street. I turn over on to my back and give them the finger as I pull for altitude.

Their precious teamwork goes out the frickin' window. The yellow one immediately turns and goes bounding away on its jets. Green and Blue just kind of stand there for a moment, and then begin firing everything they've got at me.

I loop around the block in a climbing spiral and come screaming down the road that Yellow has taken off on. At the last moment it seems to become aware of me, too late to do anything. Dragging my fingers across its back as I pass, I catch a solid handhold on an ammo rack and jerk the mecha off the ground. My shoulders feel like they want to come out of my sockets but with a heave I set it spinning, and it does a few cartwheels down the road before crashing down on a parked truck. I loop up and back to drive down on Yellow from above. The pilot manages to bring his flamethrower around fast enough to spatter me with napalm on the way in. Feet first, I crunch it down through the truck and into the pavement. The locks on the hatch snap off when I kick at them, and I've ripped the mecha open in a single smooth attack.

This one is another plug-type, and the pilot is screaming at me in horror. Yellow's arms come up to try and bat me off, but I rip the pilot out of his socket and drop him on the sidewalk. His screams go up a few octaves when I do, and I feel dirty. I *really* hate these guys, but I don't like to think about what it must feel like to have live nerve connections severed like that. But what can I do? They're *killing* people.

Just as I'm thinking this, something flashes off to my left. I whirl, ready to fight. It's a photographer standing not fifteen feet from me. He snaps another picture of me standing atop the destroyed mecha.

"Get inside, idiot!" I shout at him.

"No way, this is gonna make my Pulitzer," he says from behind the viewfinder.

In the time it takes him to blink I've crossed the distance

between us and shattered his camera all over the ground. "There, now you don't have any reason to stay out here."

He shouts some truly inventive profanity at me, but I'm already leaving him behind and approaching Mach 1. There are three mecha remaining. I come around the corner at about thirty feet off the ground, and almost instantly a laser beam melts the windows next to me and punches clear through the corner of the building. The beam tracks toward me to correct, dragging a line of fire and destruction behind me, and but I'm across the street and out of sight in less than a second. A second is all I need. I get a glance at them and figure out my next step.

The last three have decided to stick together and make the best of it. The red one is trying to tip half the torn boxcar up on its end and use it like a bucket to hold as much cash as it can. Green is the one that shot at me, so I figure it must have some advanced sensors to be able to track me through these buildings. Blue is standing back-to-back with Green, covering the other approach.

So. Destroy Green.

I dig as deep into the lattice as I can and pop the sound barrier like a soap bubble. The world goes green and black around the edges as I take a turn at forty Gs. My shock wave bounces cars and shatters windows. At almost two thousand miles an hour I circle the block and tear back up the street toward them. At these speeds, the air itself is trying to burn me as the friction flash boils my sweat away into steam.

Blue is waiting and throws a blizzard of tracers my way. Some I roll around, others I batter through. Ruby lasers lick out from Green's shoulder turrets as it tries to turn around in time to bring its main weapons to bear on me. Too slow. Far, far too slow.

My fingers clamp down as I pass Green, getting me a hold of a solid, shoulder-jerking grip as I angle my flight down. My feet hit pavement and I pivot my momentum through my ankles and knees. My back and arms straining, I whip Green up and over, slam it down so hard that cars leap into the air all around us. Even as tires are still hitting the shattered pavement, I'm up on the front of Green, machine-gunning punches into the armor around its hatch to bust it open like the other ones. The hatch pops off and I fling it away. The pilot is dazed, her eyes unfocused and glassy.

Blue's claw seizes me around the chest and whips me away from Green. Dammit. The ground comes up to smash me once, twice, three times until I'm able to get an arm free from Blue's fat, stubby claw, rip one of its fingers off, and squirm from its grasp. Blue hoses me down with stinging rivers of bullets that tear and pull at me. The pilot is still leaning on the trigger when I rush in and crunch the barrels of its machine guns; I can hear them jam and backfire deep inside the machine. Scrambling up the front of Blue, I start jackhammering my fist against the lip of its hatch.

Blue's jump jets fire and it body slams me against a concrete pillar next to the entrance to an office tower. My ribs creak and the breath explodes out of me. Blue reverses thrust; I slide down the pillar in a daze and just manage to flit out of there before the whole area explodes in dust and stone chips from a burst of autocannon fire. Orange tracers fall away behind me as I boost for speed to come around the block again.

But no. I hang in midair on the other side of the tower. The air is flat and acrid with smoke. The air raid sirens wail in the distance. The fear and the anger urge me on, tell me to attack, attack, attack, but I have to pause. I need to think.

I can't keep coming straight at them down the road. They'll be expecting that, and these three seem to be sticking together enough that getting in and ripping off hatches isn't a real good idea. I need to pull their teeth first, and I need to approach them from an angle they're not watching. A thought occurs to me, and I decide to do it at the same moment I realize how dangerous it will be. I'm gonna go through the building. It's a risk—they might start shooting into the upper floors of towers in response, but I have the advantage now and I need to keep it. I need to keep them off balance.

A wall-sized window shatters into turquoise gravel as I punch through. Office furniture and a few huddled workers whip by me. Idiots! What are they still doing out on the office floor? At a time like this, they should be hiding in a stairwell where the concrete walls will keep them safe. Haven't they ever lived in a city before? A vortex of shredded paperwork is sucked up in my wake, and I explode out the side of the building in a cloak of shattered glass. My attack comes from almost directly above the mecha, and Blue barely registers my presence before I land on its shoulders and begin tugging at the barrels of its autocannons. These are powerful weapons, but they're not designed to resist someone like me torqueing on them. With a shriek they bend upward, useless and twisted. I dart away with a snap-flutter of my cape. Red is raising its grenade launcher as I charge. Just as it starts coughing rounds at me, I get in close and rip the ammo feed out. Slipping around to Red's back, I pop up into the air and give each of its shoulder-mounted missile racks a solid kick. They burst open like wet grocery bags, dented and split missiles spilling out and clattering to the ground.

With a few heavy stomps I crack Red's hatch open and rip the pilot out. Tossing him screaming into the upturned half of the boxcar he was dragging—a loose pile of cash is like a pillow, right?—I charge Blue before it can get any ideas.

Blue gets its arms up in time to parry my first blow, and we trade punches for a moment, a real titanic slugfest with echoing bangs like sledgehammers on cast iron. It manages to force me to the ground and I'm stuck dodging blows and punching shins. My boots gouge divots in asphalt as I land punches, and Blue's fist makes my cheek pop and sing with pain. Finally I catch its fist, a huge clawed finger in each hand, and twist it to the outside. I leave the ground, and rotate in place so I can keep twisting. The arm seizes up, strains, and rips off in a spurting fountain of hydraulics. Blue staggers and its good arm goes to grasp at its stump. While the pilot is distracted by the pain of losing an arm linked to his nerves, I get the hatch off and pull him out. The blue mecha falls over, and I set its pilot down gently in the crook of its arm. His face is pale, and his eyes are distant.

Green is on her feet again, and by the fury in her eyes I'm guessing getting her hatch torn off isn't enough to stop her. We stare at each other across thirty yards of broken asphalt and destroyed cars. She flexes her mecha's fingers, clenches them into fists bigger than my head. "I am going to kill you, kid. I'm gonna pull you apart and pop your skull!"

She's got guts, I'll say that much for her. The world goes streaky for a moment and then we're nose to nose.

"Nope."

Her hands are coming up to smash me even as I rip the last pilot from her socket and twist up and away.

The green mecha falls over with a clatter and bang. I set the pilot down—she's about as thrilled as the rest of them, hissing and grunting in helpless agony—and wobble on over to sit on the leg of a fallen mecha. Aside from the moans of the pilots, there is a sudden quiet on the scene, far quieter than I ever expected to hear downtown.

So that's it, then.

My first big fight.

Combat is not what I thought it would be.

My cape is tattered with autocannon holes. My gloves are cracked, my knuckles split and bleeding. My burns sting, my head throbs, and my ribs ache. There are bruises everywhere.

And I'm *starving*.

Slowly, the rest of the world begins to intrude. I hear choppers overhead, and look up. The news helicopters have decided to get up over the downtown core and stare down with their zoom lenses. Crap.

My throat clenches and I zip off the street, through the shattered windows of a bank, and get far enough in to be out of sight from anything in the sky. Something is wrong. I feel anxious and tight, and my guts are churning. The shakes start at my hands, a tremble moving inward toward my core. My knees are knocking and I sit down heavily in a plush chair in the waiting area. There might be vomit soon. I begin to sob, and I couldn't explain why if you asked. I'm not scared, and the pain isn't so bad, but all I can do is hug myself and shudder through it.

There's footsteps on broken glass, and I look up. A cop noses around the corner, face pressed down behind the sights of a carbine. When she sees me, she straightens up in surprise and lowers the weapon. "Are you okay?" she asks. "Is it over?"

I take a shaking breath to steady myself long enough to speak. "Yeah, that's all of them, I think, and now I'm crying for no reason."

The cop smiles faintly. "That's the adrenaline. It happens to everyone." She squeezes the mic on her shoulder and mutters some code words back to the other police officers.

"Oh, good." I gesture at the destroyed mecha with my thumb. "For a moment there I was scared they were going to think I was a wimp."

She snorts. "Breathe deep and slow. It will pass." I follow her advice, and when I'm a little steadier she says, "So you're the new Dreadnought?"

"That's me," I say. "What's your name?"

"I'm Officer Phạm," she says.

"You shouldn't have been so close," I say. "I was having a hard time with them. They could have killed you."

"It's been silent for about ten minutes." Officer Phạm crosses the lobby and pokes her head out the other shattered window to get a look at the downed mecha. "The sarge sent me in to get a look."

Ten minutes? No, it hasn't been that long. I look up at her, confused.

"Time will get away from you," she says. "Good work, by the way."

"Thanks." I sit up straight. There's something I need to check. My hand goes for my cell phone, but it's just a fistful of shattered plastic in a belt case now. "Are the news choppers gone yet?"

"You're kidding, right?"

"Dammit." I stand up and take a tentative step toward the window to try to see where the choppers are focused. "My mask got shot away. I really don't want them to get a close-up of my face."

Officer Phạm grimaces. "We can have a cruiser brought up

and drive you out of here. Throw a jacket over your head and nobody will ever know."

Tempting. Very tempting. But with the stress crash fading, I'm starting to think clearly again. Now is not the time to be running away.

"No. There's something else I have to do. In fact, get the word out that people should stay in their shelters—I don't think this is over. Get someone to call the Navy and tell them these guys might have had a submarine in Puget Sound, too." I walk toward the window she came in through. The choppers are all filming the downed mecha, it looks like. Going out the other side of this building should be safe-ish. "Oh, and you're going to find one of these pilots up on a roof somewhere; I forget which building, sorry."

"Where are you going?"

"I need to find out what the hell's happened to the Legion."

# CHAPTER THIRTY-FIVE

Up through the air like a shot, through the sound barrier, and across the skyline. I'm barely at cruising speed before I have to pull back and decelerate to come to a jogging touchdown on the landing pad at Legion Tower. Something's off. It takes me a moment to place what's wrong, but then I notice the landing lights are all dead. Wind tugs at my cape, and the tower is silent and dark. For maybe three or four seconds.

Then the machine guns start up. Art deco moldings clack open, miniguns unfold, and scarlet streams of tracers break themselves against me. One gun smashes apart under my fist, the other my foot, and it's done almost before it started. No more guns pop open to shoot me. It's amazing how fast this kind of thing becomes second nature.

The door I kicked in last night still hasn't been replaced. When I tap an elevator button, nothing happens, as if the machine gun welcome mat wasn't enough to tell me I'm not a guest of honor. The elevator doors resist me when I try to slide them open. A few solid kicks crumple them inward with a screech and crunch. The shaft is black and silent. This is starting to creep me out now. As I'm falling down the elevator shaft, a white beacon flares to life above the doors to the thirty-fourth floor. I grab the lattice to stop my fall, and watch it carefully.

"Danny, get in here," says Doc Impossible over a speaker. The doors slide open, and I'm drenched with relief. The airlock is waiting for me, and I try not to let the anxiety get to me as I wait for the sterilization beams to work.

"Doc, what's going on? How come you guys haven't answered anyone's call?"

"We're under attack. The Legion is out of action." Doc Impossible's voice is low, resigned. "I think I've got her contained, but…oh. Damn. Well, it doesn't really matter now, does it?"

The happy anime face pings its approval at me, and the airlock's inner door cracks open with a thunk and hiss. A trail of scarlet blinkers in the floor leads through the halls of Impossible's lab, first down this hall, then that one. The walls are drab and dark, and the gloom is only partially held back by harsh emergency lights every dozen yards or so. Doc Impossible's pug sticks its head around a corner, sees me, and scuttles back into the darkness.

"What do you mean, 'out of action'? Where are you?" My footsteps tap dully against the ground. I didn't notice before, but the ground is plastic. It was softly glowing, making everything underlit like some technoglossy wonderland. But now it's just flat, off-white panels that my boots *tup-tup* against as I walk. Except for the little trail of blinkers, the floor is dead. Like the walls, like everything in the building.

"Busy. Follow the trail. Calamity has been asking for you."

"You said we were under attack."

"It's bad," says Doc Impossible. Her voice is coming from everywhere, nowhere. "Utopia has fortified herself in the main computer core. It won't be long now."

"Won't be long until what?" I ask as I get to the door the scarlet blinkers are leading me to. It whooshes open, and Calamity shoots me directly between the eyes.

"Ow!" My hand shoots up to rub the bridge of my poor, battered nose. It's still tender from the walloping I got from those autocannons. "The hell was that for?"

Calamity's arm drops back down to her side like the gun is suddenly too heavy for her. "Sorry, Danny," she says in the Sarah voice. She's lying in a hospital bed, shirt removed but her whole chest wrapped in soft white bandages. Her arm is gone at the shoulder—no stump, no nothing, just gone. A square of gauze is taped over her left eye, and her face hangs slack with weariness. "Thought you were another one of those things. Nice colors."

"Thanks. What things?"

"There, that." She gestures with her gun, to something near the foot of the bed. It's Doctor Impossible, sprawled out like a corpse, except—a jolt goes through me, all the way down to my fingertips. It's Doc Impossible except her head is missing from the lower jaw on up, and there are fiber-optic wires and smashed circuitry where there should be blood and skull. Her body lies in a puddle of its own white circulatory fluid. "That thing came in, pointed a gun at me, and then, bang, ate its own bullet. Explosive-tipped, by the looks of it. Didn't think I'd get lucky twice, thus the hollowpoint hello. Did you know she was a robot?"

"Why would a robot be a nicotine addict?" I look at the ceiling. "Doc, what's going on?"

Her voice floats down from nowhere. She's quiet, and sounds dazed, like the effort to guide me here was one last grasp at lucidity and now she's sliding, sliding down into the black. "I thought I'd removed all the back doors, but now I wonder if that was only a memory I was meant to have."

"Do you have any idea what's going on?" asks Sarah. "I don't even know what day it is."

"It's Thursday, maybe eleven in the morning." I tell her briefly about the fight downtown, about how the Legion wasn't answering its calls, how other than the miniguns on the roof, the tower seems completely dead, and about the attack Doc mentioned when she was still making sense.

"Clever bitch must have lied to everyone," says Sarah. "She told her goons it was going down next week in case one of them squealed, so we all thought we had more time."

"Doc!" I shout at the ceiling. "I need you!"

"How much of me is a lie?" she says.

"Please, come in here!"

Her voice seems to notice me for the first time a long while. "I can't. My new body isn't done yet."

Sarah shrugs her good shoulder at me. "Robot. Told you."

"I'm not a robot," says Doc irritably. That's good. Irritable is good.

"Then what's with the dead robot on the floor here?" I ask.

"I'm an *android*. I—oh. Oh, Danny, I'm so sorry. I didn't…I thought there was more time."

"Doc, what's going on?"

There is a long pause, and I open my mouth to repeat the question, but she speaks again. "Utopia is my mother. She built me, six years ago. I promise, I didn't know she was my mother until last night. I told you I was running from someone, right? That's who, but I didn't realize she'd taken a new name and face until you told me she knew who you were yesterday. How could she know? Even if she saw you—and I don't think she did because she'd have killed you on the spot—but even if she did, how does that get her a name? She learned it from me. She must have *let* me go, and kept a back door into my programming so she could slip into my mind any time she chose. She could wear me like a glove, if she wanted."

Something tumbles into place and locks. At the time, I was freaking out and didn't really pay attention, but I remember what Utopia said to me. She said she'd killed *two* Dreadnoughts.

I was there when she killed the third Dreadnought last month, but the second Dreadnought was killed by a kaiju, not a person. Which means she as much as told me who she is.

Not a supervillain, but *the* supervillain.

"Oh, shit."

"What?" asks Sarah.

"Utopia is—"

"Mistress Malice, yes," says Doc Impossible.

Sarah says a few things that could strip the paint off a battleship.

"She built me as a culmination of her project to create a true artificial intelligence, to prove consciousness can exist on a synthetic substrate," says Doc. "I was step one of her plan."

"What's she doing?"

"If what I think I know isn't some kind of double bluff, I think she's trying to upload herself. I have always had a fascination with neural-electrical links, which is strange now that I think about it because I've never had neurons. She must have been nudging me, all the time, always there, she was—"

"The plan, Doctor," says Sarah.

"Oh. Right. Once she proved consciousness could exist in a digital environment, she'd want to migrate her own mind into such an environment. But that's not easy to do, there's a lot of theory of mind questions that need to be solved; if she just made a software copy of her brain, the program might think it was her, but would it be? My mother is the world's biggest narcissist, so there's no way she'd let a digital copy of herself have all the fun. She needed a way to be sure it was *her* inside the machine, not a knockoff. The neural prosthetics I was developing can be repurposed to convert her brain into a computer one neuron at a time. Once her brain is fully digitized, her mind will be software. The connections were there, I just…didn't see them. God, I'm so stupid."

Sarah and I trade glances. She looks as lost as I feel. "That's it? She just wants to be a computer program?"

"No," says Doc Impossible. "She wants to rule the world. This is a means to an end. As self-aware, self-editing malignant stream of code injected into the internet, she could take control of everything from online banking to nuclear launch codes. She could store a thousand copies of herself in darknet servers all over the world, and become impossible to kill."

"Oh," I say.

"I vote no," Sarah says.

The heavy, hanging defeat returns to Doc Impossible's voice. "It doesn't matter. She's already won. When I realized I was compromised, I created a copy of myself inside my backup servers, and set it to recompile from the kernel up while doing a checksum against every segment of code. This would hopefully create a clean version of myself, one free of her control. That's the version that's speaking to you now. But Sarah was still in serious condition, and I couldn't leave her alone while my debug program ran."

A wall flickers to life, and a video feed begins to play. It's the conference room, shot from up high in a corner. The Legion is sitting around a table, waiting for something. Doc Impossible enters, carrying a small round device.

"I made a mistake. I let the compromised version run for a few more hours to keep an eye on her. We all thought we'd have more time."

In the video, Doc Impossible is speaking to the gathered Legion. They lean in, interested in what she has to say. She sets the small device down in the center of the table and steps back. Valkyrja is looking up at her and asking a question when it happens. Little jets of gas spurt from the device, a cloud like a greasy heat smudge fills the air.

"Mother used my body to ambush them. She puppeted me. I don't know where she got the nerve gas."

Valkyrja's mouth is hanging open, cheek muscles bunching and spasming as she flops out of her chair and begins to jerk. Carapace leaps up from his seat, but Doc Impossible points what looks like a car key fob at him and his armor falls right off in pieces. Almost instantly, he's crumpled to the ground and choking on his own vomit. Magma is on his feet, staggering toward Doc with his hands out, but trips over his own feet and goes down. He doesn't get back up. Chlorophyll isn't fazed by the gas. He grows thorns like claws all over his fists and charges with a shout of rage, but Impossible pulls a gun and shoots him just above his left eye. His head bursts open like bloody cabbage. His leg jumps once, twice, as he lies there at the edge of death. Graywytch's robes have come alive with burning sigils. Her bird is twitching on the ground next to her, and she's slashed her arm open with a ceremonial dagger, the blood spattered around her at every point of the compass. Doc Impossible's body raises its gun and fires at her again and again. The bullets slam into air and burst into shrapnel. Graywytch's lips curl back and she spits words at Doc's body. Utopia lowers the gun, says something in reply, and leaves.

"Carapace and Valkyrja are confirmed KIA. Magma probably is, too. Chlorophyll is immune to poison, but likely won't survive much longer without medical aid. Graywytch is in a protective circle, but if she were able to leave her zone of safety she would have done so by now."

"No." It's not true. This is a trick, a lie, some kind of test. It's not true. *It's not true.*

"It happened, Danny. The Legion is gone."

I look at Sarah. She'll know what to do. She'll know how to make it better.

Sarah stares back at me, lost in horror. That, more than anything, is what makes it real to me. My knees grow weak, and I sit down heavily in a plastic chair next to her bed.

"Mother then came down here to kill Calamity, but the clean version of myself finished initializing and managed to contest control of my body long enough to shoot myself," continues Doc. "I have an independent security system for this level, as well as a Faraday cage around the whole lab. After I severed the datalinks to the rest of the building, she could not intrude again. But I'm trapped here until my new body is finished fabricating."

"How long until she's finished uploading herself?" I ask the question but it sounds like it came from someone else.

"I can't tell from in here. Minutes, probably. No more than an hour."

"There's still time to stop her," says Sarah, but she sounds like she's voicing a hope, not a conviction.

"No, she's won. She's behind a security system that was built to keep out someone like Red Steel. You could punch through the vault walls, Danny, but they'd discharge their voltage into you, and electricity is one of the few things that you're almost as vulnerable to as anyone else. They're powered by the building's main reactor, but that's inside the vault, too. She's won. I'm sorry."

There's a hole in the bottom of me, a hole everything is

draining out of, leaving me cold and empty. Too late. Too slow. Too weak. I wasn't good enough, wasn't strong enough. It's over. Mistress Malice, Utopia, whatever she wants to call herself—it doesn't matter. Soon she'll be able to call herself Empress, if she wants. They're all dead, and I'm alone. The creeping, bubbling shame of it takes hold as I realize I'm scared, not for the world, but for me. She's going to kill me. What's one more Dreadnought but just another notch in her belt?

Sarah perks up. "Wait, what kind of reactor is it?"

Doc Impossible sounds nonplussed. "Supercritical light water fission, why?"

"Then it's got to have a coolant loop, right? I can't imagine you could fit even that in the secured zone."

"No, but the coolant has its own…wait, the security for that hadn't been upgraded on schedule. It's on a different system, but main security has a placeholder dummy script in its place. We had to hack it that way to keep the alarms from going off all the time, and then just never got around to actually fixing it. She probably doesn't even know the hole is there."

"Can you un-sever your datalinks?" asks Sarah.

"Yes, it's just an analog break switch—"

"Well, that's a plan then, isn't it? You turn off the security, and I go down and cut the coolant pipes. That will scram the reactor, and while the system is switching over to the backups, Danny—" Sarah stops, smiles. "Dreadnought goes in and wrecks Utopia's day."

"That could work," I say.

Sarah throws off her blankets and swings her legs over the side of the bed.

"Wait, you're not healthy enough to be moving around," says Doc.

"I ain't dead yet," snarls Calamity. "Point me to some explosives, I mean to return a favor."

• • •

Calamity's breathing is heavy in my ear. The earbud radio still smells like emulsion from the fabricator. We didn't have time to tune them properly, so her mic is picking up all sorts of extra noise. I can hear every cuss and exertion as she claws along the serviceway deep in the building's guts. There's a junction she's got to get to for this to work, but it's deep in a rat's nest of pipes and passageways. Hands and knees only, but she's short a hand.

"Almost there," she says, and it sounds like she's speaking from inside my head.

Doc Impossible comes on the line. "Remember, you need to set them to detonate in sequence, so—"

"I was paying attention, Doc," grumbles Calamity. She goes on to repeat something Doc said about shaped charges, word for word to rub it in.

I'm standing in a hallway on the same level as the main computer core. Actually, it's the middle floor of the five-floor complex that houses the core, reactor, nanolab, and secure vault. The computers inside the Legion's tower are some of the most advanced on Earth, and contain a lot of the most sensitive and secret information imaginable. The vault holds…well, nobody's really sure, but everyone knows it's not just for the Legion's use. A lot of private groups pay to store sensitive stuff here, too. After all, what's safer than a building full of superheroes?

The main core complex is housed in an enormous armored citadel set within the tower. It's a shell of solid steel larger than most houses. Much larger. Its walls aren't strong enough to keep me out, but they're designed to zap anyone who touches their bare surface with enough voltage to seriously ruin my day. When the reactor does an emergency scram to avoid a meltdown, there will be a break in the current while the system switches over to backups. I'll have 2.3 seconds to punch my way through nine inches of armored steel. I've picked out the section I'm going to attack and carefully pulled the drywall down.

Now I stare at the target down a long hallway: a bare spot on the wall. The emergency lights splash harsh black shadows against the walls.

"Hey Doc, I've got a question," I say.

"Go ahead." Her voice has a slight crackle as it comes over the radio link.

"Why does an android need to smoke?"

"Addiction.ini," says Doc Impossible.

"What?"

"I thought…I thought maybe an addiction would make me more human," she says. "Like I could be what I wanted to be. Not what she made me. But I was wrong."

"Oh. When we're done here—"

"All set," says Calamity.

"Okay, get out of there," says Doc. The really nerve-wracking part is we don't know how much time we have left. Could be an hour. Could be two minutes.

"Yes, Ma." A few minutes after that, she says she's reached a safe spot to detonate from.

I take a runner's stance and line up.

"Dreadnought?" Calamity asks.

"Yeah?"

"Best of luck."

I smile. The world's about to end, but somehow she doesn't seem worried. I don't know what I'd do without her. "See you on the other side, Calamity."

"Going in five, four, three—"

"Wait!"

"What?"

"Are you going to detonate it *on* one, or the beat *after* one?"

A clearly transmitted sigh. "The beat after."

"Okay, let's go."

"Five, four, three, two…"

On *one* I dig into the lattice and push off.

Calamity is saying *mark* at the same time a shudder goes through the building.

The hallway rushes and blurs around me. The power fails and the switchover begins as my fist hits the wall with everything I have behind it. It sounds like if you hid inside a dumpster and someone beat on the outside with a cinder block, but louder, *much* louder. Shock waves of tight-packed pain shoot through my knuckles and up my wrist. The wall buckles inward, a shrieking floor-to-ceiling dent a foot deep. A tenth of a second later, my other fist hits, and joins its song to the tremendous, incredible noise. My fists blur like hummingbird wings, a rolling cacophony shakes loose ceiling tiles, and then I'm through. The armored walls fall away, and I burst into the main computer core.

Utopia is there, chestplate open, firing her glittering beam straight through my chest.

There's no pain, not at first. No, it's more like a sense of wrongness. There's something missing, or maybe something where it doesn't belong. There's a detonation from far behind me where the inversion beam is carving a tunnel through the building. Hot wind presses my cape to my back and makes dust devils out of rubble.

When I look down at my chest, I see a neat little hole about the size of a golf ball. It's charred around the edges, and I think it goes all the way through. I open my mouth to scream, and the wound whistles as my scorched, punctured lung begins to leak. The scream dies as a horrified gasp.

Then the pain comes. It comes in crashing tsunami waves, endless and heavy, drowning all thought, obliterating all sense. Something jolts my knees, and I realize I'm falling around the time the floor smacks me in the face. I writhe and gasp.

"Very good, Danielle," says Utopia. "You almost made it."

She shoots me again.

# CHAPTER THIRTY-SIX

The world peels away and leaves behind a scarlet haze. Someone is dragging me by my ankle. My head is knocking against stairs. The pain is everywhere, everything. A white bar of agony is punched through my chest. Another through my gut. With my eyes closed, I peer into the lattice and examine myself. If I could, I'd scream.

I'm *unraveling*.

The lattice is a hard white net against absolute black. The strings of reality are infinitely thin and infinitely bright. Everything is a knot or a twist in the lattice. Every bird in the sky, every song on the radio, it's all in the lattice. I'm not different. My body is a pattern of twists and ties and wraps and bindings. But now there are two holes punched straight through. And at the edges, the lines have snapped. They drift and wave in a current that isn't there, and as they shift, they unkink, untie, unknit themselves. My pattern is growing loose, a cascade of reactions spreading out from the wound. *This* line is slack so *that* knot comes undone. *These* twists are slashed, so *those* tangles start to slide apart. And every shift, every unraveling, is agony.

"Danielle, can you hear me?" someone asks from far away. A moan is the best reply I can manage. "Please try. I may have overdone it."

It's Utopia. That's right. I was supposed to fight her. I drag my eyes open, and shove them into focus. We're in the main computer core. A vaulted ceiling above a deep pit with catwalks around the edges. And in the center, a computer that's made as much of glass as it is of metal. Utopia steps up to a console, lifts a crown of wires tethered by a cable to the main core, and places it on her head.

I'm propped up against a console, a few yards away from her. My tongue is thick and dry. It takes me a few swallows, but I croak out a "Stop."

"I'm afraid that's not going to happen. You have delayed, but not prevented my ascension. If you can hold on, however, I might be able to save you."

"What?" Something gives way inside me, and I clench against a horrible sensation of draining, like someone has pulled a stopper from a jug and *glug, glug, glug,* there goes my life. The sensation passes and I sag. My skin has gone clammy and tight.

"I was serious when I said I try to avoid unneeded killings." Utopia really seems to believe that.

"You tried to shoot Calamity. You tried to shoot her in her bed."

Utopia is quiet for a moment. "Yes. Well. Your presence here shows it would have been better for me if I had." The lights in the core begin to blink, and holographic screens project images of her brain. The nanomachines are swarming inside her skull, mapping all the connections.

"You're Mistress Malice." I try to get my arm under me and push myself to my feet. If I can get to my feet, I might be able to…I don't know. Something. I've got to do something before I die. She killed Valkyrja, and Magma, and all the others. She has to be punished for that. I can't let her win. My shoulder erupts with pinching, tearing, slicing pain when I put weight on it. It feels like there's a colony of carnivorous termites carving their way into my joints, chewing on the sinews. I cry out, a feeble squeak. Strongest girl in the world, yep. That's me.

"'Mistress?'" She looks over at me and smiles. "No. I never called myself that. Blame the newspapers. I was only Malice. But that was another life."

"Doesn't look like it." My voice is thready. My chest aches with the effort of speech. One lung feels heavy with fluid, a strong, steady pull at the ligaments. Everyone knows what pain on their skin is like. But this pain, it's different. It's *inside* me. There's no escaping it. It fills me up.

"I told you, this is to save us all. Nemesis is coming."

"Keep telling yourself that. Murderer." Every word is a battle. I can feel myself slipping back into the darkness, and I know this time I won't come back.

"Danielle?" She sounds so far away. "Danielle, listen to the sound of my voice. Stay with me. Please. If you die—well, it would be a waste. It would make the next phase of this needlessly difficult."

In the blackness of the lattice, I see the damage accelerate. It won't be long now. My pattern begins to slump apart, to fray and snap under the strain. I'm not just dying, I'm breaking up.

No.

No, I don't think I'm going to accept this.

I'm not going to die on my first day of freedom.

*There.* That thread is linked to the others around it. I can see the other half of it, see where it tore apart and began to unravel. A strange focus comes over me, and I just…grab them. I grab the threads and I yank them together—

—a spurt of blood—

—a flash of new pain—

—and the snapped thread leaps back together, like magnets.

Nausea flushes through me. But the thread holds. And now, one of those holes in my pattern has a bright white line crossing it. I seize another broken thread, and join it together again. Ice and knives saw at my bones. Every thread I pull on comes with a new injury. I'm better at handling the lattice directly now than I was when I saved the jetliner, but I'm still not good enough to keep from hurting myself. I pull on another, and another. Match-head flares of pain each time, burning brighter with every tug of the lattice. A new pain, a different kind. Cold and deep, erupting in strange places. My kneecap. My chin. My toe. It's too much. A rib snaps, and I'm sure it must have been audible. I cry out.

Utopia is looking at me.

"It hurts," I say. "I'm scared."

Two lies, both true.

"Hold on, Danielle," says Utopia. She taps some commands into the computer. "Listen to my voice. If you can stay with me for a little while longer, I can save you."

"How does…" I swallow back some nausea. "How does taking over the internet help me with the holes in my body?"

Got to keep her talking. Got to keep myself present. I grab another snapped thread, pull it tight, join it with its severed half, and watch it twist itself back into shape. The agony is astounding. Something cracks and grinds in my wrist. Every repair comes at a cost. Every cost comes with interest. But it's only pain, and pain doesn't kill.

Utopia looks up. "Oh, is that what my daughter thinks I'm doing? She lacks vision. I suppose I only have myself to blame for that. No, once I've uploaded myself, then I will then upload *everyone else*." She gestures at the computer core, a giant construct of gleaming steel and faceted crystal. "This is all hypertech now, but I've been developing methods to deploy this process with base-line technology. Nobody will be left behind. By necessity, the mass production process will be more destructive than the one I'm using here, but by the end of the year even the most recalcitrant subjects will be brought to heel. We're all going to leave our bodies behind and live in a simulated environment of my own design. Virtual reality of the purest sort, indistinguishable from the physical world except there will be no crime. No hunger. No *death*."

"A utopia." I clench as a particularly nasty spasm takes me, and then relax, gasping and full of cold, spiky aches.

She smiles. "Precisely. And it will save us from Nemesis, too. Nemesis is dangerous because of the quantum instabilities it causes. Those instabilities are triggered by observer effects. No observers, no effects. In the world I'm building, humanity will only be able to observe what I allow them to, only think what I give them permission to think. Until I am God, nobody is safe."

"Doc was right. You *are* a narcissist." Pull another thread. My left pinky cracks and I hiss.

"It's not ego if you can back it up, dear. In a few minutes, I'm going to be deity, and you will be my first priestess. Even if I have to edit your personality to fit."

"Yeah, no, I don't think I'm really down for that," I say. Something is wet and salty on my upper lip. I wipe my nose and my hand comes away smeared scarlet with blood. Eh. Whatever. Finish the rest later. I get to my feet. My gut and chest are tight and painful, but it's the dull throbbing of a wound beginning to heal. "But tell you what, I'll fight ya for it."

Utopia turns to look at me. She takes a step back and her chest plate snaps open. The world goes to streaks around me and then she's stumbling back against the railing, my fist inches deep in her chest, gripped around the glowing azure speck hanging between her lungs. It's heavier in my hand than I expected.

We lock eyes. Utopia's face twists with the kind of fury that kills people.

With a sharp tug, I rip the weapon straight out of her chest. A tangle of tubes and wires comes with it, wet and snapping. Her back arches; she goes up on her toes with a rattling gasp of pain. The fragment of exotic matter flares in my hand, painfully hot, and I toss it away. I hit her, once, twice. Dents in her metal. Cracks in her plastic. She crumples, and I tear the wire crown from her head, rip its cable from the computer. Utopia's eyes are glassy, her jaw is slack, and she's twitching randomly. I smash her arms. I break her legs.

And then…

…and then it's over.

The holographic screen is flashing big red PROGRAM ERROR warnings. Sparks jump from the ripped cable. Utopia, Malice, whatever you want to call her, seems to reboot and tries to sit up. With my boot on her neck I helpfully direct her face back to the floor.

I've won. My body begins to unclench, and little jags of pain run through me. Wounds and injuries hurrying to make their report. But I've won. The relief is overwhelming.

I tap my earbud radio. "All right, Doc. I saved the world. Can I get some food now?"

# CHAPTER THIRTY-SEVEN

Doc Impossible retakes control of Legion Tower's systems and flushes the nerve gas from the briefing room. Her robots go in and spray everything down with a decontamination agent, and then the paramedics pour in to see if they can save anyone.

Valkyrja is dead. So is Carapace. Magma is alive, barely, and eight paramedics strain themselves to heave him up onto a creaking gurney and rush him out of the building. He'll be flown to Hawaii and dunked in a volcano to recuperate. Doc tells me he'll be up and about in a month or so. Chlorophyll is alive, too, but brain damaged. It's unclear if he'll make a full recovery. His sister Aloe is on her way to take custody of him, which might get a little interesting when she arrives, what with being a supervillain on parole and everything. Graywytch came out of the whole business without much worse than a slash on her arm, a slash she gave herself to power a spell. She disappears into her condo on one of the lower levels without so much as a *thank you*. Bitch.

I come out of my first battle with five broken bones, three bone bruises, a dozen lacerations (mostly on my knuckles), deep bruising across forty percent of my soft tissue, two second-degree burns, and four perfectly circular scars. Two in front. Two in back. Most of the bone injuries were self-inflicted. Healing by yanking on the lattice isn't something I'll ever do for fun.

The Navy is sweeping Puget Sound, but I don't think they'll find anything. I doubt there was ever a real escape plan in place. When the mecha got to the shore and realized they'd been set up, whatever they would have done about it would have still played into Utopia's desire to use them as a sideshow. All those lives tossed away, just to distract any capes she didn't take care of on her own. Whatever excuses she makes for herself, even if she believes them, Utopia is no different from Malice. I'm looking forward to testifying at her trial.

The police insist on coming inside and taking a statement from me while I stuff bulging mouthfuls of pizza and salad in my face. I'm not bothering with single slices and starving myself right now. If this body is my physical ideal, then it's *my* ideal, and right now that means I'm going to eat as much as I want. Who cares if I stop looking like a supermodel? I just saved the whole goddamn world.

The painkillers Doc gave me have me a little bit floaty, and at first I don't want to tell the cops my real name. One of the detectives rolls her eyes, pulls out her phone, and brings up CNN.com. It turns out that photographer's memory card survived what I did to his camera. Oops. The front page is splashed with a huge photo of me standing atop a defeated mecha. One foot is higher than the other, resting on the boxy bulge of an ammo rack, and in a real-life cliché that's almost too twee to believe the breeze has pulled my cape back behind me a ways. It's tattered with cannon holes, one corner sliced off by a beam saber. I'm looking straight at the camera. My lip is split and the eyes belong to someone I don't recognize. The headline shouts DREADNOUGHT RETURNS.

*There was heavy fighting in downtown New Port today as a teenage girl wearing Dreadnought's livery squared off with five walking tanks…no comment from the Legion Pacifica, but police and paramedics have responded to Legion Tower…the death toll currently stands at—*

I stop reading.

That's it, I guess. Every news organization in the world is going to be trying to find out more about me, and it's only a matter of time before someone recognizes my face and calls in to claim the bounty on my name. So much for a secret identity. So much for ever backing out of this life. Maybe I should feel worse about this, but I don't. A thrill of giddy fear, and then it's gone. I'm Dreadnought now. No takebacks. Might as well get on with it.

I give them my statement and ask them to send some cops to protect my parents until I can work something out with the Feds to get them into witness protection. They're quick to agree, and it occurs to me that right now I could ask the city government for just about anything and get away with it.

Almost the instant after the cops are gone, Calamity slips in and sits down next to me. She's got her pants on, scorch marks and all, but the shirt is some cheap disposable thing Doc printed up for her. It was white but has gone zebra-striped with grime. I hadn't realized how much I wanted to see her until she showed up, but now she has, and everything seems brighter.

"You did it," she says.

"*We* did it." I gesture at the pizza box and mumble around an enormous bite something to the effect that she can have some of she wants. She takes a slice and picks at it.

Now that there's no tension keeping her tight and wired, Sarah begins to slump.

"How are you doing?" I ask.

Her eyes get wet and she screws her mouth shut. I go to hug her, and she shifts away from me. So instead, I take her hand and I squeeze it, and after a moment she squeezes back. We stay like that for a long time.

"I lost my arm, Danny," says Sarah. Her voice shakes. "What am I going to do without my arm?"

"Keep saving the world, I imagine."

Calamity doesn't cry, and that's why I look the other way just now. So she can keep saying that, like it was true.

• • •

Doc Impossible finds Sarah and me curled up together on a couch in the lounge. Doc's new body moves stiffly, and her skin seems almost translucent in places. When she enters the room I try to sit up straighter, but Sarah is draped over me and fast asleep. She's heavy and warm. Her face is at peace.

"Your suit is next in the fabber," says Doc. Her voice sounds wet, like she hasn't broken it in yet. "Should be ready in about ten minutes."

"Cool," I say, trying not to blush. "Uh, cool."

Doc holds up a phone. "Also, your parents have been calling nonstop. Do you wanna talk to them?"

Again, I hear the door slamming behind me. Time to slam one right back. "Fuck no."

Doc nods and takes the phone off hold, turning on her heel to head back down the hall. "No, she can't come to the phone right now. Yeah, superhero stuff. I know, I know, kids these days. Anyhow, have you considered getting a lawyer? Restraining orders can be *so* embarrassing…"

• • •

My new supersuit reeks of matter fabricator emulsion, and it's still warm to the touch. This one has a high collar, but no mask. There's no point anymore, after all. The breaks in my bones have already begun to fuse, the pain receding to a dull throb in the background. Still, I can't walk without a limp yet, so for now I'm flying everywhere, just a few inches off the ground. I've practiced the speech twice, and I hope that will be enough. The street in front of Legion Tower is crammed with news vans, police cars, even a SWAT truck. The cops have kept the media away from the building, but when they see me floating down the broad steps, the horde of reporters and camera crews simply duck under the police tape and rush to meet me. They flow around the outmatched cops like a river around rocks. Long before I'm ready for them, they've crowded around me. Cameramen jostle for position, and field correspondents shout questions. Their boom mics are like a cage hanging over me. It takes a moment for the initial rush of questions to subside. When it's more or less quiet, I begin.

"My name is Danielle Tozer. I'm Dreadnought." Pause while the photographers strobe their flashes and the reporters shout more questions. I lift one hand for silence, willing it not to tremble. The reporters quiet and the camera flashes drop off in frequency. I look down at the notecards in my hands and see how they're jittering. *Stop that*, I think, and they do. "I have a statement to make about today's attack, and then I'll answer a few questions. Mistress Malice didn't die in 1961; she went underground. Earlier this month, she reemerged calling herself Utopia, and murdered the previous Dreadnought. Today, she attempted to begin the process of turning the entire human species into software simulations that she could control. Depending on your definition of death, this would have involved the murder of everyone. Had she succeeded, whatever remained of us would have been forced to worship her as a god. I stopped her, and she is now in police custody. While I was fighting her troops downtown, she ambushed the Legion. Carapace and Valkyrja are—" My voice hitches. The cameras strobe in ecstasy. A deep breath steadies me, and I can continue. "They're dead. Magma and Chlorophyll have both been seriously wounded. Doctor Impossible is resigning from the Legion Pacifica for personal reasons. According to the Legion's bylaws, further decisions about the team's status will have to be deferred until a quorum can be assembled.

"I want people to know that even with the Legion out of action for the time being, they still have someone looking out for them. I've lived in New Port all my life, and I'm not going anywhere."

For some stupid reason, they start clapping. My eyes get a little wet and itchy.

That's it. That's the end of the speech. Here's where I'm supposed to start taking questions. But there's something else, something I wasn't sure until just now I was going to say. "And one more thing. I'm not telling you this because it's important, but because I know you'll hear about it eventually and I don't want anyone to think I have something to hide."

The clapping dies off and they push the microphones in closer.

"I'm transgender, and a lesbian, and I'm not ashamed of that."

More camera flashes. More shouted questions. A few reporters rush off to get a head start on writing, as if they suddenly know all they need to about me. Idiots. The headlines, some of them at least, are going to be gross. Too many people are going to react like Graywytch. And if I ever wanted to reconcile with my family, that chance has been likely just been sunk. But it doesn't matter. Saying it out loud gives it power and my nervousness fades away. I feel good. Whatever happens now, I can deal with it.

Because I'm Dreadnought.

And I think maybe I could be a good person.